31472400162776

"What happens when a family of Long Island witches is forbidden to practice magic? This tale of powerful women, from the author of the addictive Blue Bloods series, mixes mystery, a battle of good versus evil and a dash of Norse mythology into a page-turning parable of inner strength." —*Self*

"*Witches of East End* has all the ingredients you'd expect from one of Melissa's bestselling YA novels—intrigue, mystery and plenty of romance. But with the novel falling under the 'adult' categorization, Melissa's able to make her love scenes even more . . . magical." —MTV.com

"De la Cruz has, with *Witches*, once again managed to enliven and embellish upon history and mythology with a clever interweaving of past and present, both real and imagined . . . [It] casts a spell." —*Los Angeles Times*

"De la Cruz is a formidable storyteller with a narrative voice strong enough to handle the fruits of her imagination. Even readers who generally avoid witches and whatnot stand to be won over by the time the cliffhanger-with-a-twist-ending hits." —*Publishers Weekly*

"Fantasy for well-read adults." —Kirkus

"A sexy, magical romp, sure to bring de la Cruz a legion of new fans." —Kelley Armstrong, *New York Times* bestselling author of the Otherworld series

"Fans will be delighted with the next entry in her new adult series. A compelling tale of powerful magic, romance, betrayal and suspense." —Library Journal

winds
of salem

winds of salem

a witches of east end novel

melissa de la cruz

HYPERION

New York

Library of Congress Cataloging-in-Publication
Data

De la Cruz, Melissa.
   Winds of Salem : a witches of East End novel/
Melissa De la Cruz.—First Edition.
        pages cm
    ISBN 978-1-4013-2470-4
    1. Witches—Fiction.   2. Long Island (N.Y.)—
Fiction.   I. Title.
    PS3604.E128W56 2013
    813'.6—dc23

                                    2013010165

                    FIRST EDITION

        10   9   8   7   6   5   4   3   2   1

SUSTAINABLE Certified Sourcing
FORESTRY
INITIATIVE   www.sfiprogram.org
             SFI-00993

THIS LABEL APPLIES TO TEXT STOCK

We try to produce the most beautiful books
possible, and we are also extremely concerned
about the impact of our manufacturing process on
the forests of the world and the environment as a
whole. Accordingly, we've made sure that all of the
paper we use has been certified as coming from
forests that are managed, to ensure the protection
of the people and wildlife dependent upon them.

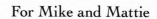

For Mike and Mattie

Jealousy is always born with love,
but does not always die with it.

—François, Duc de la Rochefoucauld,
Maxims

Once upon a time in North Hampton . . .

∿

In a rambling colonial house in a little elusive town by the sea on Long Island's northern and easternmost tip, a silver-haired witch named Joanna Beauchamp lived with her two daughters, Ingrid and Freya. Blond and brainy, thirty-something Ingrid was the local librarian, while barely-out-of-her-teens Freya was the wildest bartender who had ever mixed drinks at the North Inn's bar. The women lived quiet, solitary lives, suppressing their natural talents in adherence to the Restriction of Magical Powers. The law was handed down from the White Council after the Salem witch trials effectively ended the practice of magic in midworld after Freya and Ingrid were hanged in 1692.

Immortals, the girls returned to life, scarred by the experience and wary of the mortal world, and small-town life continued apace for centuries until the day Freya won the heart of the very handsome and very wealthy philanthropist Bran Gardiner, whose family owned the Fair Haven estate on eponymous Gardiners Island. Helpless against the force of her desire, Freya celebrated her engagement by having a torrid affair with Bran's younger brother, Killian, he of the dark, smoldering good looks and devil-may-care attitude.

Following Freya's lead of throwing caution to the wind, the witches soon unleashed their full powers—Joanna, whose specialty was recovery and renewal, brought the dead to life. Ingrid, a healer who could tap into people's lifelines and see the future, began to dole out her spells and charms to any patron with a trying domestic problem, and even gave the mayor's wife a powerful fidelity knot. Freya, who specialized in matters of the heart, served up heady potions, and every night at the North Inn became a wild, hedonistic romp. It was all a bit of harmless, innocent, enchanted fun until a girl went missing, several residents began to suffer from a rash of inexplicable illnesses, and a dark menace was found growing in the waters off the Atlantic, poisoning the wildlife. When the mayor turned up dead, the finger-pointing began, and for a moment it felt like the Salem witch trials all over again.

But these were no ordinary witches, and Fair Haven was no ordinary mansion. Rushing to untangle the mystery, Ingrid discovered archaic Norse symbols in a blueprint of Fair Haven manor, but just as she was close to cracking the code, the document disappeared. Freya discovered she was caught in a centuries-old love triangle with Bran and Killian that harked back to the days of Asgard itself, when she was pursued by her true love, Balder, the god of joy, and his brother, Loki, the god of mischief.

Soon, Norman Beauchamp, Joanna's long-lost ex-husband, was back in the picture, and everyone was trying to save not just their little town, but all the nine known worlds of the universe from *Ragnarok*, the doom of the gods.

Because once upon a time in Asgard, the Bofrir bridge connected the kingdom of the divine to Midgard, the mortal world. One fateful day, the bridge was destroyed, and the mighty strength of all the gods' powers along with it. The culprits of this heinous act were said to be Fryr of the Vanir and his friend Loki of the Aesir, two daring young gods whose childish prank wrought terrible consequences. Accused of trying to take the bridge's power for themselves, Loki was banished to the frozen depths for five thousand years, while Fryr, the god of sun and harvests, was consigned to Limbo for an indefinite period, as his crime had been the greater one. It was Fryr's trident that had sent the bridge to the abyss.

With the bridge destroyed, the gods were separated. The Vanir (or as they were known today, the Beauchamp family, gods and goddesses of hearth and earth) were trapped in Midgard, sentenced to live their lives in mid-world as witches and warlocks, while the Aesir (the warrior gods of sky and light, mighty Odin and his wife, Frigg) remained in Asgard, but both of their sons were lost to them for thousands of years. Their sons were Balder and Loki, Branford and Killian Gardiner. It appeared Loki had poisoned *Yggdrasil*, the Tree of Life, and unleashed the doom of the gods, so Freya banished him from their world.

Fryr was Freddie Beauchamp, Joanna's long-lost son and Freya's twin, who suddenly appeared to Freya in the alley behind the North Inn one evening with unsettling news. He had escaped from Limbo, and revealed that he had been framed for the destruction of the Bofrir and knew the identity of the real culprit.

No, it wasn't Loki. Not Bran Gardiner at all, but Killian Gardiner, the god Balder, who was responsible for its destruction and Freddie's imprisonment.

Determined to prove her lover's innocence, Freya turned Killian's boat, the *Dragon*, upside down to follow her brother's wishes. She didn't find the missing trident, but one night, she found something else: the mark of the trident on his back, which proved Killian did indeed have the weapon in his possession.

Meanwhile, Ingrid was falling in love for the first time in centuries with Matthew Noble, a sweet police detective. But romance between a virgin witch and a mortal was complicated, not to mention a rowdy band of lost pixies caused further havoc by robbing treasures from the great homes in the area. Ingrid was forced to choose her loyalties—to the mortal who loved her, or to the magical creatures who only needed her help.

Back from Limbo, Freddie spent his time shagging coeds and playing video games until his attentions were focused on the lovely Hilly, the goddess Brünnhilde. Only one thing stood in his way: her father, who manipulated Freddie into signing a document that bound him to marry his daughter Gert instead.

Joanna had problems of her own, as a charming widower and her ex-husband competed for her attentions, while a troubled spirit made contact with her, to warn her that a powerful evil was bent on destroying the Beauchamps—an evil that had begun all the way back in Fairstone in the seventeenth century, with Lion Gardiner, Loki in yet another incarnation.

The pixies confessed to stealing the trident and placing it on the *Dragon* to incriminate the innocent Killian, but it was too late as Hilly's sorority sisters, the Valkyries, had already whisked him away for punishment. Freya was still in shock at his sudden disappearance when she, too, was snatched away from North Hampton, a noose appearing around her neck . . .

Which meant that she had been taken back to Salem, and unless her family could figure out a way to rescue her from the darkness of their past . . .

Freya was cursed to relive the witch trials all over again . . .

The girls will not stop. They babble and fling their arms, or become deaf and dumb. When anyone approaches, they hide in corners or under the furniture. Physicians, ministers, and men of Salem Town have come, and they advise fasting and prayer from the community. Fasting and prayer.

But their fits grow worse still. Yesterday they made animal noises, Abby crawling on the floor like a pig, while Betty mewed like a cat. They carry on in such a fashion it is impossible for them to go about their usual employment that delivers them from the temptation of idleness. Ordinarily, they are known to be exceedingly pious and good, docile little girls.

Finally, at a loss, Griggs was called, and as fasting and prayers had proved futile, the doctor declared the girls "under an evil hand." The villagers could only come to one conclusion: the girls had been—

bewitched.

—*Freya Beauchamp,*
May 1692

5

salem

spring
1692

chapter one

A Violet War

æ ♆ ↄ

Late March in Salem Village and the early spring flowers
were in full bloom—the yellow, purple, and white crocuses
of the meadow, the lily of the valley in the woodlands, brilliant
clusters of grape hyacinth and daffodils the color of baby chicks.
Violets proliferated along the ponds and rivers all the way to the
town harbor, and everything was peaceful in the vale as fat hogs
lolled in their pens and cattle and sheep grazed in green pas-
tures.

Inside the small wooden houses of the village, servant girls
groped for their clothing in the pitch-black, rising before the
cocks crowed to revive the dying coals in the hearths with a
quick blast of the bellows. The womenfolk donned layers of petticoats and shifts, lacing up their bodices and putting on their
white caps, while the men and boys pulled on their breeches and
boots to set to work.

In one particular household, a farm on a substantial property
on the village outskirts, encompassing part of the Great River
and Indian Bridge, the maids did their best to keep their master's
temper temperate, or at least not blustering their way. The farm
belonged to one Mr. Thomas Putnam, the eldest sibling and
leader of the Putnam clan, a handsome but austere man, with a
near-perpetual somber cast to his brow. Thomas was one of the

wealthiest and most influential men in Salem Village, although to his dismay and chagrin, not the most *prosperous*. That title belonged to land-rich families like the Porters and his half brother, Joseph Putnam, who also had a finger in the mercantile business of the port of Salem Town.

But such taxonomies were neither here nor there at the moment. Mr. and Mrs. Putnam and their children slept tranquilly as the house servants and farmhands began their daily work. On this fine morning, two young maids, Mercy Lewis and Freya Beauchamp, filled large baskets with dirty linens and cookware to wash in the nearby river. Mercy, a sixteen-year-old orphan, had seen her entire family slaughtered by Indians in the Eastward two years earlier. Freya, a year younger, had also ended up in service after she had arrived at the family's doorstep one day, fainting dead into Mercy's arms.

Freya knew her name but had no recollection of her past or her people. Perhaps she had survived the smallpox and lost her memory to the fever. Or maybe, like Mercy, she had seen her family killed, and the horror of it had caused her to forget. When Freya strained to look back, she saw nothing. She did not know where she came from. She knew the dull ache she felt in her heart was the absence of family, and she knew that she missed them, but for all she tried, she could not remember her mother or father or a single sibling. It was as if her past had been erased—taken—lost as leaves spirited away by the wind.

All Freya knew was that Mercy was a friend from the start, and for that she was grateful to have found a place in the Putnam home. With the large farm and several young children underfoot, the family had gladly taken her in as an extra hand.

The laundry and dishes assembled, the girls stepped out of the house and onto the dirt path, baskets balanced on their hips. Freya's red hair, startling as a sunset, glowed like a halo in the early rays of light. Of the two, she was the more striking one, with her rosebud lips and creamy skin. She had a lightness to her step and a quick, beguiling smile. While Mercy was pretty, with pale blue eyes and a high forehead, it was not her scarred cheek or hands that made her less so, but a tightness to her person that showed in her pinched lips and wary expression. The older girl tucked a wayward strand of blond hair that had fallen out from beneath her cap as she stopped by a bed of flowers, setting her basket on the ground. "Go ahead, pick one," she urged Freya as she knelt on the ground, "pick a violet, and let us have a violet war!"

"No, dear, we mustn't tarry. Poor Annie is all on her own!" Freya said, meaning the oldest Putnam daughter. "We can't leave her to tend the little ones by herself while Mistress is bedridden." The lady of the house often took to her room to recover from the many tragedies of her life. Like her husband, Ann Putnam had been disinherited by her rich father, with his wife and sons seizing permanent control of his wealth. Her failed battle in court against them had left her bruised and embittered. Worse, soon after her three beautiful nieces died from a mysterious illness, one right after the other, and her sister, the girls' mother and her only close friend, died as well, most likely from a broken heart. Their loss had left Mrs. Ann Putnam frail of body and spirit.

Freya reminded Mercy that there was no time for idle pastimes such as picking flowers. There was much to do still: the rooms swept and scrubbed, the butter churned, the ale checked, the kindling gathered, supper cooked. "Not to mention we must make more soap and those golden candles Reverend Parris bid for his altar. We need—"

Mercy laughed and put a finger over Freya's mouth to shush her and pulled her down to join her on the grass. She was tired of hearing about their endless chores.

Freya laughed as well, but covered her mouth with a fist, worried that someone might hear them. Her bright green eyes glinted at Mercy. "What on God's green earth is a violet war anyway?" she asked as she placed her basket next to her friend's.

Mercy smiled. "Choose your violet, and I'll show you, cunning girl!"

Freya blushed. Mercy knew all about Freya and her talent with herbs—it was their closely guarded secret. But then the mistress knew, too, and she hadn't sent Freya away. When Freya had first arrived, she had heard Mrs. Putnam complain of headaches, so she had gone into the woods and picked peppermint, lavender, and rosemary to make a potent brew that instantly eased her discomfort.

The mistress was grateful, but she warned Freya that Thomas mustn't know of her gift. Mr. Putnam was a devoutly pious man, and he might mistake Freya's talent for making physics as the devil working through the girl. Not that it had stopped Ann from asking for another and another. "I miss my dear departed sister and those poor dead children," she would say. "Girl, could you make something for the pain?" Freya always obliged.

Ann also frequently asked Freya if she could see into her and Thomas's future. Would there be more land, more money?

Freya had heard from Mercy that their master and mistress had both been cheated out of shares of their inheritances from their fathers. Ann wanted to know if anything would change in this regard. Freya tried hard to please her, but she could not glimpse into the future, just as she could not glimpse into her own past.

As Mercy watched, Freya chose a perfect violet with dark, rich purple petals, plucking it at the base of its stem. Mercy did the same with her fire-scarred fingers.

"Hold up your violet and make a wish," Mercy instructed.

"Perhaps we shall wish for two other girls to do our work," she said with a naughty smile.

Freya chuckled as she closed her eyes, contemplating a wish. Truly she did not mind having so much to do. It was folly to wish their lives otherwise. Work was important to the community and to their household. No, there was something else. Something else that she knew would not easily be wished away, and she was not entirely convinced she would desire its removal either.

The other day, Freya had discovered she could make objects move without touching them. She had made the butter churn itself just by thinking that she had to do so. When she saw the handle turning on its own, she almost screamed. Later that afternoon the same thing happened with the broom, sweeping the room as if possessed by a spirit. Freya tried to stop it but could not help but feel thrilled at the sight.

What was wrong with her? Could it be that the devil had possessed her like the Revered Parris warned from the pulpit? She was a good girl, devout, like all the girls in the Putnam household. Why had she suddenly been invested with such power? This gift? Did she even want to wish it away?

"SILLY GIRL, HAVE you made your wish yet?" asked Mercy, staring curiously at Freya, who had opened her eyes.

She hadn't made a wish at all, but now she did: she wished that she and Mercy would be like this always, the best of friends, and that nothing would ever come between them. "I'm ready."

Mercy instructed her to wrap the stem of the violet, where it curled beneath the petals like a bent neck, around the part of her own stem that curled the same. The girls interlocked their flowers.

13

"Now pull," said Mercy, "and whoever lops off the other's head—the flower—will have her wish."

The girls pulled at the stems of their interlocked violets, moving the flowers this way and that. It was Freya's violet's head that went flying off.

Mercy raised her victorious violet with her scarred hand. "I got my wish!" she cried.

Freya was glad for her friend but felt wistful just the same. "Come on now, let's go."

Mercy rolled onto her side, staring dreamily up at Freya, as she pressed her violet into the cleavage of her bodice. "All right. But first, I must tell you a secret."

"A secret!" said Freya. "I do love our secrets."

Mercy grinned. "There is a new young man in town. I saw him training with the militia in the field by Ingersoll's Inn on Thursday."

Freya batted her pale red lashes at her friend. "And?"

"A dashing youth with dark hair and green eyes," Mercy added. "I can't wait for you to see him! For aught I know, he is already promised to another maid, but you must see how very handsome he is."

Freya thrilled at the description. "Do you think he will visit the Putnams?" she asked.

"Maybe, but we will most likely see him in church."

With that pleasant thought, they both rose and followed the path to the river.

LATER THAT EVENING, after dinner and prayers, after the bread had been made for the morning and placed in the oven door by the hearth for the night, and the little children put to sleep, the girls lowered their rope beds in the hall, their work finally done for the day. The beds hung about a foot apart. They shook out their blankets and lay in the flickering light of the fire.

Mercy reached out her hand, and Freya interlocked her fingers with her friend's. They should know better. What if the master awoke and saw them holding hands? He would not approve of such a display of affection. He might misinterpret it. But they interlaced fingers nevertheless, the way they had hooked their violets together earlier, until slumber seized them, and their hands fell apart.

chapter two

Of Plums and Pie

E arly the next morning, Thomas Putnam drove the girls to
the meetinghouse in Salem Town, traveling a good way
across hillocks, rivers, inlets, and rocky terrain. Legal proceedings involving villagers still had to take place in Salem Town, as
the village was not yet fully independent, to his continuing annoyance.

Freya and Mercy had been summoned as witnesses in a case
between two quarreling goodwives. The whole affair had been
the talk of the village for an entire year now. The girls would be
providing evidence against Goody Brown, the defendant, who
lived near the Putnam farm. Mercy had once been in Goody
Brown's employ, while Freya often went to the Brown household
to buy or trade baked goods for the Putnam house. It was Mercy
who had volunteered their services to Mr. Putnam, as she sur-
mised that he was weary of the bothersome talk between the
women and eager to bring it all to an end. He had seen to it that
Mercy and Freya would be called as deponents. Mercy was
thrilled; the clever girl knew the trip would mean some time off
from work and the opportunity to visit the town, which Freya
had not yet had occasion to see. Freya felt rather guilty about
Mercy's machinations, although she knew the girl meant well.

They sat meekly next to their master on top of the carriage as it wobbled along the pebbly road. Thomas was tall, good-looking, and broad shouldered, with a commanding, booming voice. He ruled Salem Village as he ruled his household, but he disliked going into Salem Town for it was somewhat outside his jurisdiction. The new families who had land by the port were becoming increasingly more prosperous than older farmers like himself, and they had been abandoning the old Puritan ways, to his disapproval. The very thought of Salem Town alone filled him with bitterness. It was there that his father had lived with his second wife, Mary Veren, the wealthy widow of a ship captain, marrying her while his own mother's dead body had barely grown cold. Mary soon gave birth to his loathsome half brother, Joseph, who eventually reaped much too much of the property that was rightfully Thomas's.

He comforted himself with the thought that at least he had secured the appointment of the reverend. Mr. Samuel Parris was finally ordained, which meant the village could at last have its own church with a minister who could give communion and preach to covenanted members rather than just a congregation. With their very own church in the meetinghouse, the villagers no longer had to travel twice a week—a good three-hour walk—to the port town to worship, as missing church was a punishable offense.

He drove wordlessly, a dour expression on his face, the girls beside him, their caps and blouses recently laundered and scrubbed in the river and left out in the bleaching sun to look their brightest. They dared not utter a word unless Thomas addressed them. There was a breeze, but the sun was sweet against the girls' cheeks as the wheels rolled and squeaked over stones in the road. They crossed a creaky bridge over a river, planks groaning under the wheels as they reached their destination.

The meetinghouse was packed with plaintiffs and defendants,

although there were many who came just for the entertainment, squeezed into the pews and galleries or standing in the back. A year ago, Goodwife Diffidence Brown had bought ten pounds of plums from Goodwife Faith Perkins. Goody Brown made pies with the plums and sold the pies at the market. The following week, Goody Brown claimed her customers returned to her stall to complain that the plum pies had been inedible, tasting as "putrid as rotten fish." Brown alleged that every customer who had bought a plum pie clamored for a refund, which she promptly gave. The allegedly bad plums had caused Goody Brown "tremendous grief and financial loss."

When Goody Brown complained to Goody Perkins about it, Goody Perkins refused to make restitution on such hearsay. "I gave you fat, juicy, sweet ones. There is nothing wrong with my plums and, as everyone in Salem Village knows, you are a lying hag, Goody Brown." She didn't believe Goody Brown's story one bit. Most likely Goody Brown was hard up and trying to make a few extra pence. It was not beneath her. A scuffle and some pulling of hair ensued.

Goody Perkins then claimed that when Goody Brown left her doorstep, Goody Brown "fell to muttering and scolding extremely," and Goody Perkins heard Goody Brown clearly say, "I will give you something, you fat-looking hog!" Goody Perkins claimed Goody Brown had cursed her, and that she was a wench and a witch. For almost immediately after, Goody Perkins's baby stopped nursing and fell ill, and she almost lost the infant. Then one of her sows "was taken with strange fits, jumping up and down and knocking her head against the fence, and appeared blind and deaf," and died in a "strange and unusual manner." This spring the trees in her plum orchard had not bloomed, and she feared she would have no plums to harvest.

The magistrate, a spice merchant whose loud sighs made it

clear he had better things to do, harrumphed and quieted both plaintiff and defendant, who had begun bickering at each other again. "Order in the court! You goodwives are giving me a headache." The people in the meetinghouse tittered. "Order!" he called again, then requested the bailiff usher in the first deponent: Mercy Lewis.

The magistrate glanced up at Mercy and in a bored voice said, "What saith the deponent?"

"I do not know what I *saith*, Sir Magistrate. Is there a question?" asked Mercy. More laughter from the galleries. Mercy glanced at Freya, who smiled encouragingly back at her.

"Well," said the spice merchant, flashing his gold tooth. "Has the deponent witnessed the defendant, Goodwife Brown, do anything unusual? *Maleficium?* Did she ever do any harm to you while you worked for her? Is she a cunning woman?" He frowned in a way that looked as if he were trying not to laugh. Then his face went solemn, and he glared questioningly at Mercy.

"Maleficium?" she asked.

"Latin for *mischief, wrongdoing, witchcraft!*"

"Goody Brown—she does possess unusual strength," said Mercy. "She can carry many sacks of flour at once."

The gentlefolk in the meetinghouse laughed again.

The magistrate sneered. "Anything else?"

"Once, with the other servant of the Putnam household— where I now work—Freya, we visited Goody Brown, and she lied to us. She tried to cheat us when we bartered for flour, adding stones for weight, she did. She can be greedy. I saw much of this firsthand when I worked—"

"Next witness!" yelled the magistrate, cutting Mercy off as he looked back down at his papers.

Mercy was ushered away, Freya brought forth. Unlike Mercy, Freya did not want to make any accusations. There were enough cantankerous relations in the village as it were, and she certainly did not want to get herself into trouble or cause bad blood between herself and other villagers. Yes, it was her opinion that Goody Brown was lying about the plums. But Freya also knew for certain that Goody Brown was no witch, a very grave and dangerous accusation—the penalty being the noose. If anyone here were a witch, it was Freya herself, and this made her cheeks burn as she was sworn in, remembering what had happened with the butter churn and then the broom.

"What hath this deponent to provide as evidence?" asked the magistrate.

Freya shrugged, her cheeks now a similar tint to her strawberry curls that fell from beneath her cap. The sun shone through the windows now and Freya felt overheated. The meetinghouse, crammed as it was, had grown pungent, rank with odor. She felt as if she couldn't breathe.

"Anything that could point to Goody Brown employing witchcraft? Have you seen her *collude* with the devil, perhaps?" asked the magistrate.

"I have seen no such thing," she said.

Thomas lowered his head in the front row, feeling embarrassed by his servants. Bringing them here had been a waste of everyone's time. Clearly his girls were not much help in moving this case along.

The magistrate, a pragmatic and forward-thinking man, was not entirely disengaged from the proceedings and did derive a certain amount of pleasure from debunking the phantasmagorical imaginings of country folk. "I would like to call forth my own witness," he declared as Freya was accompanied to her seat. "Mr. Nathaniel Brooks, please rise and step forward."

A din rose in the meetinghouse as a tall youth came forward. He strode with ease and confidence to the front, hat in hand, standing in a relaxed and guileless manner before the magistrate. His ebony hair fell just above his shoulders, and his emerald eyes caught the light.

"Please tell the court where you live," said the spice merchant.

"Presently, I live in Salem Village with my uncle, a widower, who needs a hand on his farm," said the youth. "I haven't been in the village very long." He smiled, taking his time, glancing around the meetinghouse. For a fleeting moment, the youth caught Freya's eyes. She felt a jolt from his stare. But just as quickly, the lad looked to the magistrate.

"Now, Mr. Brooks, where were you on the afternoon of Wednesday the twenty-sixth of June, 1691. Do you remember?"

"Why, yes, I do. I was at the market, purchasing a plum pie."

The spectators took in a collective gasp.

"I very much like plum pie and wanted one for dinner," continued the youth.

The people in the meetinghouse laughed.

"And does the witness see the maid from whom he purchased said plum pie in the meetinghouse? Is she present?"

"She is," said the youth. He pointed to Goody Brown. "There she is. It was her plum pie I bought."

The spectators leaned forward, whispering, anxiously awaiting what might come next. The magistrate waited, relishing creating suspense. Finally, he spoke. "And did you, Mr. Brooks, eat said plum pie?"

"Yes," said the youth with a smile. "Yes, sir, I had the pie for dessert that very evening."

The spectators leaned farther forward.

"And how would you, Nathaniel Brooks, describe this plum pie?"

Nathaniel looked out at the people in the pews and galleries, taking his time. His gaze met Freya's and their eyes locked again. He smiled. She smiled and her cheeks flushed.

The magistrate cleared his throat. "Nathaniel Brooks? Will you please answer the question carefully? *How did you find this plum pie?*"

Holding Freya's gaze, as if the remark were directed at her, Mr. Brooks replied, "*Quite sublime*, Sir Magistrate! In fact, Goody Brown mentioned that the pies were made with the best plums of Salem Village."

Again came a loud collective gasp, and afterward everyone began to chatter.

"Order!" called the magistrate. The room silenced.

Goodwife Faith Perkins was smiling, feeling somewhat vindicated. Goody Brown was indeed a liar but perhaps that didn't exactly make her a witch, either. After all, she herself had exaggerated a bit about her baby and the sow.

The magistrate gave his verdict, chastising both women. The only crimes here, he summarized, were lack of neighborliness, greed, and wasting his time. The case was dismissed, and he was done for the day. The meetinghouse adjourned.

As FREYA FOLLOWED the crowd outside to the fresh, briny air of the harbor, her heart beat hard in her chest as she recalled young Mr. Brooks daringly making eye contact with her. She had been instantly struck—smitten, as if every sense in her body came alive at his glance. She spotted Mr. Putnam by the carriage, speaking to Mr. Brooks and another young man. Something flashed in her memory and for a moment she saw Mr. Brooks in his bright linen shirt, opened at the neck, revealing a tanned swath of skin—and his hands were wrapped about her waist, pulling her toward him—then it was gone.

"There you are!" said Mercy.

"Yes," Freya said in a daze.

They stood in the shade of a building. Mercy followed Freya's gaze to Thomas and the two youths across the way.

"Goodness! There he is!" said Mercy.

"Who?" asked Freya.

"My handsome youth. The one I told you of, with dark hair and green eyes."

Freya looked at her friend in a panic. "The witness?" she asked. "Nathaniel Brooks?"

Mercy laughed. "No, no, the other one, his friend. James Brewster. Isn't he lovely?"

Freya smiled, relieved.

James Brewster looked up, caught her eye, and winked.

What cheek!

Even from this distance Freya could see that James Brewster did have green eyes but a yellow green, like an inquisitive cat's. James's hair was dark as well, as Mercy had described it, but a sandy brown with light streaks, whereas Nathaniel's was a raven black.

"Did you see that?" Freya asked.

"See what?"

"Nothing." Freya shook her head, suppressing a smile. Life had certainly become much more interesting now that they had glimpsed the two young men.

Mercy offered Freya her arm. "Shall we?"

Freya nodded and the two girls crossed the street.

23

chapter three

Secrets

و‌ص ⚵ ܒܝ

"Do not despair, my brothers and sisters, for there are also true saints in the church," Reverend Parris proclaimed from his pulpit. Here he gave Thomas Putnam a subtle nod. It was lecture day, noon on a Thursday, and the reverend was giving one of his interminable, unrelenting, and punishing sermons. The psalms had already been sung in a most monotonous and tuneless manner, parishioners echoing back the deacon, prayers recited. And now Parris was going on about the devil trying to infiltrate the church and how one had to align oneself with God Almighty. Parris always found reason to chastise his parishioners. "The church consists of good and bad, as a garden that has weeds as well as flowers . . ."

Parris's long dark hair flailed around his shoulders when he railed on about the devil. He had large brown almond-shaped eyes and a long, slim aquiline nose. A good-looking man whose bitterness made him ugly, as he was full of envy, especially for the merchants who had succeeded in business where he himself had failed in Barbados before coming to New England. Thomas Putnam had found an ally in the reverend—they both harbored an intense dislike for the people of Salem Town. Parris's words reached a fever pitch as his tithing man strode up and down the aisles with a stick, prodding those who nodded off or using the feather end to tickle fidgeting women beneath the chin.

"Here are good men to be found, yea"—again a glance at Thomas, Captain Walcott, then Mr. Ingersoll, who ran the inn, all in the front row—"the very best; and here are bad men to be found, yea, the very worst." He looked up to the ceiling here, not selecting any particular culprit for the bad ones, knowing they themselves would know who they were.

Freya and Mercy stood in one of the galleries along the wall, with the Putnam children lined up beside them, first Ann Junior, then the rest, tallest to shortest. Ann surreptitiously reached for Freya's hand. Freya squeezed it tightly to reassure the girl.

Nathaniel Brooks and his friend James Brewster stood across the way in the opposite gallery, hats in hands, heads bowed, as was Freya's. Now and then, Freya's eyes lifted, meeting Nate's. Was he really staring back at her? She felt Mercy elbow her once as if to note he was indeed. Freya's body grew tingly. Nate's black bangs fell over his left eye. He was ravishingly handsome. When Thomas had driven the four young people back to the village from their court day in Salem Town, Nate had helped Freya out of the back of the carriage, chivalrously reaching out a hand. His grip was firm, strong yet gentle. A surge of energy passed between them as their hands and eyes met. Freya thrilled at the memory as she looked back to the reverend, a smile playing on her lips.

Freya noticed that the good reverend was preaching against covetousness when just yesterday she and Mercy had brought him the gold candles he had requested for his altar. She glanced at Nate, who rolled his eyes. Was he having similar thoughts? She glanced at Parris for fear they might get caught sending each other these silent missives. Confident that the reverend had not cottoned on to her glances, she looked back at the boys' pew. This time, it wasn't Nate who was staring back at her but James.

LATER THAT AFTERNOON, Freya donned a cape, slipped the hood over her head, grabbed her basket, and wandered off into the woods. Once a week, the servants in the Putnam household were afforded an hour for solitary prayer. She wended through the pines, oaks, and beeches down a path, kneeling to pluck an herb or flower now and then. Few dared to venture out so far, knowing the native settlements were near, and the kidnapping of villagers was not uncommon. Freya was not afraid of the natives, however violent the stories she heard. Some called them savages, heathens, or devils. But she had also heard that their white captives often refused to return to their old lives after they were rescued. They preferred the native culture of all things— the freedom from all the rules and codes one had to follow in Puritan society. She had a feeling she would like that freedom as well.

The villagers' fear granted her privacy and Freya let her mind roam however she wanted. In these woods *she* was free. She could breathe.

She heard branches crackling and quickly pivoted around. A deer leaped between the trees. She smiled at the doe and continued along the light-dappled path until she came upon a clearing. On the border of the meadow, she found a huge outcropping of stone, where she sat for a bit. She noticed a nearby dog rose bush. She got up and strode over to it. The roses were still just little buds. They would blossom in June, delicate petals the white pink of a maiden's cheek. Once the petals fell they would turn into rosehips later in the summer—which would make for a good marmalade and a potent cough syrup. Freya reached out, whispering a word she didn't quite understand, and the little bud came off its stem as if plucked by an invisible hand, dropping into her outstretched palm. She felt a thrill, then caught herself. There was someone behind her. She stood stock-still. Had whoever it was seen what she had just done? Had she been caught?

"*Rosa canina*," came a low, soft voice. "That's what they are called."

She turned, pricking a finger on a thorn, dropping the small bud. James Brewster stood in the clearing, smiling.

"You pricked yourself!" he said, and took her hand to wipe the blood trickling down her wrist.

"Oh!" she said, taking her hand back and biting on the puncture, squeezing out a last drop of blood from it. "What are you doing here?" she asked, looking up at him.

James spoke hurriedly. "I'm sorry, Miss Beauchamp, I didn't mean to startle you. Forgive me, I saw you wander off into the woods while Brooks and I were helping Mr. Putnam with the new barn. I had to go to the river to gather stones. When I got there, I saw Miss Lewis with the eldest Putnam girl. The little one fell into the river and hurt herself. She called for you. 'Only Freya can fix it,' she said. So I ran until I found you. They fear they will be in trouble from Mr. Putnam as the girl is supposed to be home, tending to the children."

"Goodness!" said Freya. She gathered her basket, and they quickly made their way across the clearing.

As they walked together, James asked her about herself and Freya told him about how she appeared at the Putnams' doorstep one day.

"You don't have family?" he asked.

"Not that I remember. Mrs. Putnam thinks I must have suffered from the pox, which is why I lost my memory."

"That is grievous indeed. To lose our memory is to lose our identity."

"I am a fortunate girl," Freya said. She said it so often she almost believed it. "The Putnams took me in and I have a home here. How do you find Salem, Mr. Brewster?"

"Please, call me James."

"James," Freya said with a smile.

"It is . . . interesting," he said. "Before we came to Salem, Brooks and I lived in Europe. We are naturalists and are often in the forest, where we study flora and fauna, the multifaceted aspects of nature. In a word: *science*."

"Oh dear," Freya said, eyes sparkling. "I don't think the reverend would like to hear that."

"Which is why I can trust you with our secret?" James smiled.

"Of course." Freya nodded. That he had revealed something so dangerous to her brought a huge sense of relief. Despite having Mercy, she realized how very alone she had been until this moment. As close as they were, she did not think Mercy would understand about the true nature of her gifts.

James smiled at her and she smiled back, thinking that he was indeed very handsome—and perhaps if she had seen him first in the meetinghouse instead of Nate, perhaps her affections would lie with him—but as it was, her heart was already full of a certain Mr. Brooks. But she was grateful for his kindness and his wise words that hinted of a world beyond Salem. The sun pierced through the clouds and beat down on her hood. She pulled it back and fixed her cap, still smiling at James.

"There she is!" he said.

ANNIE SAT IN the grass by the river, her back propped against a boulder. Mercy was crouched at her heels, holding the girl's ankle, one foot raised upon her thigh. Annie wore nothing but her shift and skirts. Her wavy brown hair fell loose and damp over her chest, clinging to the shift. Mercy had washed the mud off the girl's woolen bodice and linen cap, then placed them on a bush in the sun to dry. She had strung the young girl's boots up in a tree, and now they dripped and dangled in the breeze.

"Freya, my Freya!" Annie cried as she and James came running.

James turned his back to the girl so as not to embarrass her.

"Don't worry, James," said Mercy. "Annie's a wee girl." Mercy wanted to be able to gaze at the object of her affection and not at his back, albeit attractive as well.

"Are you sure?" he asked.

"Turn, will you!" she ordered, so the lad had no choice.

Freya had kneeled beside Mercy and Annie. "You look a fright!" she said to the girl.

Annie began to whimper. "I'm so very sorry, Freya. I promise not to fall again. I promise!"

"You are always falling, aren't ye? We might have to give you a cane," reprimanded Mercy.

"No!" yelped Annie.

Freya studied the girl. Annie was a difficult child. She often shrugged off her duties caring for her mother and siblings to spend time with the servant girls. Perhaps she was resentful of being the eldest and burdened with the responsibilities—but that was the way things were, and Annie should know it was her duty, Freya thought. No one was exactly happy with her lot, but they all made the best of it.

Annie was invariably hurting herself or getting in trouble with her father, and they would then be obliged to defend her, sometimes even having to tell a sinful lie to do so. Annie would thank them, telling them how much she feared but loved and revered her father. Freya liked her but also pitied her. There were times she caught Annie gazing at her in such an odd fashion it made her nervous. But perhaps Annie was just young, and her life certainly wasn't easy with a mother who was always ill and having such an austere man for a father. They had plenty, all that they needed, but somehow it never seemed enough. There was no warmth in that house.

"Let's see what we have here." Freya lifted Annie's skirt and observed her red and swollen ankle. "Ah, it's nothing!" she said. She had James hand her the basket in which she had gathered herbs during her walk, and asked him to pick some of the lamb's ears that grew along the river. When he came back she rubbed the leaves he handed her with some arnica, then she held the crumpled bits around Annie's ankle, whispering a short incantation.

Annie sighed with relief. "Your hands are so soothing."

James and Mercy watched, and when Freya removed her hands the swelling had gone down and Annie could walk again.

"A cunning girl!" said James, looking admiringly at Freya.

Mercy placed a finger at her mouth, then warned him, "Not a word of any of this!"

He promised he wouldn't say a thing, then gathered his rocks and returned to the barn, leaving the young women, who did their best to make Annie presentable in her damp clothes.

chapter four

In Bloom

"It is all so heavenly!" Mercy remarked as she strode through the stable, lifting her skirts, then filled the horse's trough with water from a bucket. All morning the maid had been going about her work with a smile on her face.

Freya laughed at such a comment as they stood amid horse dung. With a smile, she inquired, *"Heavenly!* How so?"

They were inside the Putnam stables, taking care of Thomas's prized Thoroughbred. The master wanted to ride the animal later that day. A stable boy and a few of the farmhands were responsible for cleaning the stalls, picking the mud and stones from the horses' hooves, shoeing, washing, feeding, and riding the horses, but Thomas wanted to make certain his stallion was especially well groomed—that the leather of his saddle and bridle gleamed as brilliantly as his coat—and had assigned his maidservants to the task.

Freya brushed the Thoroughbred's forelock, a palm at the warm muscle of his neck, peering inquiringly at Mercy. She ran her other hand down the white diamond along his nose, let his velvety lips nibble at her palm. The horses stirred in their stalls, flicking their tails, dropping their hooves, exhaling noisily.

Mercy placed two hands over her heart, sighing audibly. "I am madly in love, Freya!"

She had suspected Mercy was going to say this. "James?" she asked.

"Yes, James, James, James!" Mercy twirled around with the water bucket, letting the name ring out.

Freya was genuinely happy for her friend, for she knew how such feelings were, how one wanted to cry them out like this. "That is wonderful!"

"I know it is crazed of me to think—for I am of lower station—but I do believe he loves me, too," Mercy continued. "You know . . . the way he looks at me. Have you noticed the way he looks at me, Freya?"

Freya hadn't. She had, however, noticed the times James had smiled at her, the teasing glint in his eyes. This was disconcerting where Mercy was concerned. It would seem James was a shameless flirt. Freya wasn't about to hurt her friend by telling her this. She was no good at telling a lie, nor should she sin so improvidently. "I will pay more attention from now on!" she promised, not knowing what else to say.

Careful not to soil the hems of their skirts, the maids closed the door to the Thoroughbred's stall and went to treat the leather of Thomas's tack with rags soaked in mink oil. Mercy took charge of the saddle balanced on a beam, while Freya retrieved Thomas's riding bridle from a wooden peg, then brought it over to a bale of hay where she sat down.

As Freya ran the cloth along the leather reins, she whispered, "I have a confession, too." She blushed with happiness, making a very pretty picture as a ray of sun slanted through the opened doors upon her apron, mauve skirt, and white petticoats peeking through above her leather boots.

"A confession?" said Mercy. "That sounds serious."

Freya smiled, biting her lip. "I, too, am in love!" she said.

Mercy ran over and crouched beside her friend, gathering

her skirts, grabbing Freya's hands. "You must tell me everything! Who is the lucky lad? I had no idea!" Love had given Mercy's large blue eyes a sparkle, softened her mouth, and reddened her cheeks. She was almost beautiful.

"Why, Mr. Brooks, of course! You knew, did you not?" Freya asked in a skeptical tone.

Mercy laughed as if this were the most hilarious yet agreeable thing she had ever heard. "I didn't. I swear! You hide it well, I must say." She tucked a curl into Freya's cap and ran a hand along her friend's cheek, but Freya lowered her head, suddenly distraught. "What's wrong?" Mercy asked.

"It's what you said earlier . . ." Freya sought to find the words. "I, like you, am enamored of someone much beyond my station. He comes from a wealthy family and has traveled to Europe and back."

Mercy tapped her on the knee. "Oh, stop that, you wench! You are considered the fairest maid in all of Salem Village and Salem Town! Many speak of your beauty. I will hear none of that from you! Anyhow, it matters little nowadays. Men of high rank marry poor lasses like us here in the New World. Don't ruin this for us. I am so very happy we are both in love! Tell me! Tell me everything!"

Freya wanted to tell everything to her friend—who was so like a sister to her—and felt a great wave of affection for Mercy at that moment. But she held back, and the cresting sentiments crashed painfully within her. It wasn't caution or mistrust, but something whispered to her to keep her true feelings a secret, and she felt guilty for it, but still, she listened to that voice. So she told Mercy nearly everything—about each little glance she and Nate had exchanged at church. Mercy listened voraciously, nodding her head at all the details. But there was one thing Freya kept from her friend.

33

That very same morning when she had woken in her rope bed, she had found a small, coarse-grained card tucked between the blanket and her chest, with the swirling letters *NB*, a sideways *δ* beneath them. There was no note, but the seal told Freya everything she had to know.

NB for Nathaniel Brooks! He had been inside the Putnam house! Perhaps he had been there late at night for business with Thomas, up in the paterfamilias's study while everyone slept. He had stood over her while she slumbered! Had he run his fingers along her brow maybe? Just the idea of it caused her to shiver.

He had wanted her to know he had been there, and was thinking of her. She trembled with excitement even as she was loath to share any of this with her beloved Mercy.

chapter five

Mr. Brooks and Miss Beauchamp

ꕔ♆ꕔ

After supper at noon, Freya finished her chores and helped Annie with the children, reading the Bible to them before they napped. She told Mercy she would take the wash to the river by herself. Her friend needed to give her scarred, chafed fingers a break. With her basket of laundry and pots and pans, she took a shortcut, plodding along toward the river. When she got there, she worked quickly, cleaning and scrubbing, then returned the roundabout way through the meadow, where James had caught her unawares that day. As she walked she lost herself in the splendor of her surroundings: the wind rustling through the trees, the verdant grass springing beneath her boots, the fragrance of wild roses.

James had mentioned he and Nate often came to these woods, and while she had hoped, she truly did not expect to see her love, so when Nathaniel Brooks stepped onto the path, he took her by surprise.

He was a sight to behold: elegant, tall, slim, self-assured as he walked toward her, an amused smile twitching on his lips. He wore a blue linen shirt, open at the collar, black breeches tucked into heavy boots, his hat angling over an eye. His face was clean-shaven, and his dark hair shone brilliantly in the sun as he removed his hat to greet her.

"Mistress Beauchamp!" he called to her as they approached. "We are well met! Fancy seeing you here!"

"Mistress!" she echoed, laughing. "Miss is more like it for I am not goody yet. Or just Freya, if you will." Her words appeared to come easily enough, but her heart was in her throat. Most likely, she thought, there was too much color in her cheek.

Nate stopped a few feet away. They both froze. His mouth opened as if to speak, but he refrained. They laughed at their awkwardness, and Freya relaxed a bit, her shoulders dropping. She studied the swell of his lips, the rich, deep green of his eyes.

"I received your card," she said.

"What card?" he asked, with a naughty glint in his eyes.

"How did you know I could read?" She wasn't being coy—she genuinely wanted to know. Perhaps he could tell her something about herself. Perhaps he had recognized her from the life she'd forgotten.

He pursed his lips then smiled. "I did not know of your literacy, but if I did, I would say it is your haughty and refined manner that would have given it away."

"Really!" She let out a laugh. "Haughty? Refined?"

"Yes, like a lady, a woman of high standing, a princess or a queen." He grinned.

"Why thank you very much, *Mr. Brooks*," she said facetiously.

He took another step forward. " 'Tis nothing! And you must call me Nate!"

"Is that all you wish to tell me? That my comportment is haughty? That I behave as if I am above my station? A mere servant like myself . . ." She lowered her eyes. She knew she should behave more humbly, but at the same time she believed his palpable attraction allowed her some latitude. Although she *was* taking a risk by being impudent.

"No," he said. "Not at all." He moved closer so that they stood inches apart. "But I am glad you are here. Ever since we first met I have harbored a deep desire to be with you, to *know* you . . . I didn't mean—" He had embarrassed himself, Freya knew, for to "know" a woman was to know her intimately.

She looked into his eyes. "What didn't you mean?" She attempted not to laugh. It was fun to make him squirm a bit.

He took a deep breath and lowered his head. "I didn't mean any impropriety to your person."

She would like to think Nate's interest in her was more than just the licentious feelings of a young man of privilege for a pretty servant girl. "You are forgiven, Nate." She smiled, swaying as she clasped her hands. "I should take your leave, as I must return to the farm soon or else someone might come looking for me."

"May I walk with you?"

She nodded. "Let me get my basket."

He rushed toward it. "Allow me!"

FREYA AND NATE walked silently in tandem, crossing the meadow. They entered the path in the woods. He held a bramble up for her and she ducked through. They had grown shy, as if there was nothing more to say or they could think of nothing. Neither could find the right words. Then the sight of Nate carrying a woman's basket made Freya giggle.

He stopped in the path, turning to her with a wounded look. "Why are you laughing?"

She laughed more. She couldn't stop, her bosom quaking

above her bodice. "It's just funny," she said, "a handsome, tall lad like yourself carrying a maid's basket!"

He gave her a stern, squinting look, then in a huff dropped the basket at his feet, the pots and pans making a terrible clatter.

"The basket!" she said, looking down. What was wrong with him? She was about to kneel to retrieve it, but he reached over and clamped her at the waist with two strong hands, holding her fixed in place, just as she had foreseen when she first saw him.

They stared at each other. Freya's heart rebounded inside her chest. She wondered whether she had made a terrible mistake letting this young fellow accompany her alone through the woods.

Then his shoulders began to shake and he was laughing, and she realized it had been a joke, a play at seriousness, at annoyance, and she laughed, too, incredibly relieved. He let her go. They smiled at each other. He stepped aside, closer, and grabbed her maiden's cap, holding it aloft with a mischievous grin. When she made a leap to grab it, he bounded away, taunting her with the cap, waving it in the air.

"Stop!" she said, but he only laughed.

She made another attempt to nab it, but he caught her shoulder with his free hand, and swung his hand with the cap around her waist. They stood still. She inhaled him. He smelled of work, mud, and the woods. He felt as solid as the pines around them. Nate whispered in her ear, the words rushing. "How beautiful you are with your red hair along your cheek." He pushed a curl out of her face as he said this, seeing how the sun lit it up, then placed her cap back on her head. "Miss Beauchamp, I fear I have . . ."

"Freya, my name is Freya."

"Freya then," he said softly.

Freya wanted him to hold her longer and to hear what he had

to say, but regardless of her dislike of Salem, she still had to live within its rules, and she broke the embrace regretfully before he could finish what he was going to say.

"I feel the same way . . . yet . . ." She shook her head and looked around the empty forest.

He nodded, releasing her from his embrace. He understood the rules as well as she.

chapter six

The Proposal

F reya ascended the flight of creaking wooden steps to the study, holding the candlestick aloft to find her way. Mr. Putnam wanted her to meet him there once she was finished with her work. As much as Mercy told her not to worry, Freya fretted. She had never been called to his study before. Surely, she must have done something wrong.

Now that she thought about it, she had performed a multitude of crimes. Perhaps someone had seen her and Nate together in the woods the other week and reported it to her master. She would surely get the lash—that is, if Mr. Putnam wanted to take care of her misdeeds himself. What if he suspected her of witchcraft? Had the mistress of the house mentioned her efficacious physics? What would happen if she had?

She stood at the door, spying the flickering candlelight in a crack in the wood. Thomas was in there, waiting for her. With a trembling hand, she tugged her skirt, righted her cap, then held her head up and knocked quietly so as not to wake the household.

She heard him cough. "Come in!"

"Mr. Putnam," she said once the door was closed. She curtsied, even though he wasn't looking her way.

Thomas sat at his desk, writing in a ledger, briefly glancing up as he dipped his pen in the inkwell, then continued to write.

"Freya," he said. "Give me a moment." He blew on the ink. His face was expressionless, giving nothing away.

Freya kept one arm at her side while she held the candlestick. He flicked his eyes up at her. "You may put the candlestick down."

She walked to a small table to set it there and returned to her spot in the middle of the room, clasping her hands at her apron.

"You may look me in the eye," he said.

She lifted her chin but not too proudly so as to provoke more severe a punishment. Her eyes met Thomas's piercing ones. They were an icy blue.

He clapped his hands. "I have propitious news!" he exclaimed.

"Propitious?" she echoed, surprised. This was not what she had expected. She had been awaiting her doom. Nor would she ever have anticipated the man's apparently favorable mood or to be made privy to any kind of news, propitious or otherwise.

Thomas shrugged. "I was surprised myself!" His eyes roamed her body, sizing her up. She felt a bit like cattle. He smiled. That was a first. "Well, to get straight to the heart of the matter, *so to speak*"—here he smiled again—"Mr. Nathaniel Brooks has asked for your hand in marriage."

Freya started. She stood dumbfounded for a while but sought to hide all the emotions stirring within her. She wanted to run down the stairs and wake Mercy to tell her the tremendous news immediately. She attempted to suppress a smile, and her mouth curled into a frown. "Why . . . why . . ." she fumbled as Thomas studied her. "I don't know what—"

"You don't have to say anything," he interrupted. "This is most excellent and providential for you as well as me. Though it might seem displeasing to you at the moment—you are but a girl, and a young one—this means you will be a rich little wife soon. I am happy for you!"

She had obviously concealed her feelings well. This news was anything but displeasing to her. She hadn't been able to stop thinking about Nate since she had first glimpsed him, and she held on to the memory of his arms around her waist. What relief to know there would be no more reason to conceal their affections now that he had asked for her hand!

"You are fortunate. They are a prosperous family," Thomas continued. "They own much land, seafarers as well as farmers and involved in commerce. As much as the latter ires me, I cannot deny that they are influential in the port. This would be a helpful alliance, one that might give me more sway in Salem Town. And it would also, of course, be a tremendous step upward for you." He shook his head, laughing to himself. "To think just a little while ago you were an orphan on our doorstep!"

Dazed, Freya didn't know what more to say. Thomas had dipped his pen in the inkwell once more. She curtsied, about to take her leave, and went to retrieve the candlestick.

"I am not finished," he said.

"Oh!" She turned.

"Not a word about any of this. You know how the villagers chatter, but I do want you to get to know Mr. Brooks of course. However, don't let him know I have informed you of his intentions. I have simply told him I will consider the offer and dowry." He wriggled a bit in his seat. "The utmost discretion must be applied, Freya. Mr. Brooks has seen you in the meetinghouse and is very fond. You are pious and chaste, and I trust you to remain so. Not a word to Mercy either. I know you two are intimate, but she is prone to wagging her tongue, that one. For now, this is between you and me until told otherwise. Agreed?"

Freya nodded. "Yes, sir!" she said, breathless, and left the room.

THE NEXT MORNING, Freya woke to a drumbeat in her chest. Mercy snored softly, her blond hair falling over her face, her scarred hand dangling off her rope bed. There was just the faintest hint of light beyond the small, darkly tinted windows.

Freya rose, lit a candle, dressed, retrieved the bread from the oven, and put her bed away. She took a moment by the hearth and said her prayers. She prayed that the Putnam household be kept safe and continue to prosper. Then she asked that she see Nate most expediently, that same day if possible. She finished her prayers with a rushed "Amen."

Outside in the moist darkness her senses were assaulted by the scent of blooming wisteria. The vines with their grapelike flowers twined up the awning on the side of the wooden house along which she groped for her way in the dark.

Ever since her discovery in the lean-to when she had first churned the butter just by thinking it, she had begun to rise early before anyone else on the farm. She needed this time alone each day to continue to practice her skills. Today she wanted an even earlier start so she might eventually steal away to the woods and perhaps happen upon Nate once more. She believed he would accept her talents. He was kind and learned; he would not cast her out for being what she was. His friend James had not judged her when her touch had healed Annie's ankle by the river.

Besides, when she practiced her skills, she felt almost dizzy with an intense joy at the power of her talent. Perhaps what she was doing *was* witchcraft, the occult, magic—all considered odious, wicked, abominable, the insidious design of the devil. That was what everyone believed. But did that make it true? Freya

43

didn't think so. It felt good and pure and wholesome. What she was doing would brand her as a witch and get her hanged, but it was beyond her control. It came so naturally, and she couldn't help herself. She needed to do it more and more.

She rushed to the cowshed. She could barely see the path in the grass. Inside, she moved quickly about because she had learned to feel her way around by now. She wended through the large, shifting bovine bodies. Without her having to use her hands, the cows began to splash steamy streams of milk inside the buckets she had placed beneath their teats.

Eggs lifted from the hay inside the chicken coop, flying into her basket as the hens let out surprised clucks. Next, she rounded the farm to the lean-to structure, where she would check on the fermenting hops, bottle some ale for supper and dinner, then churn the butter, using witchcraft to get it all done quickly. She was full of energy, her incantations leaping from her lips in winding whispers. She had no idea where the words came from—she just knew them. They made her light-headed, intoxicated. Perhaps love enhanced her magic.

On her way to the lean-to, she heard her name in a loud whisper.

"Freya!"

Nate! He was here!

She turned and walked toward the voice. It came from a copse of leafy trees. She heard a branch crackle underfoot, and James Brewster stepped out from the shadows, his clothes rumpled. He took her in with a deep breath.

"Oh, James!" Instantly, she was embarrassed by the disappointment in her tone. She was, of course, delighted to see James.

"Freya!" said James again.

She remembered her agreement with Mr. Putnam to exercise utmost discretion regarding her and Nate. She wasn't about to betray her benefactor. Mr. Putnam was so kind, and she must remain loyal and not say a word about her engagement.

"What are you doing here?" she asked.

"I was on night duty at the watch house, so I am returning to the Brooks farm to get some sleep." He yawned, covering his mouth, and stretched his arms. His cotton shirt lifted, revealing a smooth swath of skin. Freya blushed. He beamed, his eyes glinting. He was as handsome as Nate, to be sure.

"I see! You were the one to keep us safe in our beds."

"Indeed," he said. "Safe from the *savages*!" He widened his eyes. "I don't quite see them that way though. I rather like those savages." He put an index finger to his lips and made a shushing sound, and winked at her.

Freya made a face. "If people heard you, James, they might accuse you of idolatry or even devil worship!" she teased. She was one to speak. If only people had seen what *she* had just been up to.

"Smart you are!" he said. "Very modern!"

"Modern?" The word was familiar to her, but she couldn't remember what it meant. She knew she had heard it a long time ago, somewhere in her foggy past.

"Ahead of the times," James explained.

"Like you," she said keenly.

"Perhaps," he allowed with a small smile.

She was going to ask him more but heard noises from the house. The family would wake soon and Mercy would be out here as well. She felt a strong affection for James suddenly. Nate's dear friend and Mercy's love. Perhaps one day the four of them would be as close friends as she and Mercy were. Freya would like that.

Without thinking, she pulled him close and kissed him on the cheek.

"Well!" he said, shocked.

Laughing, Freya spun away and ran back to the farm.

45

north hampton

*the present
new year's eve*

chapter seven

What Dreams
May Come

∽ ♆ ∾

"H ey, what's going on?" came a low rumble at the end of the
line.

The sudden sound of Matthew Noble's voice made Ingrid
Beauchamp's pulse quicken, even after all this time. "Hey, Matt,"
she said. "It's going." In the background, she heard the sounds of
the North Hampton Police Department: papers shuffling,
phones ringing, the kind of laughter that went along with work
horseplay, static crackling from a walkie-talkie, and a guy whin-
ing about his stolen car. Detective Noble was still at the precinct
and Ingrid hadn't left work either. After all the librarians had
gone home—including Hudson Rafferty, the world's oldest in-
tern and her dearest friend in the world, the hugely pregnant
Tabitha Robinson, and a few new clerks—Ingrid had locked the
front doors, turned off the lights, and retreated to her archivist's
office at the back.

"You haven't answered any of my calls. I've been trying to
reach you for hours," he said.

"I'm so sorry." She glanced at her cell and saw that he had

tried earlier and also left a text. She must have forgotten to turn the ringer on her phone back on after closing up shop.

"Hmm," reflected Matt, "why do I keep hearing that from you lately, Ingrid?"

They usually checked in with each other as soon as library hours ended, if not before, but ever since December when Freya had been whisked back to Salem through the passages of time, their relationship had been placed on a permanent hold. It barely even had a chance to begin. It was January, a few days after New Year's Eve, which had been a grim celebration at best, and Ingrid could not afford any distractions. There was too much at stake—who knew what was happening to Freya back there? Ingrid was consumed with books on seventeenth-century Salem Village politics, before, during, and after the witch-hunt fervor. There was no time to return calls or texts, much less for a relationship.

Ingrid couldn't help but revisit Freya's last moment before she was taken, that awful night at Mother's house. Her sister had been standing by the fireplace, still in disbelief over how Killian had been torn away from her just as she had found him again after centuries of pining. Freddie, their brother, had reassured his twin that they would do everything to find Killian and bring him back. But Freya had not answered; instead she had turned silent, her eyes filling with shock. She appeared to be staring at something that terrified her. Her bright green eyes had clouded over, becoming dull, as her face blanched. She gasped and choked. It all happened within seconds. Ingrid had risen to her feet, moving forward to help. But there was nothing anyone could do. As Freya brought her hands to tug at her neckline, Ingrid saw the invisible rope cutting into her throat, squeezing it and leaving a red mark.

Then she was gone. Her sister was gone.

Ingrid knew what had happened the minute she had seen the rope burn at her sister's neck. Gallows Hill, 1692. When the two of them had hanged for witchcraft. It was happening all over again. Somehow, someone wanted Freya back there. Back to Salem Village and all its horrors.

Ingrid pulled the rubber band out of her hair to lessen the pinch at her temples. She anxiously scratched at her scalp. "I keep saying sorry, Matt, because I *mean it.* You know I wish I could be spending my time with you instead, but I can't, not until we find her. But don't worry, I think I'm getting closer."

"The dreams?"

"Yeah, I had another one," she said, and shuddered.

"Ingrid? You okay?" asked Matt.

No, she wasn't. She had drifted off again while talking to him. "You know, I don't think it's fair to you to be with me when I'm so distracted."

Matt let out a breath. Ingrid wished she could feel the warmth of it against her face and neck. She felt herself almost give in and tell him to pick her up so they could spend the night together. Instead a silence hung between them, fraught with tension.

Her love for Matt had not waned. If anything, she loved him more than ever—for his patience and always being there when she needed a shoulder to lean on, solid as a pillar. He encouraged her when she lost hope of finding Freya, and was as helpful as a mortal could be in this situation. He didn't understand everything about her background or her family, but he had accepted her for what she was. A witch.

"Why don't you give me a call when you're wrapping things up?" Matt said. "I'll pick you up and drive you home."

She stared at the books piled on her desk, all different sizes, stacked in towers, then the one open under the circle of light cast by the desk lamp. "I don't know . . . I'm not sure when I'll be finished. I wouldn't want to hold you up or wake you if you've gone to bed."

He laughed. "Come on, I just want to see you. Anyway, I'm still at the precinct doing paperwork. We just wrapped up a case."

"While I didn't even ask how you're doing . . . I'm so sorry."

"There you go again. I'm fine."

"I really miss you," she said, but even as she did, she'd grown distracted by the pile of books in front of her.

Matt was silent. "Let's talk later," he said.

"I promise this will get better, and we can spend more time together."

"Sure." He remained on the line but was silent.

She waited a little longer but that was it, so she said good-bye, and they hung up without saying their usual "I love you"s. Ingrid felt empty and awful from the way the conversation had ended. Their relationship was constantly being stalled by something or other. She lowered her head and began to read, then realized she had read an entire page and not retained a word. Because what if Matt grew used to her absence and stopped missing her altogether? The poor guy couldn't wait forever, could he? He couldn't wait forever for her to . . . well, to sleep with him, for one. They weren't teenagers. She wanted him as much as he wanted her. She wanted him more than anything. He was the one for her. Except, there was just one thing.

He was mortal.

He would only get hurt, or she would, there was no getting around that. She would only pretend to age, but he would die, leaving her alone forever. While Matt seemed to accept her differences easily, it was a revelation to Ingrid to find she was the one with doubts, perhaps because she knew exactly what their relationship would mean for her in the end. So she had pushed him away, using Freya's disappearance as an excuse.

She thought about the dreams. In the first, Freya stood alone in a field of wheat. She saw the village in the distance and recognized it. Salem, with its dark square homes, beneath gigantic clouds moving fast through a blinding blue sky. The sleeves of her sister's saffron-yellow blouse beneath her dark mauve bodice rumpled in the wind. Her cap fluttered against her sun- and wind-kissed cheeks, as she held it in place, her palm against her crown. Her sister looked so young, she couldn't be older than sixteen. There was panic in her eyes. The dream ended there.

In the second installment, Freya stood in the field again. She was whispering something. Something Ingrid couldn't hear.

In the third dream, Freya was screaming as the wheat field went up in a great whoosh of orange flame, black smoke licking at the great blue of the sky. The fire consumed the field, moving quickly behind her sister. Freya came running, closer and closer, larger and larger, until she passed Ingrid, but they didn't touch.

Ingrid had woken in a hot-cold sweat.

That had been the last dream.

Freya was trapped in Salem Village. Freya was in danger and there was nothing Ingrid could do about it.

Her eyes ached. She squeezed them shut. In Salem, witches had been hanged, never burned. In fact, no witch had ever been burned in the Americas. However, the flames meant something. The fire expressed urgency. Time was running out. Little progress had been made.

The Beauchamps' magic had grown feeble, Ingrid knew; it was a candle at the end of its wick. Her mother, Joanna, could not muster the strength to reopen the passages of time however much she tried. Freya was trapped in seventeenth-century Salem while Ingrid and her family were trapped here, unable to return to the past and rescue her.

Ingrid began reading her book again. The Salem witch hunt in 1692 had been an anomaly in its intensity, concentration, scale, and death toll. It lasted one year and ended almost as abruptly as it began. Nineteen had been hanged. One man was pressed to death by stones. Four perished in jail awaiting trial. More than one hundred people in Salem and its surrounding communities (mostly women, but there were men and children as well) had been accused and forced to languish for months in prison under horrific conditions in dark, wet, cramped, stinking, rat-infested cells. They were hungry, thirsty, dirty, shaved, manacled to walls, pricked and prodded for "witches' teats"—nipples or birthmarks or moles where one's familiar supposedly suckled, proof one was indeed a witch.

How could she help her sister? Was there a way to prevent the crisis that spread like wildfire from happening again? What had caused it? What was the spark? It had all begun in the home of Reverend Samuel Parris, when his daughter Betty and young ward, niece Abigail, began having strange fits. That was the beginning. Ingrid would start there.

For reasons Ingrid didn't understand, she couldn't find her own or Freya's name recorded in any of the documents or history books. There was nothing about the Beauchamp girls who had been hanged on Gallows Hill. The fact that they were not in any records was puzzling yet heartening. Maybe it meant that the past had already been altered somehow? And that Freya was safe?

The burning field of wheat and her sister in the middle of it . . .

Ingrid grabbed another book and read, pushing past a wave of weariness. There were three facts about the history of Salem that were of great interest to Ingrid. One, that the Reverend Parris was instrumental to the Salem witch hunt, spurring it on and fanning the flames; two, that Thomas Putnam and his clan filed the most accusations against witches with the court; and three, that Joseph Putnam, Thomas's younger brother, was one of the few Salem residents to speak out against the witch hunts. The brothers had been fighting over their inheritance, Ingrid knew, with Thomas feeling as if he had been cheated out of his. Ingrid always suspected Salem had been about more than just witchcraft.

The phone rang again, startling Ingrid. She picked it up.

"Hey," said Matt, "just calling to say good night. I'm heading to bed unless you want me to pick you up."

Ingrid didn't answer.

"That's what I thought." Matt yawned.

"I'm sorry."

"Don't be," he said.

She wanted to tell him she loved him, but somehow his silence made saying those words too daunting.

"Night, Ingrid."

"Night," she said, then hung up. She stared at the phone for a moment, feeling a pang, then plunged her nose in yet another book.

chapter eight

Brother Time

Sunlight pierced the curtains, falling over the *C* of Joanna's body beneath the duvet, illuminating the strand of silver hair that fell over her lips. She woke with a start and blew at the lock of hair and pressed her eyelids shut again. She did not want to wake up, not yet. This wasn't the way to greet the day, so full of anxiety and dread.

Joanna had gotten her beloved son back, only to have her youngest daughter ripped away from her, tugged back through the passages of time, a noose at her neck. Freya . . . beautiful, free-spirited Freya, back in the dark ages. Puritans. There was a word for those people but Joanna would not use it. She was comforted by Freddie's assurance that he believed Freya was alive and well for now—he would feel it if his twin were dead, he had told her.

Still, she was a mess.

Her body ached from using her magic to break the passages open but it was no use. The passages of time were sealed. Baking couldn't even help her out of her funk: her pies came out sunken and burned. She had so little magic left in her fingertips she couldn't even restore them to their rightful plumpness. During the day, Joanna could barely eat, and in the evenings, she'd taken to ordering from Hung Sung Lo's for the family, the mediocre North Hampton Chinese take-out place.

At least she wasn't alone. She snaked a hand between the sheets, reaching for reassurance, warmth, comfort, to pull his body into the curl of hers and make the feelings go away. But the spot beside her was empty, cold.

"Good morning, gorgeous!" boomed a voice at the bedroom door.

Joanna sighed with relief. She sat up and saw her husband in the doorway, already dressed in jeans and a bright cotton plaid shirt. He was clean-shaven, his silver-and-black hair standing a tad awry. "Hello, darling!" she cried.

Norman was holding a breakfast tray, beaming at her. She saw a small vase holding a rosebud, a stack of croissants and muffins, butter, jam, orange juice, and a cup of coffee, the steam highlighted by the morning light. The creases in his forehead and cheeks had turned into grooves. They were both aging as their powers diminished and they worried about Freya. Despite it all, Norman kept up a good front. He made a valiant effort to cheer up Joanna when needed. She couldn't help but beam back at her man, feeling a teenage crush all over again, a surge of blushing bliss.

He walked toward her.

"Don't you look handsome this morning." She smiled.

He dismissed the comment with a scoff. That was also what she found so attractive about him—he had no clue just how handsome he was, even if he was rumpled and worn out, like an older, more weathered James Bond.

He sat on the edge of the bed, handing her the tray. The curve of his neck caught her eye. She could take a bite of him right there instead of eating this divine breakfast he had brought her. She was grateful that they had decided to give this another go.

They were trying. Actually, they *weren't*.

That was the thrill of it—they didn't *have* to try. There was

57

nothing to fix; it was easy and tender. This kind of love, the love-of-one's-life kind of love, was the only cushion for pain during a crisis such as this one. Joanna propped the tray on her legs, still smiling admiringly at Norman. If it weren't for Freya gone, she would have thought, *Magic be damned. I am happy to live as a mortal, with my husband.*

"You are one to speak, old girl! In this morning light, you look as stunning as the day we first met on that beach, even though you claim to feel . . ."

"Like crap?" finished Joanna.

"Yeah, I didn't want to ruin the moment." He frowned, then reached and squeezed her hand, and they kissed.

"What a lovely breakfast, fit for a queen!" she said, when they pulled away. She looked at the offerings. "Where did you get all this?"

Norman cleared his throat. "An idea struck me last night, and I didn't get much sleep. I was down in your office working, and I went to the bakery when it opened."

Joanna grabbed a blueberry muffin and sniffed it. It was still warm, freshly baked, and to her surprise, its scent jump-started her appetite. She bit into the warm, buttery, crumbly moistness. "Mmm."

"I thought that might give you a lift since you haven't had time to bake."

"So thoughtful!" She couldn't get enough of the muffin.

Norman told her of his plan. His brother Arthur had popped into his head in the middle of the night. Arthur Beauchamp worked with the Wolves of Memory, the historical keepers of the passages of time.

"How is dear old Art?"

"I don't know. I haven't heard from him in ages. But I did find him online." He told her Arthur was still teaching at Case

Western in Ohio. Yet when Norman had tried calling his line this morning, the phone rang and rang. No voice mail. Then he couldn't get through to anyone at the university, and for nearly an hour had struggled to find his way out of an endless labyrinthine loop of voice-activated options.

Finally, he found a cell number and called that—it went straight to voice mail, so he left a message, but he wasn't even sure if it was his brother's cell phone because the message just repeated back the number he had dialed. Then when he tried that same number again, a message said the number was no longer in service. Something or someone appeared to be preventing him from reaching Arthur.

There was only one solution. They needed to hit the road and head to Cleveland to find him.

"We're driving there?" asked Joanna.

"Why not? We can break it up. Drive five hours, find a motel, drive another five. How about it, Jo?"

"A road trip!" She removed the tray from her lap. One muffin and a few sips of coffee, and she suddenly felt invigorated. She and Norman were taking action, not simply despairing and sitting back. Inspired, she began to make preparations for their journey. Yankee practical, she thought: thermoses with coffee, crackers, cheddar and brie, fruit, nuts. Joanna loved thinking about projects in terms of food.

Arthur—of course! The old timekeeper had to possess the key to the passages she couldn't unlock herself.

"You're a genius, my dear! But I do hope Arthur's all right. I hope nothing has happened to him."

chapter nine

The Newlyweds

F reddie heard the shower turn off, followed by Gert's loud sigh. The little New Haven off-campus apartment had walls that were so insubstantial that whatever anyone did in another room could be heard as if you were standing side by side. He could tell that she was annoyed because he had used all the bath towels again without putting out new ones. He had made a mental note, of course, to do some laundry and throw some in there, but it had slipped his mind when he put on *Warhammer* and just *had* to get to the next level.

"Freddie!" called Gert.

Gullinbursti, Freddie's piglet familiar, snorted against his foot as if to tell him to get moving. "I know, Buster," said Freddie, throwing the remote down on the little black couch, among popcorn kernels, crumbs, magazines, and fast-food wrappers. "I know I know I know!"

Married life. You had to get your wife immediately out of a jam if she were in one. That was how one showed everlasting love.

"Dammit!" he muttered to himself.

All the towels were dirty. He hadn't done the wash. He smelled one and decided she wouldn't notice. He was supposed to keep the house running while Gert was studying for finals, but he had stuff on his mind and had been busy, too. He was worried about Freya. It had been so long since she'd disappeared and the family seemed to be getting nowhere. If anything, his anxiety over his twin had driven him to play even more video games.

There was also his volunteer work as a firefighter. The local firehouse had given him a ton of shifts because—as Fryr, the sun god, which they didn't know about, of course—he had a knack with flames. Fighting fires, observing RECEO (Rescue, Exposures, Confinement, Extinguishment, and Overhaul), was hard work, exhausting, and by the time he got home, he was just too tired to throw a load into the washing machine. Of course there had been a clean one for *his* shower after a day at the station with the boys and tromping around in flames in that heavy bunker gear. He felt just a tad guilty at that.

"Freddie!" Gert screamed.

"Uh-oh," Freddie remarked to Buster. "Here goes nothing." Best to play dumb. In a couple of leaps (everything was within a couple of leaps in this apartment), he made it to the bathroom, opened the door, and spied his beautiful wife hiding behind the shower curtain, dripping wet and looking angry.

He smiled. "Here you go!" he said in the lightest, most cheerful tone as he handed her the used towel.

Gert took a sniff and gritted her teeth. "This stinks! God, Freddie! I asked you to wash the whites—I left Post-its, I texted . . ." She shook her head. "Go! Close the door."

Dejected, Freddie went and sat on the couch and turned off the TV. He should clean up the place. That would make Gert happy. He rose, ambled to the kitchen, got a garbage bag, and began throwing out everything that appeared superfluous: old magazines, newspapers, take-out bags, empty Chinese food containers, and so on.

Lately, things had just gotten too tense in this cramped apartment. He and Gert argued incessantly over the most mundane things. Who cared if the bathroom sink and mirror were spattered with toothpaste? Who cared if Freddie couldn't find a video game after Gert had done the straightening up? They had both gotten so petty lately. They fought about the tight quarters, but they were together, and wasn't that what was most important? Sometimes the brawls ended in mad, hungry sex, but lately it was just pointless arguments with no make-up sex afterward. How lame was that? He and Gert had been married for less than two months, and their marriage was already in the dumps.

He had to *do* something about it.

"All right!" he said. "I'm vacuuming."

Freddie got the vacuum out of the narrow cabinet in the kitchen and plugged it in. In the living room, the machine sounded as loud as a Harley. No wonder they never used it. Buster ran for his life into the bedroom, where he hid under the bed on which Gert was now studying, books sprawled all around her.

In the living room, Freddie had begun to use the bare metal tube to suck the crumbs out of the couch. That felt satisfying. Then Gert was upon him, hands on her hips.

"What are you doing?" she boomed over the machine.

"Um . . . what does it look like?"

Gert flicked the button on the vacuum cleaner off. They stood in a silent face-off. Freddie admired his wife, thinking she looked incredibly hot standing there with her warrior face, a small glimpse of her true nature as the *jötunn* goddess Gerðr. He wanted to do her right there and then. He was so hard up, and sort of getting hard at the thought. But then she spoke.

"Can't you see I'm studying? What are you doing—trying to sabotage me?"

"What? No!" he said. "I just thought you would appreciate some cleanliness and order around here."

"What I would appreciate is a clean towel after a shower when I don't have time to wash any!"

There was no winning. But Freddie was the bigger man. He wasn't going to get into it and explain that he had decided to turn a new page and that doing laundry had, in fact, been on his agenda. First, he had decided to fix the pigsty aspect of the place (Buster had nothing to do with it . . . but he didn't want to think about their *other* little problem—or more like *problems, plural*—at the moment, which was probably one of the main reasons Gert was so tense). He would get her what she wanted. He would be a model husband. He decided to give his spouse some space for now, take a walk and pick up some groceries. He would fix this marriage even if Gert had given up.

63

HE PUT ON a cap, a coat, and gloves and walked outside, striding quickly down the sidewalk, the sun in his face. It was a beautiful winter day, and he cut across the park, admiring the silhouettes of the empty tree branches, and Freya surfaced in his thoughts. What was she doing now? He could almost sense her. It was a reassuring feeling, like a second heart beating in his chest.

At the store, he bought laundry detergent, paper towels, sponges, and three different cleaning products—one that was purple and had a whimsical Spanish name, Fabuloso. The pretty cashier batted her thick black eyelashes at Freddie. As he bagged his items, he winked at her. In turn, she licked her lips. Even if Gert thought he was lame, it was nice to know he still had it going on.

He stopped by what looked like a little hole-in-the-wall. The window read FOOD SHOP. The place was run by a chef who made delicious dishes he knew Gert loved. Freddie chose eggplant Parmesan, beet and goat cheese salad, quinoa with lentils, and green beans in olive oil and garlic. They had been eating so much junk food lately—maybe that was the cause of their foul moods. Too many French fries and milkshakes. Too many fried mozzarella sticks. Hadn't his mother always said that eating well meant feeling well?

Last on his list of errands, he purchased a small chocolate cake, a bottle of Cabernet, and a bouquet of lilies. The flowers reminded him of Gert on better days. Suddenly, he felt terrific. He felt Fabuloso. The evening was going to be A-OK. He was going to win Gert back. It was ridiculous that their relationship had come to this so quickly. Their vows might have been exchanged at gunpoint, after he had blown his chance to be with her stepsister Hilly (Brünnhilde, whom Fryr had loved since time immortal but could never have), but he did love Gert. He was even monogamous for a change. He had just thrown away the receipt with the cashier's number on it.

When he returned to the apartment, it appeared his wife had the same idea to get them back on track. A better idea, even.

"I'm so sorry, Freddie, I have been such a bitch lately. After you left, I cleaned up. I feel like an asshole," Gert said as she greeted him at the door in a satiny white peignoir.

"I've been the asshole," said Freddie.

"We both have been . . . It's just having the pix—" she began, but Freddie didn't want to be reminded of *that*, so he pressed a finger to her lips. He showed her what he had bought, thinking they could have an indoor picnic.

"Oh, Freddie!" Gert gasped, and she pulled him into a kiss, pressing her body against his.

Freddie became instantly hard again, aching to be inside his sexy, bitchy wife, for the hot, sweet sensation of their lovemaking. The force of their kisses sent them toppling onto the couch, groping, pulling, pushing at each other, panting heavily.

Gert's peignoir had fallen to the floor at this point, and they couldn't get Freddie out of his clothes fast enough. She tore off his T-shirt. Freddie bent over to pull off his shoes, as she gripped impatiently at his leather belt to get the big brass hipster buckle undone.

One of Freddie's Chuck Taylors hit a wall, while the other flew into the air over the back of the couch.

"Got it!" came a hoarse voice, and the clap of a sneaker caught in midair.

"Ergggggggh!" said Freddie, half undressed, grabbing the peignoir off the floor to hand to Gert.

"They're here?" she said, sitting up, donning the robe. "I thought you said they went skiing!"

"They were supposed to," said Freddie, glaring at Sven, who was holding up the sneaker, as the other pixies bustled into the apartment, carrying skis, snowboards, snowshoes, and what looked like the handles of a snowmobile. Freddie shook his head.

Sven, whose hair was now turquoise, looked as scruffy as he usually did, cigarettes tucked in the sleeve of his T-shirt, which featured the grim reaper holding a scythe standing among cute puppies and a penguin with a bow tie. Val sported a spiky crimson Mohawk, a blush in his cheeks from carrying five pairs of skis up the three flights. Irdick, the round-faced one with the pale platinum hair, cried out, "Hey, Mom, Dad, we're home!"

The girls—fair-haired Kelda in *Lolita* heart-shaped sunglasses and dark, olive-skinned Nyph in star-shaped sunglasses—giggled. "Yeah, um, hi!" they said in unison.

"Oops! I think we interrupted something?" Kelda peered above her heart-shaped lenses at Gert, who was tying the belt of her short robe. Then she looked at Freddie, still shirtless, his hair mussed.

Gert shook her head but the pixies were not having it.

"We totally did!" Nyph snickered. The pixies were ageless and immortal, but had a childlike air, like a group of loud preteens.

"Gross!" said Sven.

"Sorry!" Kelda said, giggling even more.

"What are you doing here?" asked Freddie, disgruntled. "You promised to go on a ski trip! What the hell?"

Gert was incensed. "I lent you my car, for God's sake! Can't Freddie and I have the place to ourselves for once?"

"Yeah, about the car . . ." said Irdick.

"No!" said Freddie, knowing what was coming. "You didn't!"

"Yeah, we did," said Sven.

"T-t-t-totaled," said Val.

Gert screamed, a scream that lasted forever, ending in a single sharp note that made everyone cover their ears.

The pixies, who had been Ingrid's wards, had somehow become Freddie's responsibility. He wasn't sure how that had happened. Something to do with Ingrid having to concentrate on her research, and soon they were just underfoot. Ever since they had moved in a few weeks ago, his marriage had deteriorated. The pixies were supposed to have stayed away the entire weekend, finally giving them a little peace. But here they were again. It was a total nightmare.

Talented thieves who had gotten Killian in trouble in the first place, they were in charge of stealing back the trident from whoever had taken it (they swore they couldn't remember who had assigned them the task of stealing it from Freddie originally), but after a few days on the yellow brick road, they claimed to have "lost the scent." They were waiting to pick it up again. No one knew when that would be. They were useless, total mooches, not to mention the messes they made and that they never lifted a finger to clean. All they wanted, as Sven put it, was to have "some goddamned fun."

And now they had totaled Gert's antique Jag, the only thing Mr. Liman had ever given his adoptive daughter.

Freddie sighed as he picked up the phone to call the insurance company.

chapter ten

The Most Important Girl in His Life

That morning a note had been left on the kitchen table for Ingrid. "Gone to find Uncle Art in Ohio. Love, Mom and Dad." It was Saturday night, about six in the evening.

When Ingrid had called Joanna's cell earlier, her mother had sounded harried. What could have been so urgent while they were still on the road? Those two were behaving like delinquent teens taking off on a joy ride. Ingrid wished they had told her what it was about—but she decided to stop worrying for now. Her parents could take care of themselves. She had something far more pressing on her mind.

Matt was on his way. They had made special plans for tonight and she hoped it would go smoothly—no awkwardness, discomfort, or fumbling. It was her way of making it up to him for not being available lately.

Ever since Ingrid had returned to the elusive little seaside town to be closer to her family after years of living abroad and working in American universities, she had remained in the room upstairs next to Freya's in her mother's old colonial. She spent so many hours at the library that she hadn't the time to look for an apartment. Plus, she had been comfortable here, with her mother and sister for company, and for a while it had been a treat to have the entire family together again, with Freddie back and even their father, Norman, welcomed into their old homestead. But as the maxim went, good things never lasted.

Tonight, though, it was really quite perfect that she had the house to herself, logs burning in the fireplace, scented candles lit. She had prepared dinner and set the table in the dining room. Perhaps she should flick more lights on? Would that be better? She decided to turn the ones in the dining area on, dimmed, in addition to the candlelight, so they could see each other while they ate. She headed upstairs, passing her griffin, Oscar, in the hallway, his lion's tail looping around her ankle.

"Oh, no, this won't do, my dear, you have to be out of sight this evening. You are just too scary even though you're a pussycat." She grabbed him by his feathery scruff and brought him to the pixies' old haunt up in the attic. "Sorry," she said sadly, locking the door. "Not tonight. Another time, perhaps." She returned down the stairs. *Yes, witches do possess familiars, but they certainly do not suckle them. Good gods!* thought Ingrid. *How gross. They really got so many things wrong back in Salem.*

She went inside her bathroom. "Yikes," she said, glimpsing herself in the mirror. She had worn her hair down, as Matt liked it, but it looked a fright—witchy, really. She ran a brush through it, then sprayed it with some serum Freya had recommended so that it looked glossy and smooth. Ingrid smiled at her reflection. There was a pink flush in her cheeks, her gray-blue eyes shone, but her lips looked pale. She found a berry-red lipstick, but when she put it on, it looked too scarlet.

She dabbed her lips, then finished them off with a touch of

69

gloss. "There!" She didn't look half bad, she thought—not too pale or bookish or bland.

The doorbell rang and she started, losing hold of the perfume bottle, which fell to the sink. She placed it back on the counter, deciding against it. *Too overbearing.*

Everything had to be perfect tonight.

Tonight was the night!

Downstairs in the front foyer, she took a deep breath. She steeled herself and opened the door.

Matt Noble stood in the doorway with a shy grin. "Hey there!"

Ingrid tingled all over at the sight of him.

Then she turned to the girl beside him. "Maggie! How are you? It's so great to meet you—I've heard so much about you from your dad!"

Tonight was the night Ingrid was finally going to meet the most important girl in Matt's life. His daughter.

"Likewise," said Maggie, giving Ingrid an impressively firm handshake for a twelve-year-old. Maggie looked unabashedly at Ingrid, her big brown eyes aglitter. And she was *so* pretty. Beautiful was more like it, but more olive toned and exotic looking than freckly, Irish Matt. "What a pretty dress!" Maggie said. "Is it vintage? And you have such great hair!"

"Well, I could say the same to you." The child was delightful. "I always wished I could be brunette." Ingrid nodded.

"The proverbial grass is always greener," said Maggie.

"Exactly!"

"Um, I'm here," piped Matt.

"Oh, right!" remarked Ingrid.

"But please, I don't want to interrupt the lovefest." He grinned.

Maggie giggled.

"Come in," said Ingrid, and once Maggie strode through the door into the house, she and Matt took a moment to exchange a kiss.

His cheek came around to hers, tenderly nuzzling it, and she felt his breath on her ear, which made her melt. "You've got this one!" he whispered.

"I hope so, I'm nervous," she said, then softly, "I've missed you!"

"Tell me about it!" he boomed.

MAGGIE WAS A quiet, watchful child but, at the same time, engaged and inquisitive. She was polite but also confident. Over dinner, she asked adultlike questions, sometimes encouraging the conversation if there was a lull. Matt's daughter sought to put people at ease, and Ingrid felt grateful for it. She felt insecure about her cooking—she was no Freya in the kitchen. Had she over-grilled the scallops? Was the reduction of blackberry vinegar too tart or too sweet? Did Maggie even like scallops?

"As a matter of fact, I'm a pescatarian. I don't eat red meat," Maggie reassured her. "It's perfect. Really! These are so moist and yummy."

Ingrid laughed, sipping her wine. "So is it an ideological or health choice to be a pescatarian?"

"Ideological to a degree but also a texture thing. The texture of meat makes me think of the poor animal. I worry about lobsters, but I just love the way they taste. Have you ever read David Foster Wallace's essay?"

"'Consider the Lobster'?" asked Ingrid.

Maggie nodded, batting her eyelashes. Matt winked encouragingly at Ingrid. She had scored points. "It does make you think. So sad about the author's suicide. Dad says he was a genius but he hated all of his footnotes." She laughed. She was indeed a precocious child, thought Ingrid. "So Dad says you're doing some research on Salem? The witch hunts and trials?"

Ingrid was a little taken aback and looked to Matt for reassurance. She wasn't sure how much the young girl knew about her background.

"Maggie's always been fascinated by the macabre, haven't you, kid? I thought I'd tell her a little about your work . . . as an archivist and history scholar." Matt coughed.

"I've been digging into it a little—trying to see if I can figure out what was the spark—what started it . . ."

"It was the girls, wasn't it?" asked Maggie. "Girls my age."

Ingrid nodded. "You're familiar with the story?"

"A little. I know it started with girls having weird fits."

"Yes, Betty and Abigail. It was in the parsonage, the house of Reverend Samuel Parris, Betty's father and Abigail's uncle, where they started having those strange convulsions. When they wouldn't stop, rumors began circulating that the girls were bewitched. Things took a bad turn when one of their neighbors, Mary Sibley, decided to take matters into her own hands, asking Parris's Caribbean Indian slaves, Tituba and her husband, John Indian, to bake a witch's cake."

"What's that?" asked Maggie, her eyes full of wonder. She had pushed her plate aside to lean forward toward Ingrid.

Ingrid looked to Matt. She smiled uncomfortably. "I don't know if I should . . . It's not particularly appetizing."

"Go ahead, she can take it."

A witch's cake, Ingrid explained, was to be used for countermagic. It was to be baked with some of Betty's and Abby's urine, then fed to Parris's dog. If the dog became seized with fits, it would prove that dark magic was at play. Or the animal might also run to the witch responsible for the girls' fits, thereby pointing out the culprit.

"So what happened?" asked Maggie, breathless. "Did the dog lose it?"

Ingrid shook her head. "Mr. Parris found the cake as it was cooling, before it was actually fed to the dog. He beat Tituba to a pulp once he found out what it was and chastised poor Mary Sibley in church before all the parishioners, stating that with Mary's actions, 'the devil hath been raised among us.'"

"Sheesh!" commented Maggie, and Matt laughed at the expression.

"Parris's position in the village was tenuous, and he wasn't a well-liked man. I think he might have been afraid that his girls would soon be accused of being witches themselves. If that happened, he could lose his job, his home, everything. So he did what he could to shift the focus off his girls, off himself. But with his words to his parishioners, in a sense, the devil *had* been raised. At that point, other girls in the village began having fits, too. Hysteria spread like a contagion. But now Parris needed a culprit, someone to take the blame. He badgered Betty and Abby to tell him who exactly had bewitched them."

73

"And did they say?"

Ingrid looked down at her hands. She had lived through the history she was retelling, she knew how it ended. "Sadly, yes. Many people were imprisoned and hanged."

Maggie shivered. "Do you think any of it was real? Do you think the girls might have been . . . cursed somehow?"

Before Ingrid could answer, Matt cleared his throat. "Speaking of witch's cake, I'm having a terrible hankering for dessert. You make us anything, Ingrid?"

Ingrid smiled at Matt's little inside joke.

"But, Dad, Ingrid hasn't answered my question," Maggie admonished.

INGRID SUGGESTED THEY go into the kitchen for ice cream, strawberries, and whipped cream first before she answered Maggie. She passed around the bowls and took a bite before addressing the issue. "Do I think the girls' fits were real? No, of course not. They were faking it. In my opinion, it probably started out as a prank that got out of hand and the girls couldn't recant their statements without being punished themselves. By the time they did take back their words, it was too late. So many of the victims had already perished. The remaining accused were eventually released but still had to pay the jailer's fees . . ."

"Ugh! That's awful!" Maggie scooped up the melted ice cream at the bottom of her bowl, mulling it all over. She attempted to hide a yawn. "I wonder what gave them the idea to even do such a thing."

Ingrid had been wondering that herself and had recently come across a document that had proven to be very revealing: a pamphlet published in 1689 by an obscure Boston clergyman, a minister who went by the name of Continence Hooker. *An Essay on Remarkable, Illustrious, and Invisible Occurrences Relating to Bewitchments and Possessions.* But they would be here all night if she got into that, and she knew at this point that Maggie wouldn't be adverse to the idea. She couldn't do that to poor Matt.

"It's hard to believe girls could cause so much trouble, huh?" Maggie asked.

"Not too hard." Matt smirked.

Ingrid nodded. Girls had done this. Young girls, prepubescents, adolescents, innocent of the consequences of their actions. It was hard to believe they had desired to cause so much pain, so much evil. Could they have been manipulated somehow? Used? She wondered . . .

"Well, it's late, and it looks like we're all tired," she said. "I gave you an earful! Maybe another time we can talk about it more?"

Maggie nodded as she took a last scoop from her bowl.

Matt tilted his head. "Well, I better get this one home to bed."

Maggie looked at her father, scrunching her forehead. "I'm not tired!"

Matt laughed. "Sure you aren't, Pidge."

"Pidge?" asked Ingrid.

"Pigeon? There's a kid's book about not wanting to go to sleep," Maggie explained.

"It used to be her favorite."

"Dad still thinks I'm three years old," Maggie said, rolling her eyes. "Fine, let's go. Ingrid, where's the bathroom?" she asked.

Ingrid told her, and when she turned to Matt she had a new appreciation for him. He was a good father, devoted, loving. She had the urge to lean over the table and kiss the freckles on his nose. It appeared he had the same idea, as he put his hands on her face and kissed her gently.

After he pulled away, they stared into each other's eyes, elbows on the kitchen table. "Did I do okay?" Ingrid asked.

"Better. She's crazy about you! Like I told you she would be."

Ingrid smiled. She'd always wanted a daughter, and she had to remind herself that Maggie already had a mother.

chapter eleven

Of Gods and Men

By Sunday, Joanna and Norman had made it most of the way across Pennsylvania but not quite to the border of Ohio and had stopped for the night at the Happy Hunting Lodge, a bed-and-breakfast off I-80, smack in the middle of the snowy woods. The two-story centuries-old brick-and-wood salt-box appeared run-down from the outside, but the interior was clean and cozy.

The walls of the room—the "Gleeful Newlyweds Suite" of all things—were lemon, decorated with small oval- and square-framed sepia photographs of stocky-looking men and women with squinty eyes. There was a heavy, antique wooden bed made up with crisp white cotton sheets. In the bathroom, squeezed into a triangular wedge beneath the sloping roof, the brass fixtures gleamed, as did the glossy white claw-foot tub. Joanna found it heavenly to sink inside, washing off the dust from the road. After a long soak, she threw on one of the complimentary plush terry robes.

In the bedroom, she stood over the dresser, her wet silver hair a twist over a shoulder, as she lined up Norman's evening meds, extracting a pill from each container—high blood pressure, cholesterol, and so on. Altogether, he had four different pills to take. Being immortals didn't make them impervious to the ailments of age, and these days they found themselves especially vulnerable with their magic ebbing.

She looked out the window into the darkness of the woods, where a thin stream threaded through the trees. An owl hooted. Norman lay on the bed with an abstracted expression, his hands clasped behind his head.

"Remember the first time we walked to the Bofrir?" Joanna asked as she sat on the side of the bed, offering him a glass of water and the pills in her palm. Everything that was happening now had started back then, in Asgard, when the bridge was still standing. They were Nord and Skadi, gods of the sea and earth, back when the universe had begun, when everything in the nine worlds was new, and even their love was a nascent discovery, fluttering eyelashes against cheeks, a very first kiss, delectable, sweet, untainted. They had walked the Bofrir, that rainbow path wrought of dragon bone, the vessel that entwined the powers of all gods within, connecting Asgard to Midgard.

"Remember?" she repeated.

Norman sat up and took the pills silently. He placed the glass on the bedside table next to his phone. "My body might have weakened, my magic waned, but I am not senile yet, Jo." Lying back down, he took in a breath. "I remember, we stared across that great abyss, wondering what it was like on the other side."

"And now we're stuck here, unable to return," she said.

"Well, would you? Go back?" asked Norman. "I mean now, having lived in Midgard? Would you want it any other way?"

The last was a challenging question. The bridge's destruction had imperiled their lives—the lives of gods as well as mortals. As paradoxical as it was, she wouldn't trade her experience in Midgard for anything. "I love it here," she concluded.

"Yes," said Norman. "This is home now."

"But *why* did it happen? And what exactly happened that

day? We still don't know." Joanna sighed, frustrated. The bridge had been destroyed and now Killian Gardiner—the god Balder—had been accused as the culprit and seized by the Valkyries. But if anyone believed Killian was truly behind it, Joanna had a bridge to sell them.

"Well," he said, "we do know that Freddie was there, since his trident destroyed the bridge and was found in its ruins, and that Killian was a bystander. Killian attempted to shift the time line to bring the bridge back, but he couldn't. He also tried to keep Loki there, but of course he got away. Neither Freddie nor Killian saw what really happened though. Or they don't remember. Or their memories were tampered with."

"It's Loki, it's always been Loki," Joanna said. From the beginning her suspicions always ran toward Bran Gardiner, better known as Loki. Freya had seen to it that he had been banished from North Hampton, but where was he now? The dark god of mischief had a vendetta against Freya and her family. Loki had been sent to the frozen depths for his part in the bridge's demise, and Joanna was sure he was behind Freya's disappearance as well. She looked at Norman, her blue eyes shining in the dimly lit room.

Her husband nodded. "It does appear that Loki's powers prevailed and he can travel through the passages of time as he wishes. But no one actually saw him destroy the bridge, so no one knows what really happened."

"But it had to be Loki. His powers increased, he can move between worlds; it had to be him."

"Not necessarily," replied Norman with a frown.

"You have an alternate theory?"

"I might."

"Care to share it?"

"Not yet," Norman said, and it was clear he was thinking of

that long ago time, when they had been young and in love. Oh, the suitors she had had. Joanna smiled to herself. She could have had the most powerful god in the universe, but she had wanted Norm.

They fell silent. The owl outside their window had quieted, too, and the only sounds were of the wind through the forest and the old B and B creaking on its stone foundation. Norman's cell rang, and they both jumped.

Norm glimpsed at the caller ID. "It's Art!"

"Oh, thank the gods," said Joanna.

It was strange to hear his brother's voice, which sounded so tired and gravelly. "Art! How are you? You sound as if you've been living in a cave!"

Joanna could hear Arthur's muffled response, but she couldn't make out the words. She stared inquisitively at Norman, egging him on to tell her something.

"Huh!" Norm turned to Joanna. "Well, what do you know? . . . He's hiding out in a cave in Ohio." He signaled to Joanna to grab pen and paper from the suite's desk, and when she brought them over, he scribbled down the directions his brother gave him.

79

chapter twelve

The Salon des Refusés

G ert and Freddie's living room was filled with cigarette smoke that coiled upward to the ceiling. Someone had brought a small vintage record player that scratched out John Coltrane's *Blue Train* in the background, a bluesy, moody, slipping, sliding tempo.

Gert's friends from school had dubbed these smoky, candlelit get-togethers their Salon des Refusés. The French term was usually meant for a gallery displaying art rejected by the mainstream, but in this case it was these kids who saw themselves as the unaccepted masterpieces. They were splayed about the apartment, eating olives, crackers, and cheese, drinking red wine, languidly smoking cigarettes. They all came from wealthy families, but they liked to affect an impoverished air. Discussing Sartre, Camus, Nietzsche, Kierkegaard, and Heidegger, they thought themselves incredibly soigné and sophisticated.

Sam, with a thin mustache and soul patch, lay sideways on a beanbag, peering out from behind Ray-Ban Wayfarers. Beside him, cross-legged, sat Gert's sister Cassandra, a.k.a. Swanwhite: long, pallid, anorexic thin. She had become part of the crew since she began dating Sam, whom she'd met at a campus party Gert had invited her to last semester. She didn't say much but looked the part. There was another couple, a young man with a scraggly beard and a woman with boyish-short hair and bright red lips, whose names Freddie couldn't remember.

Freddie thought the pretentious bunch mostly harmless, although the worst among them was Judith—a philosophy major who sported a slanting jet-black bob with uneven feathery bangs high above her wide forehead. The voice that issued from her crimson lips was icy and mocking, especially when directed at Freddie.

Judith took a drag from her cigarette and exhaled slowly. "So tell us, Fred, when we talk of *existence preceding essence*, what meaning exactly do you find in being a fireman?" She had a touch of an unidentifiable accent, which Freddie chalked up to coming from Fakeland. "Does it help quell the doldrums? Bring some significance to an otherwise senseless and absurd existence? Or is it simply that you are fulfilling a little *boyhood* fantasy?"

The kids in the room laughed.

Freddie was very annoyed. Normally her barbs amused him, but this time he wasn't going to take it. "Well, Judy," he said, taking liberty with her name as she did with his, "you pride yourself on being such a feminist and yet you say 'fireman' instead of the more up-to-date and gender unspecific *firefighter*?"

"Ooh!" said the room, impressed.

"Touché!" said Judith. "But you still haven't answered my question."

Although she was just trying to impress everyone in the room, Freddie found her question stupid. It didn't really deserve an answer, but if she was going to press him he was going to answer. "Being a firefighter *is* probably as meaningful as it gets, Judy. I save lives."

"Aha!" said Judith. "Lives that perhaps don't need or want to be saved!"

Freddie couldn't quite believe what he was hearing now.

"That's what it all comes back to," piped in Sam. "In the overwhelming face of the absurd, there is only one major question we must ask ourselves—"

"Whether to live or die," finished Cassandra. Sam leaned over and kissed her—his good little student.

Gert, who was sitting on the couch, coughed. "You guys are getting morbid."

Finally, thought Freddie, his wife had decided she'd had enough of their nonsense. "Yeah, that's totally idiotic," he added. "If you're in a house that's going up in flames, all you want is to make it out alive. The urge to live precedes everything." He laughed. "These are all just empty intellectual concepts— theoretical, speculative. They have nothing to do with real life. Firefighting is *life*." There. He had said something intelligent and *meaningful*. He could keep up with these college kids, even though they acted as if he were beneath them. He looked to Gert for approval, but she rolled her eyes.

"My friends are not morons," she reprimanded.

He hadn't said that, and he couldn't believe Gert wasn't taking his side.

"No, we're not," said Judith, smirking in a way that meant she was about to hit them with her SAT scores again—or brandish the name of their university like a cudgel, as if Freddie gave a rat's ass. "And why . . ."

"Why what?" What did Gert see in these people? Just then he spotted Kelda and Nyph peeking their heads out of their bedroom. Gert had asked them to stay out of the way for the evening. They mouthed something to Freddie, but he couldn't make it out. "Excuse me," he said, and left the room.

"He still hasn't gotten rid of his little friends?" Judith asked Gert as Freddie strode toward the pixies' room. He could hear her continuing to poison his wife's mind, loudly whispering something about a grown man hanging out with teens and how that was weird and how she was worried for Gert.

Val was strumming an electric guitar that wasn't plugged in. Who knew where he had gotten it. Sven lay on the top of a bunk bed, reading Raymond Chandler's *Farewell, My Lovely*, while Irdick was taking a nap in the lower bunk.

"What?" Freddie asked Kelda and Nyph, who were grabbing at his T-shirt.

"We hate Judith. We *hate* her!" Nyph said.

"Yeah," said Kelda. "She's awful. She deserves a comeuppance."

"She's Gert's friend," said Freddie. "I'm warning you guys, leave her alone."

"But why is she so mean to you?" asked Nyph. "You're the best."

"She wants him," said Irdick, rolling over.

"Obvious!" added Sven.

"Who doesn't want Freddie?" threw in Val, gliding his fingers down the neck of his guitar.

Freddie shrugged, suddenly exhausted. He decided to go lie down in his room. He hadn't gotten much sleep last night. There had been a particular nasty fire: a house in the suburbs had burned down, and they had rescued a baby and three-year-old girl. The parents were nowhere to be found. The police suspected foul play.

He lay on his bed, listening to the vapid chatter in the living room and quickly fell asleep. He woke with a start from a dream in which he had been engulfed by flames that wouldn't obey him as they usually did.

Gert hung over him, shaking him by the shoulders. "Where's Judith?" she asked.

Freddie blinked his eyes. It took a while to orient himself. "I don't know. With you? I just came in here to nap."

"Everyone's leaving now but Judith's disappeared. I thought she went to the bathroom."

Freddie reached a hand to Gert's peachy cheek and caressed it. "She probably left without telling you."

Gert turned away, rebuking his caress. "I'm walking them out."

Freddie watched her go. He listened to his wife see her friends off, then return to do her toiletries in the bathroom. Not a peep from the pixies. They must have gone to sleep or left for their nocturnal adventures. Maybe there was hope for him and Gert to get lucky tonight.

Gert returned to the bedroom. Freddie sat up to watch her undress. She pulled off her jeans, then her striped navy tee, her blond hair cascading down across her shoulders. Standing in only her underwear, her back was long and muscular. She had little depressions at the base of her spine, dimples above each buttock, which he found very sexy. She threw on an old T-shirt, climbed into bed, and turned away from him. Freddie sighed. They had turned into an old, silent, apathetic couple.

A loud thump came from farther inside the apartment, then more thumping.

Gert turned to him. "What's that?"

"Beats me," said Freddie. It sounded as if it had come from the terrace. He rose, and Gert followed him.

When he pulled the curtain away from the sliding glass doors to the terrace, Gert right behind him, they both stared. There was Judith, gagged with one of Freddie's bandannas, strapped to a chair that was now tipped against the glass so that her shoulder and forehead slumped against it. She was staring at them, eyes wide and frantic. It had probably taken her some time to inch the chair to the sliding glass doors so she could heave herself against them and make the noise. Her hair, which was

84

usually neatly styled, looked wild. She shimmied, letting out a muffled grunt, urging them to come outside.

Gert swung the door open. "Oh, my God! Judith! What happened?" She removed the gag and saw that Judith had been strapped to the chair with several of Freddie's belts.

"Those friends of yours!" Judith muttered. "The little ones!"

"You put them up to this!" Gert accused as she swung around on him. "Freddie, how could you!" she said, looking utterly betrayed as she unsnapped the belts and released her friend. "It's freezing out here! She could have died!"

But did she want to live? Freddie wanted to ask but refrained. "It wasn't me, I swear!" He called for Nyph and Kelda but they were gone.

Freddie knew the pixies were just trying to help, but at this rate they were going to help get him a divorce.

chapter thirteen

Detective Noble

M att had called Ingrid to invite her over for a Saturday-
night movie. He was all by himself, he told her, missed
her something crazy, and thought he could tempt her away from
her books by watching Hitchcock's *To Catch a Thief.*

"I'll come right over," she said, and could hear him grinning
on the other end of the line.

She was down in Joanna's study, wading through more
books for the answers, but she needed to unwind. She missed
Matt something crazy, too. Mother and Father were out there
looking for Uncle Art—surely she could take a break. Save for
meeting with Matt and Maggie last weekend, she had been going nonstop, and they hadn't spent any time alone in what seemed
eons. What kind of relationship was that? Not a relationship at
all—which he had been frequently reminding her lately.

Now Matt sat on his side of the king-size bed, while Ingrid
sat on the other, her shoes kicked off, arms looped around her
knees, a bowl of popcorn between them. It was like having to
start from scratch all over again to break through the barrier of
mutual shyness.

Matt pointed the remote at the flat screen across from the
bed. A swell of music rose, and "VistaVision Motion Picture
High-Fidelity" came on the screen superimposed over a snowy

peak. Technicolor. Exterior day: the shop window of a travel agency festooned with posters of France, behind the glass a cruise ship model, then a mock Eiffel Tower farther inside. Cars rolling past reflected in the window. The camera zoomed in on a poster: IF YOU LOVE LIFE, YOU'LL LOVE FRANCE. Cut: a woman screams at the discovery of her missing jewels.

Matt turned to Ingrid and put a hand on her thigh. "You had quite a captive audience the other night," he told her. "Maggie can't stop talking about those Puritan girls and what they did."

Ingrid smiled. "I've been obsessing about them, too."

"So how's the work going? Find anything useful?"

"A little. I think I've figured out how the girls got the idea." Ingrid unfolded her knees, reached for the remote, and turned off the television. Matt grabbed the bowl of popcorn between them and moved it to his bedside table, then he rolled over, closer to her, lying on his side, head propped up on his pillows, his hand still on her body.

Ingrid was very conscious of the feel of his hand on her thigh, its weight and the tingling sensation that sent a flush to her cheeks. The slightest touch from him and her entire body grew weak. It felt like it had been ages since they had last made out. She carefully placed a hand on his as she told him about that document she had found in the archives. Continence Hooker's essay.

"Reverend Hooker?" Matt chuckled. He scooted up to her to rest the back of his head on her lap.

Ingrid laughed nervously. For a moment, she wasn't sure where to place her hands. Matt had closed his eyes. She stared down at his head, his wide, creased forehead, the freckles splashed across his nose, the fetching cleft in his chin. He was really so handsome. "Yep, that was really his name," she said, running her fingers through his soft red hair. There. That felt natural. Why was she being so self-conscious? Could he tell? He looked like a sleepy, very contented cat. "Continence Hooker, can you imagine!"

"Better than Incontinent Hooker, I suppose, that would be a real problem," he said, opening his eyes to look at her while she told him a little more about the atmosphere of the times.

Apparently, in late seventeenth-century New England, individuals who were struck by strange fits entailing severe physical contortions and nonsensical babbling were not completely out of the ordinary. Sensational cases of bewitchment were documented by leading Boston clergymen, and these essays were published as pamphlets that became widely popular. Ingrid rattled on excitedly, "You know, they were kind of like cheapie bestsellers, like today's self-published e-books about the afterlife or alien abductions or paranormal activity."

Matt whistled the theme song from *The X-Files*.

Ingrid giggled, then went on. "The thing you need to know about these essays is that they were written for a purpose, which was to encourage a belief in the supernatural. Read, the devil." She went on to explain what she meant more specifically.

Around this time, in the last decades of the seventeenth century, figureheads of colonial society—both in the church and political office, the two going hand in hand—had grown to fear the effects of commercialism, scientific thought, and individualism on the old Puritan ideals. They believed that these insidious new ways were deleterious to morality. Ingrid concluded, "These pamphlets were designed to show what would happen if one let the devil of modernism through one's door."

Matt's eyes were closed again, and she suddenly feared that all her dry academic talk might have put him to sleep. But then his eyes popped open, bright and alert. "So you're saying these things were designed to keep the masses in line?"

Ingrid laughed. "I've certainly hooked a smart one!"

Matt smiled and brought up a hand to play with her hair.

Ingrid wasn't finished. Someone like Reverend Parris, she explained, would have subscribed to such a belief system and purchased these kinds of pamphlets in Boston, keeping them as well as a Bible in his upstairs study. "Here's the thing that gave me the chills when I put it all together. Hooker's descriptions of one young woman's fits in a household on the outskirts of Boston were nearly identical to the ones recorded by various witnesses of Abby and Betty. Not just nearly identical, but word for word, action for action, almost the same thing. The girls used the same words, same combinations, phrases, even sentences, to describe the tortures they endured and the specters and familiars they saw, as in Hooker's account."

"Could it be a coincidence?" asked Matt.

Ingrid shook her head. "If anything, these girls were lacking in originality."

"So what you're saying is . . ."

"They got the idea from a book. *This* pamphlet."

"Okay." Matt nodded. He sat up. "But remember these are rural girls in seventeenth-century Salem . . ."

Ingrid nodded, impressed that Matt saw the problem so quickly. "I know. How could they get the idea from a book? They couldn't read. They couldn't even sign their names on their testimonies. They used *X*'s instead. So there goes that theory . . ."

"Hold on, don't give up yet . . ."

Ingrid stared at him.

"The girls couldn't read . . . so someone read it to them. Someone who wanted them to know about it, or someone who didn't know what they would do . . ." said Matt.

She felt her skin tingle in excitement. "Matt, I could kiss you—of course! Someone read Hooker's pamphlet to them! But who?"

Matt smiled. "We'll figure that out later," he said. "Now about that kiss . . ."

chapter fourteen

Cavern in the Woods

By early afternoon, Joanna and Norman had arrived at the cave. Up a path through a craggy cliff, there was a wooden door set into the mouth of the entrance. They found it unlocked and it creaked open as they set foot inside.

This was no ordinary cave. The walls were indeed made of the same craggy black stone as the cliff, but it wasn't what Joanna had envisioned hearing the word *cave*. There were linoleum floors, a kitchen in the back, and a couch and bookshelves in front. To their dismay the place was ransacked—papers scattered everywhere, a computer lying on the floor, pillows sliced open, gutted, eiderdown stuffing everywhere. The fridge as well as the stove had been left open. It was a mess. They exchanged a troubled look. "What happened?" Joanna asked. They began to search the place, calling Arthur's name.

"He's not here," Norman yelled from the kitchen.

"Not here either," she reported from the bathroom, whose tub was carved into the rock.

Norm came around a counter, and they both took a seat in the dining area.

"Now what?" said Joanna in tears, her emotions having gotten the best of her. Arthur had seemed like their best bet at getting to Freya, and now he was gone.

Norman reached out for her hands. His brother had either been taken or he had moved to his next hiding spot. And someone had been here looking for something. Whatever it was, their hopes of Art leading them through the passages of time were dashed. Perhaps it had something to do with the young wolves Arthur was always talking about, some old favor that he had to do for a friend. In any event, that was another story.

Joanna looked up at him, and he wiped her tears. "Don't despair yet, Jo. There is one last resort."

She knew what he was going to say but hoped he wouldn't.

"The Oracle."

She shook her head. The Oracle was best left alone.

Norman insisted. "It might be the only way to save our daughter."

chapter fifteen

Fighting Fire with Fire

S now was melting on the sidewalks of New Haven. The little cul-de-sac was full of the scent of wet leaves and grass, along with a darker, acrid smell. The house on the end of the street was on fire. Flames licked the upstairs windows. A girl on the sidewalk was screaming that one of her roommates was trapped inside. "I know Sadie's in there. She was asleep when we left for the party. Get her! Please!"

Red, white, and blue lights flashed over the houses. Neighbors in pajamas had come outside to watch. A cluster of frat boys in flannel shirts, hoodies, and jeans commented on the action. "You think chucking that keg of beer at it would help?" one said.

"Why would you do that, dude?"

Another giggled. "The flames are awesome, man! God, I'm high."

"Me, too. You mean this is real?"

The girl, raccoon eyed and looking rumpled in a puffy jacket over a short dress, explained to the first responders that when she had returned home from the party two fire trucks, an ambulance, and three police cars were already on the scene. The truck ladders were extended and several firefighters had climbed onto the roof and were hacking away. One of the firemen sought to calm the girl down, instructing her to sit on the curb out of the way. The EMTs came over and gave her a blanket. "My other roommates are still at the party, but Sadie—she stayed home. She's in there," the girl sobbed to a pair of police officers taking notes.

Inside the house, Freddie was making his way through the smoke-filled corridor upstairs. Somewhere behind him was his team—Big Dave, Hunter, and Jennie, the lone firewoman on the team. The trapped girl had been calling out to them for help from one of the rooms in the back, but now she'd gone quiet.

The hallway seemed to go on forever, the rooms on the way empty, filling with smoke and flames. It was as if someone had splashed the entire place with an accelerant. And there was not one fire sprinkler in this campus house. Huge possible lawsuit, Freddie thought. Underneath his mask with the self-contained breathing apparatus, he could hear his breathing getting louder.

Freddie reached out a hand, pushing at the flames along one wall, redirecting them: they moved down the wall but unexpectedly billowed back. Usually they responded to Freddie's every command, the way a musician in the orchestra pit follows a conductor's baton and hand gestures: rising, lowering, fading, stopping. Tonight the flames had a mind of their own.

If he didn't find the girl soon, they were screwed. First came self-preservation, then rescue. But he knew she was close, and he needed to get to her. At this point, they would have to exit via the roof. The fire had followed them up the stairs. He remembered a recent dream in which he'd been surrounded, engulfed by flames, and realized the nightmare was presently unfolding before him. He had no power over the flame—he had become an ordinary firefighter in the midst of an out-of-control fire, a house on the verge of collapse. Sweat poured off his forehead, trickled down his neck. He heard the axes against the roof.

He moved farther inside a room. He sensed her. He could hear her heart pounding, or was that his? The carpet burned in spots. The crackling grew louder around him. He pointed his flashlight and saw an opened door, the bathroom, the girl on the tile floor, curled in a ball. Something hit hard against his helmet, falling behind him, grazing his bunker jacket—flaming debris. He quickly moved toward the girl in the bathroom. Flames leaped out at him from the side. He made a hand gesture and they rippled away, but then detached and spread, crackling and flickering, barring his way. He couldn't stop them. The fire paid no attention to him.

Dammit! He knew his magic had been losing vigor, but he hadn't been aware it had become this feeble. He needed to save the girl and get out. He moved forward, but the flames moved toward him. He lunged to the side. The flames lunged, flinging Freddie onto the floor like a wrestler, clasping a hand of fire at his neck. His mask fell off, and Freddie gasped in scalding flames. *This is it*, he thought.

Images flashed through his mind. He remembered the first time he had *really* seen Gert—that day on the campus when Hilly had broken up with him. He saw her dancing along the lamppost-lit path, her blond hair swaying, reflecting the light, the way she smiled as she turned to him.

Fire burned at his neck as the flames squeezed the air out of his lungs. He had never experienced death before, unlike the other gods, who would die and come back; he had been trapped for almost all of his long life in Limbo. He wondered if he should be afraid. They always came back, of course, but it would mean saying good-bye to this life. Good-bye to Gert for now, and who knew if he would be able to find her again? Then someone was pushing him, rolling his body, calling his name, spraying him with foam. The fire vanished, its hot weight dissipated. Jennie kneeled beside him. "Big Dave's got this one," she said. "It's okay, Freddie. You're okay. We're getting you out of here."

F REDDIE WOKE TO faint noises: beeping, whispers, squeaking, breathing. He blinked his eyes open and found himself staring up at a pale pink ceiling. His vision was blurry, the fluorescent lights too glaring. He felt his body's deadweight, so heavy on the hospital bed. He turned his head to the side, and there was Gert, staring at him with so much tenderness. She was here.

"You're awake," she whispered, rising from her chair. She came over and touched his forehead, leaned over and kissed him gently.

His throat was dry and sore, and he could barely get a word out. "Gert," he managed. "The girl . . . is she okay?"

"She's fine. You saved her. They wouldn't have known she was there if it hadn't been for you." Gert smiled lovingly at him and brought a glass of water up to his parched lips, helping him hold his head up so he could drink. "I was so scared when I heard what happened! They told me a beam fell on top of you, pinning you down! What happened—is it because we can't do anything anymore?"

Freddie nodded. His body ached, and there was a stinging sensation along his neck. *All out of magic.* Gert could feel it, too. They didn't talk about it much, but it was there—a slow transition to mortality. What did it mean?

"I'm sorry about Judith," he said. "She didn't deserve that."

"It's not your fault. The pixies confessed." A small smile played on her lips. "And anyway, it was sort of funny . . ." She laughed.

He laughed. "I love you," he said.

"I love you so much!" Gert blinked, and tears pushed out

95

from beneath her thick lashes, rolling down her cheeks. "I thought I had lost you!"

"Never!" said Freddie.

WHEN THEY RETURNED to the apartment they discovered they had the place to themselves for once, the pixies out of sight.

Freddie lay on the bed and Gert lay on top of him, her thick hair cascading over him as she gently kissed at his wounds, her lips a healing balm. He reached for the clasp at the back of her bra and took it off one-handed.

"You're such a pro," Gert teased.

He grinned as they moved together, Gert on top, grinding. Freddie felt alive, so alive, and life was good again—Gert was back.

chapter sixteen

The Perfect Family

Matt had Maggie for the weekend. Even though Ingrid had made a point of telling him she would be busy, she harbored a small, secret wish that he might call, surprise her, ask her to do something impromptu with them. The truth was Ingrid was lonely. Her research was at a standstill: while she had zeroed in on the probable source of the hysteria, there were still so many things she didn't know. *Why?* Why did the girls do it? Why did they suddenly begin to point fingers and call their various acquaintances and friends witches?

In the meantime, Joanna and Norman had gone MIA, and she had called Freddie to see if he and Gert wanted to spend the weekend on Long Island, at home, bring the pixies even—but they were all busy, too. Ingrid had visited the other week after Freddie's accident, and she was relieved to find her little brother doing well. She missed him, but as she understood it, he and Gert were having some kind of second honeymoon.

She called her best friend, Hudson, but he was in the city with his boyfriend, Scott. That was odd—hadn't Hudson mentioned on Friday as they had closed the library that he would be in North Hampton "*all* weekend long," hard at work on that dissertation for his doctorate in Romance languages at Harvard? Ingrid had helped him pick out a few salient books for his research. How many years was it now that he had been working on his PhD? Was it going on eight? No wonder, thought Ingrid, shaking her head at her friend, if he was running off to the city to go shopping when he promised to buckle down.

Her pride kept her from calling Matt and admitting she had free time.

It was noon on a Saturday. A long, solitary weekend stretched ahead. Who else might she call? Tabitha? But she remembered Tab and Chad were off on their babymoon to some resort in the Bahamas.

Dejected, Ingrid walked into the kitchen to make a sandwich. But because her rebellious teen of a mother had vanished on a joy ride, the fridge was nearly empty. An expired yogurt. Limp carrots. Old Chinese food in to-go containers from Hung Sung Lo's. *Ugh!* Part of Freya's genius was scaring up a meal when there was barely a thing left in the fridge and cupboards. Ingrid longed to hear her sister's laughter, wished Freya was in the kitchen making one of those magical meals, the two of them talking about anything that came to mind.

She needed to get out of this gloomy, quiet house. She would grab a panini at the local café, bring a newspaper, catch up on current events. She had become such a bore with her head stuck in the seventeenth century and had no idea about what was going on in the world lately. Tabitha had been appalled when Ingrid had admitted she hadn't known the actor who played a young hipster in the show *Williamsburg* had died in a plane crash last week, one of those little four-seater jets.

Ingrid had never even heard of that show.

A SCATTERING OF CLOUDS hung low on the horizon, but overhead, the sky was a clear robin's egg blue. It was cold but the breeze smelled of the sea, and there were a number of winter tourists about, who liked the cheaper rates and had been lucky enough to find their way to the charming little town. When Ingrid arrived at Geppetto's, the café at the end of the park, the outdoor tables in the covered and heated patio were all taken. The hostess came over, asking how many were joining her.

Ashamed of being alone, Ingrid glanced down. "Just me," she muttered.

The girl smiled as if she pitied her. "Great!" she said on a high note, then gave Ingrid the once-over. "I'll see what I can do." She pivoted on her heel.

Ingrid stood in line, her purse dangling off a shoulder, her newspaper in hand. She lifted her sunglasses onto the crown of her head and scanned the tables. Someone was waving. Matt. She started. He was sitting with Maggie and a gorgeous-looking brunette in big dark sunglasses. Who *was* this woman who was leaning toward Matt, whispering something in his ear, looking a little too intimate for Ingrid's taste. Maggie looked up and saw Ingrid, and began flailing her arms.

"Over here!" the young girl greeted.

Ingrid had no other choice than to make her way toward them.

"Hey!" said Matt. "What are you doing here? I thought you were busy all weekend."

"I am. I, uh . . . just needed a break and something to eat. I do have to get back to work," she lied. She patted her bun, making sure it was in place.

The woman removed her sunglasses and stared expectantly at Ingrid, smiling. Something about her recalled an elegant Italian movie star, like a Sophia Loren or Claudia Cardinale. She was the opposite of Ingrid: busty, hourglass shaped, dark, sensual looking. Matt had compared Ingrid to Grace Kelly, but next to this bombshell she felt pale, thin, and gangly.

Maggie stared at Ingrid with her big, watchful eyes. "The stuffed clams are to die for. Come, sit with us!"

Ingrid felt at a loss and the woman elbowed Matt, giving him a look. *"Matthew!"* she chastised. There seemed an ease and familiarity between them.

It felt as if the ground, which had already been shaky when she saw them, completely dropped from beneath Ingrid. Her pulse sped.

Matt looked a little uncomfortable as he made the introductions. "Ingrid, this is Mariza Valdez, Maggie's mom. Mariza this is *Ingrid*!"

"Yes, of course." Mariza smiled. "Margarita talks so much about you."

Oh right, of course, Ingrid thought. She had completely forgotten that there was a mom in the picture. Ingrid couldn't help but note that Mariza called Matt by his full name ("Matthew," which sounded so *sexy* somehow) and Maggie "Margarita"—had she been wrong in calling her Maggie? But Matt called her Maggie. The woman reached out a hand, and Ingrid shook it.

"Delighted!" Ingrid said with a smile that hurt her cheeks.

The hostess had come around with a couple to seat them at the table that had cleared beside them.

"Mari!" cooed the woman being seated as she looked their way.

"Rowena!" Mariza cried.

Rowena and Mariza fawned over each other, each saying how great the other looked. Ingrid glanced at Matt, who rolled his eyes. He motioned for her to sit beside him. Maggie continued to smile at her imploringly. The whole situation was growing more awkward by the second.

Rowena Thomas.

She had been one of Ingrid's clients back in the days when she provided her once-popular counseling services at the back of the library. She hadn't seen Rowena in a while. Shortly after Freya's disappearance, Ingrid had abandoned the "witching hour," as Hudson facetiously called it, forever the skeptic about Ingrid's "witching abilities." She didn't love Hudson any less for doubting her, but in a way her mortal friend was right. Her magic had grown ineffective, and she had begun to feel like a sham. Now her office remained locked at lunch hour, a note on the door explaining that counseling services would resume at a later date. Ingrid had made Rowena a talisman for her mother's kidney problems and also a love knot or two or three. Rowena had been desperate to fall in love.

And now, horror of horrors, Ingrid spied Rowena's date: Blake Aland, the smarmy developer whose efforts at destroying the library Ingrid had successfully squelched, the same one whose advances she had spurned. This was proof that Ingrid's magic had gone utterly awry or was plain all out. All those love knots hadn't done Rowena any favors. She and Blake exchanged cold nods.

"Ingrid!" Rowena cried out. "Oh, my God, Mari, you need to see Ingrid! She's *amaaaazing*! She totally helped me. I found Blake! Maybe she can make a special something so you and Matt finally tie the knot." Laughing, she turned to Ingrid, explaining, "We all went to NoHa High together. These two have been in love *for-ev-er*! They just won't admit it."

Ingrid looked from Matt to Mariza, who both lowered their heads. Matt was shaking his. She felt as if she had caught them red-handed.

"I wish they would finally just get hitched!" Rowena continued. "Maybe one of those hair knots of yours would do the trick? What do you think, Ingrid?"

"Sure," she said, smiling wanly. *Hair knot.* How ugly that

sounded! Like something you found clogging up the drain of the bathtub. She felt herself blanch. She wasn't feeling well at all. Perhaps Mariza and Matt *should* get married. Mariza, Matthew, Margarita—their names all began with an *M*. Mariza was beautiful and exotic—even affable and warm, it seemed. They were a family. A child should be with her real mother and father—shouldn't she?

Rowena finally left, joining Blake, who had been watching with a scowl.

Matt grabbed Ingrid's hand. "Come sit next to me. Mari was just showing me some school photos of Maggie on her phone. Have a seat!"

"We haven't even ordered yet," added Maggie.

Ingrid was so flustered she could barely make out what they were saying. There was no place for her here, she realized. Maggie already had a mother. Matt should probably be with his ex-girlfriend. They looked beautiful together, they made a beautiful family. One that should be left in peace. She looked at Matt, remembering his face from the other night, lying in his bed, their bodies pressed against each other's with only a thin layer of clothing separating them, his half-lidded eyes, looking at her with such hunger and desire . . .

No. She should bow out, leave them alone, let them find their way back to each other. It was so terribly obvious that she was a third wheel—actually, *much* worse than that—a *fourth* wheel. Ingrid was many things—a witch, a goddess, a sister, a friend—but she was not a home wrecker. She excused herself quickly, saying she had a lot of work to do, and left the three of them alone.

chapter seventeen

From the Mouths
of Babes

The yellow cab let them out in Tribeca on a narrow cobble-stone street in front of an old warehouse. They looked up at the white facade. The warehouse had been built in the mid-1800s in the Italianate style, fancier in appearance than what its original purpose suggested—to provide large spaces to store goods coming into New York City's ports. Five stories tall, with enormous arched windows set apart by ornate pilasters, the building was crowned with deep cornices now painted a gray blue.

Joanna placed her hands on her hips. Under her camel overcoat she wore a red knit dress that Norm had helped her pick out—his favorite color on her with her silver hair. "Frankly, I pictured something more run-down, less ostentatious," she said.

"You know how he is," said Norman.

The door, a copper fortress of a door oxidized with a green patina, would not budge when Joanna grabbed at the handle. Norman found the buzzer to the right and pressed the single black button.

"Scan," came a female voice from the intercom.

"Excuse me?" said Norman.

An impatient exhale crackled back at them.

Joanna moved behind Norm and spoke to the wall. "We're here to see the Oracle?"

"I know," the snooty voice returned. "You still have to scan. Use your god passes!"

"We've been traveling all day. We're tired," Joanna said. She was sick of the jaded attitudes in this city.

"We have no idea what you're talking about," Norm said impatiently.

More crackling from the intercom. "The little blue glass rectangle above the intercom. You see it?" she said slowly as if they were children. They saw it. Someone had graffitied the tag DOG EARS on it in silver marker. "Put your nose right up beneath it. Scan your eyes. *That's your god pass.* Then, if you truly are who you say, the doors will open."

They did as instructed without protest, and once their retinas had been scanned, the large brass door clicked loudly and swung open.

"Take the elevator up to the top floor," the voice enunciated in a bored tone behind them.

THE ELEVATOR DOORS opened onto a large, high-ceilinged white room interspersed with thick columns. It was early evening and the light slanted through the arched windows from the direction of the Hudson River. At the center of the room was a long glass table that doubled as an aquarium. Inside it, electric-blue and tiger-striped fish darted about in bubbling green water among undulating sea plants. Joanna glimpsed a spotted moray eel slithering out from beneath a rock. On the table lay iPads displaying covers of magazines. White orbs that looked like marshmallows functioned as seats. The walls' enormous flat screens featured video art, large abstracts of moving, swirling, saturated color.

At the very end of the room before the windows, they saw the receptionist station. A clear cube with a silver laptop and a marshmallow orb. A tall young woman in a black blazer and skirt came toward them, her black patent leather heels clipping along the shining cement floor. She wore a headset, and her glossy black hair was pulled into a big knot on top of her head.

"Cappuccino or bottled water?" she asked with a mechanical smile.

"We just want to see the Oracle," said Norman with a huff.

"Cappuccino or bottled water?" she repeated.

"We'll take water," said Norman.

"Have a seat." She extended an arm like an airline hostess toward the aquarium table. "Browse an iPad. He'll be with you shortly." She swiveled around and clipped away toward a door, pressed a button, and the door slid open.

Norman took a seat. "Squishy!" he remarked.

Joanna sat down, found her cell phone, and glanced at it. "Remind me to call Ingrid when this is over."

The receptionist was already returning, carrying a tray with two tall blue glass cylinders. She mumbled into her headset as she strode toward them. "Come with me, please." They followed her to a steel door. She pressed a button and the door slid open. "Make yourselves comfortable," she instructed.

The door slid closed behind them.

"Where's the Oracle?" said Joanna.

The room was equally as large as the previous one. There was the same kind of colorful swirling art on the walls' flat screens, but nothing else besides the large clear cube at the center. Resting on top of it was an open laptop. Norman motioned with his head at the cube. They walked toward it. Norman touched the track pad. A call was coming in. Norman clicked Answer. The video feed showed an empty bed with *Star Wars* sheets and pillows. Loud heavy-metal music blasted from the speakers.

The Oracle jumped into the frame, leaning against the mound of pillows, chomping on a burrito in a silver foil wrapper. His head was shaved with a faint black stubble, but he was still too young to need to shave his chin, being about fifteen or sixteen. He had a tattoo on his neck and wore a plain white T-shirt and jeans.

"Jo, Norm! What up, homes?" he said.

"Can you turn the music down? We can barely hear you," said Joanna.

"Oh, sure." He took another bite of the burrito, then searched for something on the bed, found a remote, and clicked it. The music went off.

"Thanks," said Norm with a frown.

Joanna pushed in beside Norm and spoke at the laptop. She noted how tired she looked on the screen. "I don't know if you've heard but Freya is stuck in the seventeenth century, and we need to get her back. We believe she's in Salem Village at a very dangerous time. Last time, well, you know what happened—"

"I know, I know," said the Oracle. "She's not the only one who's trapped in the passages. It's all messed up. There are damn sinkholes everywhere. Magic's all out of whack, there's not enough here, but it looks like there's a huge concentration of it in other parts of the time line. Salem in the seventeenth century is lit up like Christmas. A ton of magical energy there for some reason. But for now"—he took another large bite of his burrito so he had to chew awhile before he could speak again, and Joanna and Norman were forced to wait—"time's stuck. Something screwy is going on with the wolves and the Fallen and the underworld. It's thrown everything into chaos. I would be there, but I can't even teleport over to you guys, so that's why we're having to chat like this."

"Okay," said Joanna, "but what does that mean for us? We can't just sit back and wait."

Norm placed his arm around Joanna's shoulders. He needed to keep her calm. The Oracle was in one of his cheery moods, but he could get cranky and gloomy like any teen and he was not above pulling a mean prank to amuse himself.

"She just means we're here if you need us," Norm said.

The Oracle grinned. "Oh, and I forgot—with time broken, if something happens to that saucy, hot daughter of yours while she's back there, it'll stick for all eternity. Time's all screwed up so that even our immortality is in question. If someone dies while this shit is going on—they're donzo. Never coming back to mid-world." Here he leaned off the bed and disappeared from the frame, then popped back in, sipping from an oversize soda cup. "Doomed to the underworld for eternity and all that."

Joanna gasped. The Oracle was saying that if Freya was hanged, as she had once been hanged before, during the first time they had endured the Salem trials, this time she would never return. Never. It all clicked into place.

This was all an elaborate plan to kill Freya.

The Oracle must have seen the desperate expressions on their faces, because he leaned in and said, "But you're in luck because there is something you could do to get around it . . ."

Joanna and Norm huddled in closer to the screen.

chapter eighteen

Gone Baby Gone

It had been a relatively peaceful day at the fire station—boisterous, carefree high jinks among the firefighters as they performed their routine housekeeping duties, washing windows, cleaning walls, sweeping floors. Freddie enjoyed the spirit of camaraderie but he also liked the structure and discipline it brought to his life. It was nice to be part of a smoothly working team, a cog in a well-oiled machine. They checked and inventoried personal protective gear, tools, and equipment for readiness: bunker jackets and trousers, gloves, boots, breathing apparatuses, rescue equipment, hoses, hand tools, and portable fire extinguishers. Freddie wrote out a report listing damaged and nonfunctioning gear. Next came checking the emergency medical-care equipment and replenishing the first-aid supplies in the trauma boxes. Then, after a training a session, it was time to break for lunch, and Freddie found his buddies Big Dave, Jennie, and Hunter.

He was in an excellent mood. Things with Gert had been ultrasmooth since his accident. He and his friends were still fixated on what happened at the last big fire and that was the usual lunch-hour conversation. The rescued college girl, Sadie, was alive and well.

"What happened, man? You're usually our main guy," Big Dave asked.

"Happens to everyone at some point. Even fire whisperers," Jennie said sagely.

Freddie took a swig of his Pepsi and gave them a crooked smile, shrugging his shoulders.

Jennie winked at him, and for a second it did cross his mind that Jennie liked him more than just as a fellow firefighter. Now that he thought about it, she was kind of cute with those freckles and oversize blue eyes. What was he thinking? He loved Gert. Things were awesome at home.

"You healed friggin' fast," noted Hunter, reaching over the lunch table to push at Freddie's head so he could see the burn mark on his neck. The towheaded Irish kid whistled, impressed. "It's looking good, my man!"

Freddie's burns *had* healed faster than an ordinary mortal's would have, but usually such healing was near instantaneous for him. His neck still appeared red in spots.

After lunch, the lieutenant eventually sent them on a call—a rather innocuous one, it turned out. An old man had tripped down some stairs in his apartment building and pulled the fire alarm. He was fine, a tough, grumpy old guy who kept refusing their emergency medical care, pushing them away, muttering unkind epithets.

Work ended at five thirty, and Freddie walked to the gym to do laps in the indoor Olympic-size pool. It had occurred to him that swimming would revive his lungs, which had felt singed from that fire and had also been slow to heal. He had taken to going to the pool in the early evenings and gotten hooked. Fire and water were his favorite elements—*his* elements as the god Fryr—but fire had betrayed him. If his powers were diminishing he needed to compensate somehow. He had been thinking that if they were slowly becoming mortals, then so be it. He and Gert would live happily ever after and die of old age together. It wasn't so bad. They had each other. Once Freya returned, and she would—he didn't doubt it—then life would be back to normal. He'd called Ingrid the other day and found his older sister sounding awfully blue. With Freya gone, they were all on edge.

The pale light of early evening filtered through the domed skylight above the pool. Freddie loved the smell of chlorine and the moisture in the air, the sounds of swimmers splashing through the lanes, the echo of voices, and even the occasional whistle from the lifeguard.

He dove in, slicing the turquoise water with the taut knife of his body. He did the crawl, getting into a rhythm: splash, silence, breath, splash, silence, breath . . . He was pure movement. When he reached the pool's end, he curled into a ball, spun, then pressed his feet against the wall, launching out beneath the water like a rocket. His body felt agile and fit from these daily laps and all the sex he had been having with Gert lately. They had become insatiable, doing it as often as they could, wherever they could: downstairs in the laundry room against the spinning dryers and the tables used for folding clothes, in the car late at night, and once in a campus broom closet between Gert's classes. Splash, silence, breath, splash . . .

When he couldn't swim any farther, he climbed the ladder out of the pool. Panting, he removed his goggles and ran a hand over his forehead, pushing back his wet hair, shaking the water out of his ears. He rested, leaning over, hands on his thighs. His lungs stung but felt good.

He was not unaware of the other swimmers' subtle looks, men and women alike gazing at him as he walked in his navy Speedo toward the lockers. Well, let them look . . . he looked good and he knew it.

HE FELT THE pleasant ache in his muscles as he climbed the three flights up to the apartment. He unlocked the door and swung it open. His piglet familiar came running at him, as fast as its fat little legs would allow.

"Hey, guys, Daddy's home!" Freddie called.

No one answered.

He petted his familiar. "Hey, Buster, Mr. Golden Bristles! Where's everybody?" He tried again. "Hello?"

Nothing.

He checked the bedroom while Buster followed, snuffling at his heels. The bed was made but there was no Gert sitting there in a pile of books as she often did in the evenings. It was almost seven. Usually, around this time, she was here, reading and asking him to order pizza, Thai, or Chinese. Perhaps she was stuck at the library. He checked the pixies' room. Their beds were not made, messy and rumpled—he'd get on their cases—but empty, too. Had everyone gone to the movies or something? Without him? A sad thought. That new comic-book hero film *Sky Boots* had recently opened, and it was all the pixies could talk about lately. He had promised to see it with them. Freddie had actually grown used to having them around. As much as he might be loath to admit to Gert, having them as his wards did satisfy a deep craving inside him. There was something very cool about being a *dad*—so to speak. This had been on his mind recently, and he had been waiting for the right moment to bring it up with Gert. Freddie wanted to be a father, and he believed he was ready. They *were* married. Wasn't that what marriage was for?

He strode into the kitchen to make himself a sandwich, which he would eat by the window to keep an eye out for his family. He could always eat again with them if they hadn't already eaten. He was famished. As he walked to the fridge, he did a double take. On the red fifties Formica table, he saw a note. He recognized

Gert's pale yellow stationery with the faint initials *GL*, and his heart sank like a sun plummeting too fast behind the horizon.

> *Freddie,*
> *I'm sorry, I know this is unexpected and the last few weeks have been wonderful, but I need my space right now. I really need to get my degree without any distractions. I've only got one more semester till I graduate, and I have to concentrate on my thesis. I've gone to live with friends who are also studying. I hope you can wait for me. Please?*
> *—G.*

Who the hell were these friends? Judith? Or that pretentious asshole with the mustache—beard—whatever. He read the note again, irate. Just when he thought things were good, Gert pulled this one on him. What was wrong with her? She had been so loving since his accident, and he had been helping quiz her with her study cards after each one of their heated, sweaty sessions at home.

What did she mean by "distractions"? Was sex a distraction? Was *he* a distraction? He read the note a third time, not quite believing what he was reading and halfway expecting Gert to jump out of a closet and tease him for falling for a joke. But this was no joke.

He had been completely blindsided. He shoved the kitchen table, furious with himself and with her, and the note fell to the ground. He had believed they were back on track. That he was on track. Marriage. Children. Domesticity. Monogamy.

That's when he saw the purple Post-it with a smiley face that had been stuck to the Formica beneath Gert's note:

> *Picked up the scent. On our way to retrieve trident. Back soon. Please refill fridge for our return.*

We had gone to parsonage with Mr. Putnam. We were to stand around the pastor's hall, praying for the girls. It had grown dark outside. Abby and Betty were considerably more tranquil, as they had exhausted themselves. Invariably, they calmed in the evening in time for dinner and bed. Betty sat on the floor, her petticoats falling over her splayed limbs. She drooled as she stared down, her head like a poppet's that had come loose at the neck. Meanwhile, Abigail crawled on all fours, mewling.

"Who did this evil?" Reverend Parris asked.

"Tell us! Who did this to you?" Mr. Putnam cried.

"Tell us! Who was the witch?"

The more the men badgered them, the more riled the girls became. Abby rose and ran across the room. "Whish, whish, whish!" she whispered, flapping her arms, while Betty flopped on the floor like a fish.

Abby stopped at the hearth and threw a firebrand across the room, then attempted to run up the chimney as she had oftentimes done before, but Mr. Ingersoll, the tavern owner and innkeeper, caught her and held her back. She eventually calmed, then fell and rolled about, hiding herself in her skirts.

"TELL US! TELL US!" the men demanded, their voices angrier and their faces red from rage.

"She will not let me say!" Abby screamed, holding her hands to her neck as if she were being choked.

Betty took the cue. "She torments me but I will not sign her book!"

"Who is it? Who is making you do this? Who is trying to make you sign the devil's book, you poor child?" Reverend Parris asked.

Abby sat up, eyes wide, staring. Betty followed her lead.

"Do you not see her?" said Abby, pointing. "Why, there she stands!"

They all turned to me.

—*Freya Beauchamp,*
June 1692

salem

may
1692

chapter nineteen

Miracle Worker

There was never a lack for work on the Putnam farm. The
birds chirped in the trees and insects screeched and hopped
as Mercy and Freya strode along the grassy path one day in
early May. They held their baskets at their hips. They arrived at
the potato field and stared out at the endless rows, daunted. It
was already growing hot. Thomas Putnam had tasked them
with the entire field.

"It's bigger than I thought," remarked Freya.

"Yeah, well, you know Mr. Putnam . . ." Mercy blew at a
strand of hair.

Each girl took a row, kneeling in the dirt, and set about up-
rooting the spuds with their spades. They worked quietly for an
hour, focused on getting as much done as they could. Freya wiped
the sweat from her brow and neck. At the rate they were going,
they would never get this entire field and everything else done today. Perhaps they could do a third of the field if they were lucky.
There were the blackberries, ripe for the picking, that needed to
be turned into preserves, not to mention housework.

"I have a crick in my back," said Mercy, placing her hands
there as she pressed her chest forward.

"We will be standing soon enough," said Freya, squinting.

"Mr. Putnam must be crazed in his intellectuals if he thinks we can get it all done in one day." Mercy did a double take at her friend.

"What is it?" asked Freya.

"Don't you ever grow weary of it all? You are always smiling, Freya."

Freya realized she *was* smiling and felt a bit embarrassed. "Why, I have a lot to be happy for. For one, I have you." She chucked a couple of potatoes into her basket and grinned.

Mercy shook her head. When their baskets were full, they brought them to the edge of the field, where they emptied them in a bin. In the evening a farmhand would come around with a wagon on his way back to the farm. Mercy scuttled sideways on her knees to move down the row. "I have been working as far back as I can remember, ever since I was a wee girl. Yea high." She placed her palm at her breast.

Freya giggled. "That small, eh?"

"I came out of my mother's womb working, sister! A basket on my hip." She knitted her brow. "Poor Mother, God rest her soul. Don't get me wrong, I am grateful for the employment, and to the Putnams, and for walking on the rightly path of God, but I do get weary of it from time to time. My body aches and my burned hand always hurts." She closed and opened her scarred, dirt-caked fist. Her face suddenly took on a grave expression and she shook her head. They went back to work, silent and pensive for a while.

They had their differences, but Freya cared deeply for Mercy. Whenever Freya placed a hand on her friend, she could feel Mercy's suffering, a great rushing river of sorrow. She felt the terror and powerlessness of a girl hiding as the violence took place, trembling at the sound of the blood-curdling screams of her family. She saw the chaos, the peeling of skin from flesh as if from a fruit. She felt all the panic and guilt of a girl escaping a fire in which the rest of her family perished behind her. Freya wished she could conjure some sort of nepenthe for Mercy to help her forget her past, but she did not know of one. It was ironic since she herself could not recollect her own past, try as she might.

Although there was something she could do to give her friend a little respite. It *was* very dangerous but her heart went out to the maid. She could bear it no longer. It would be just another of their secrets, she decided.

Freya pressed her hands to her thighs and stood. She waded across the clumps of dirt and reached out a hand. "Come, my dear, I want to show you something."

Mercy glanced up at the proffered hand. "We really do not have time to tarry, sister."

"Do as I say," Freya said gently.

"What is there to show me in an ugly field of dirt and potatoes. Have you struck gold?" She laughed, but took Freya's hand and let herself be pulled to her feet.

"You must promise you will tell no one!" Freya said.

Mercy snickered. "Why do you look so grave?"

Freya patted Mercy's shoulder. "You mustn't be frightened."

"You know me. I have seen it all. Nothing frightens me anymore."

Freya brought her friend to the border of the field, where the trees would hide them from prying eyes. She made sure no one was near. First, she had to create a pocket to enclose them. She murmured the right words, and she felt the shift and electricity fill the air. A euphoric feeling swept over her, making her entire body tingle.

The wind swept around them, singing through the trees, raising dirt in the field. It was as if a hundred invisible hands had set to work. The spuds lifted from the earth, filling the baskets, plopping into the bins. Time leaped from one moment to the next, jarring and jagged. The bins overflowed. The wind stopped, and the dust settled.

Freya clapped the dirt off her hands. "Tell me that was much easier!" She smiled at Mercy, who was ogling her.

"It isn't possible!" she said, breathless. She ran to the edge of the field, Freya right behind her. Mercy fell to her knees, throwing her arms over a bin. "A miracle!"

"Yes!" said Freya.

Mercy gazed at Freya in awe. "You are a witch!"

"There's no such thing!" Freya said.

Mercy grinned. "Of course there isn't!"

Next came the blackberries. Rather than getting nicked and bloody hands from the thorns, the berries plucked themselves off the brambles, falling into the girls' baskets. Five lovely jars of preserves were made in the blink of an eye. The house was cleaned, spotless, and ordered within minutes without either of them lifting a finger. After dinner they put the children to bed, and once the entire family had turned in, Mercy and Freya whispered back and forth from their rope beds in the hall. Mercy wondered at the multitudes they could do in so little time and with nearly no effort on Freya's part.

"We mustn't get carried away," Freya warned. "We need to continue doing things the old way. We cannot get caught. You know what I am now, Mercy, and you know what they do to people like me. They will hang me if they knew the truth. They say this is the devil's work, but I am certain—deep in my heart—it isn't."

"I don't believe one word of it either, Freya. It is God working through you. God making miracles through my dearest friend." She reached for Freya's hand. "Does it make you weary?"

"Quite the contrary. It feels marvelous!"

The girls were quiet for a while.

"I cannot sleep," said Mercy.

"Me neither!" There was so much more Freya wanted to show Mercy. It was nice to no longer have to hide for a change. An idea came to her and she turned to her side to face her friend with a dreamy expression.

"What?" Mercy lifted her head.

Freya's bare feet landed on the flagstone floor, and the bed swung as she sat upright. "There is something else I must show you. Quickly!"

The girls went quietly, careful not to wake the house. Barefoot in their linen shifts, their hair loose, they set out for the woods, but not before Freya grabbed a broom on the way out.

They flew over Salem, the cobalt night glittering with stars.

chapter twenty

Raise the Roof

❧ ♇ ❧

It was barn-raising day on the Putnam farm, a merry occasion. Nearly the entire community of Salem Village had come to help. The men hammered away. Soon they would lift the structure. They had been working since dawn. Eventually, everyone would cheer, and then they would break to eat, drink, and mingle. Once the food was served and the shadows grew longer and the villagers let down their guards, no longer watching one another like hawks, perhaps Freya could find Nate and slip off to the woods with him, unnoticed. His words echoed in her head again: "I have harbored a deep desire to be with you, to *know* you . . ." She trembled at the thought of knowing him and wondered how soon they would be married.

For now she and Mercy helped set up the row of tables in the shade of the trees at the edge of the forest, where the goodwives of the village, along with household servants, would present their specialties—a village potluck. Roasted pig. Venison with maple syrup. Pork, apricot, and prune pie. Beef stew with peas, carrots, potatoes in a thick, sweet wine sauce. Stuffed fowl. A cornucopia. To drink, plenty of ale, cider, and wine from Ingersoll's Tavern.

Freya arranged the bread she had baked, all the while stealing glimpses of Nate out on the barn's foundation, where he and

James labored. The front of Nate's shirt was damp. His hair fell over his face as he swung the hammer. She imagined what it might feel like to run her hands beneath his shirt, to feel the hidden strength and hollows of his body.

He had not once looked in her direction, almost as if he were avoiding her. But surely he could show his affection now that he had asked for consent and she had given her hand. Then again, Mr. Putnam said no one was to know, so maybe he was only following his dictate.

Still, Freya was suddenly irritated by everything—the smell of food, her tight, heavy bodice, the incessant chatter of women gossiping around her, talking unkindly behind each other's backs while smiling in each other's faces. She felt hot and itchy, damp under the arms. She batted at a fly buzzing in her face.

Reverend Parris's Caribbean slave, Tituba, walked over, and Freya recognized her from the meetinghouse, standing with the reverend's children in the gallery. She handed Freya a fan made from leaves. "Something we do in Barbados. The leaves are not as big here as they are on my island. Here they are rather small and sad. But it will keep you cool and scare away meddlesome flies."

Freya laughed, taking the fan. "Most kind of you," she said. She was glad for the distraction. They chatted pleasantly for a while, and Freya noticed some of the goodwives—even Mercy— giving them the eye.

She knew they were thinking it was not befitting for her to talk to a slave, let alone one who was considered a savage, the devil's servants themselves. Most of the villagers already thought it strange that the reverend had not just one but two slaves: Tituba and her husband, John Indian. Servants, even indentured ones, were standard—but *slaves*! The villagers accepted the reverend's eccentricities because, after all, Thomas Putnam had seen to having him ordained as the village minister.

Freya ignored the watchful stares. She was laughing at something Tituba had said, happy to have made a new friend. She showed Tituba the array of bread she had baked, fat ones with golden crusts, pieces of bacon and corn inside, rosemary ryes, and loaves made with oats and herbs.

The men began to raise the structure, and the women moved away from the tables to gather around the barn and cheer.

Tituba and Freya remained at the tables. The Caribbean maid reached out for Freya's hand and studied her palm. "You have a way with the hearth, with creating. Your hands possess magic," she said.

Freya smiled but said nothing.

Mercy appeared and Tituba quickly dropped Freya's hand.

"What are you doing?" Mercy said, pulling Freya away. She glared at Tituba, who lowered her eyes.

"I am sorry, miss," the slave apologized.

"Mercy!" chastised Freya. "Neither she nor I have done any harm!"

"What is this?" Mercy demanded as she reached for the fan made of leaves Tituba had given her, plucked it out of Freya's grasp, bunched it up, and threw it to the ground.

Freya stared at the crumpled fan in the grass. The village folk had begun to chant as the men heaved the structure upright. Until now, Freya and Mercy had never quarreled. Freya's face turned red and she quaked all over, from anger or hurt she wasn't sure.

"I best take my leave," said Tituba, who left them alone.

"I'm very sorry," Freya called to her as Mercy continued to glower at the slave's back.

Mercy tugged at Freya's arm. "A word with you!" They took a path into the woods, whispering hurriedly back and forth as they trudged along the path.

"Those are the people who slaughtered my family!" said Mercy.

"Mercy, Tituba is from the Caribbean . . . she is not Indian," Freya pointed out.

"They are all savages! They are evil! They consort with the prince of sin and darkness."

"Tituba and her people did not slaughter your family!" said Freya. She'd had enough. They stopped in the path. The light spilled through the trees, dancing on their dresses. "I care about you greatly, Mercy. You are like a sister, and I understand how you feel. What happened to you and your family was an atrocity, but that has nothing to do with Tituba. She is just like us, a servant."

Mercy laughed at this. "You are naïve, my friend."

Freya knew there would be no persuading the stubborn girl. She sighed, dropping her head, and when she spoke her voice was full of compassion. She knew Mercy would never recover from the horror she had seen. It was etched on her body, with the scars on her face and mangled hand. "Forgive me," she said. "I am sorry I hurt you."

Mercy apologized, and they hugged, proclaiming their love for each other once more. Freya said she needed to be alone to gather herself, and Mercy agreed to cover for her. They separated, Freya strolling deeper into the woods as Mercy returned to the barn raising.

CLOUDS BLANKETED THE SUN, and the forest was shrouded in shadow as Freya walked through the tall pines. She sensed a presence and turned to look back, hoping Nate might have followed her. She spun in a circle, scanning the woods, but saw no one. It must have been a wild hog or a deer.

125

She took a path she recognized. It wound through the trees coming around to the side of the Putnam farm. She stopped in her tracks. There was the knock of a woodpecker against a hollow trunk, but it had stopped abruptly. The wind picked up. She looked up through the trees at the sky, which had turned metal gray. Again, she spun around.

This time, a tall man stepped out from behind an oak tree large enough to have obscured him. He wore a black steeple-crowned hat with a buckle, a black cape over a red shirt, and black knee-length breeches with ocher socks. The silver buckles on his long black pointy shoes shone. Freya looked inquisitively into his small dark eyes. He had a grizzled mustache and a pointy goatee. She could hear his wheezy breath rattle in his chest. She recognized him from the meetinghouse.

"Why, hello," he said, reaching out an infinitely long arm from the folds of his cape. He stood in the middle of the path, cutting off her way. "Allow me to introduce myself. Mr. Brooks at your service. It is a pleasure to make your acquaintance . . ." He smiled, his hand still hanging in the air, waiting for Freya to take it.

Freya tried not to laugh. There was something ridiculous about the man, overblown, with the foppish attire and comportment. *Mr. Brooks . . . this must be the uncle Nate lives with,* she realized, and to be polite, she gave him her hand. "Freya Beauchamp," she said.

The man took it, bringing it reverentially to his lips, pushing his cape back while bowing slightly. His dry lips made her grimace with repugnance, and she took her hand back as quickly as possible without being impolite. She curtsied. "A pleasure."

He sighed, smiling. "It is all mine. I was escaping the barn raising just now, taking a shortcut home." He placed a spindly finger to his lips to show this was their little secret. "How stupendous to meet such a lovely young maid along the way!"

Thunder roared. She heard the cries of the villagers. Most likely they were running for shelter before the rain came. She could feel that heaviness in the air that preceded a virulent downpour.

"Goodness," said Freya, looking up at the sky. "I must take my leave!"

"Yes, yes," said Mr. Brooks. "Go, child, go, get back to the farm before the tempest strikes and until next we meet!"

Freya curtsied once more, then ran as fast as she could the other way. She couldn't get away from Nate's slithery goat of a relative fast enough.

chapter twenty-one

Thank Heaven for Little Girls?

A few days later, Thomas Putnam sent Freya, Mercy, and his daughter Annie on the two-mile walk to the parsonage to deliver provisions the pastor had requested during his last sermon. The pastor had a habit of working in what he needed for his house in his railings against the devil. Stepping inside from the bright sunlight, Freya was momentarily blinded by the darkness as she and the girls entered the parsonage. The shutters had been closed to trap the nighttime cool, but the air felt thick and stifling in the middle of the day. A single candle flickered on the large wooden table.

As Freya's eyes adjusted, she saw little Betty Parris on her hands and knees, scrubbing the flagstone floor with a brush, a bucket nearby. Abigail Williams, her older cousin, had been standing over her, as if supervising the younger girl's work. Now Abby was striding toward Freya as Betty rose to her knees. The reverend's girls beamed as if the visit were divine providence itself.

"Sister Beauchamp!" cried Abby, placing a hand on Freya's

shoulder. Abby was very fond of Freya. This was a source of discomfort for her because she sometimes sensed Mercy's jealousy whenever she and Abby conversed outside the meetinghouse.

"Sister Lewis and Sister Putnam!" said Betty.

The girls joyfully greeted one another.

"Is the pastor in?" asked Freya. "We have brought meal, corn, soap, and candles!"

"Oh, no, he isn't here," said Betty. "He is out making his spiritual rounds with Mother and little Sister and Brother. They are to return at dinnertime. For now, we are all alone." She was a delicate, frail-looking girl of nine, blond with sharp, foxlike features and pale hazel eyes. There was a smudge on her forehead, soot from the chimney. The hearth, Freya saw, had been scrubbed clean. The hall was spotless, precisely ordered, and smelled of orange blossom and myrrh. Freya gently rubbed the smudge from Betty's forehead as the little girl smiled up at her for the kindness—a sweet little face with ruddy cheeks, Freya thought.

Mercy squinted, peering into the hall. "Are your Indian man and woman here?"

Abby knew of her fellow orphan's story. "Worry not, Mercy. John is out in the garden. Tituba has just now wrung the necks of two chickens and is plucking them for dinner in the back. I will not let them in until you are gone if that will make you rest easier."

"Yes, thank you, Abby," replied Mercy, curtsying.

It still irked Freya that Mercy could not see that the servants were gentle, harmless folk. Abby offered the girls a seat. She said they must be weary and thirsty after such a long walk in the hot sun. Betty took the provisions from them and put them away while Abby lit candles.

129

"We do not want to keep you from your employment!" Freya said nervously.

"No, we must not," agreed Annie.

"We know how the reverend is!" added Mercy.

Abby laughed. "Come now! You have brought provisions. The reverend would not mind if you sat for a while and had tea." She went to retrieve glasses, a pitcher of tea from a cupboard, and some hard biscuits that smelled rancid. "We can have ourselves a trifle of mischief so long as it remains betwixt us!"

"Yes!" exclaimed Annie, who sat beside Betty at the table. The older girls laughed at the childlike enthusiasm.

Scarcely had they all sat when Mercy began rambling about James Brewster. Apparently, there was much to say about the youth's looks and how she wished she could marry him and that she believed he shared her feelings. The girls listened, but Freya noticed how Abby kept glancing at her.

Finally, Freya let her gaze meet Abby's; they smiled at each other amicably. Abby's big brown penetrating eyes stared back, glinting as dark as coals in the candlelight. Abby was an extremely self-possessed girl, tall for her twelve years, busty already. Her glossy black hair fell out of her cap and her lips looked almost crimson in contrast to her pallor. One always noticed Sister Williams in the meetinghouse.

"How wonderful that Mr. Brewster has made his affection known," Abby said with a droll tone.

"Oh, he has not!" Mercy protested.

"Then how do you know he shares your fondness?"

"I don't," Mercy had to admit. "Not for certain."

Abby's smile was slightly mocking at that. "What about you, Sister Beauchamp? Has anyone caught your fancy? Or has anyone fancied you?"

Freya demurred.

"Nonsense, of course you have an admirer! You are such a beautiful maid! I would not be surprised if someone has already spoken for you!" Abby clearly meant to make Mercy feel less worthy. It was unkind.

Mercy lowered her eyes and placed her scarred hand at her face, elbow on the table, looking questioningly at Freya, waiting for her to answer.

Embarrassed, Freya stared down at her hands in her lap. This was exactly the kind of situation she sought to avoid. She laughed, making light of it all. "I'd rather not say for fear I hex it!"

"*Oh*, she said 'hex'!" exclaimed Betty. "We are not to say such words in this house!"

"Oh!" said Annie, clapping a hand to her mouth.

They all looked at one another with alarm, but then Abby tittered, and they all laughed.

"What about you, Abby?" asked Mercy. "Do you have a paramour? Pray tell."

Abby smiled. "Not all of us are so lucky to find handsome young men in the woods." She smirked. It made Freya very uneasy. What was the girl trying to tell her? That she had seen her and Nate in the woods the other day? *Little girls*, she thought, *they are so very lonely at this age.* She sensed a profound longing, a restless hunger in Abigail Williams.

Abby leaned in and whispered, "While we are on the subject of hexes, there is something someone brought the minister from Boston a few weeks prior that Betty and I are exquisitely curious about."

Mercy and Annie widened their eyes. They desperately wanted to know what it was. But Abby's words had sent a chill up Freya's spine. It was as if Abby had been waiting for this moment all along. Abby sent Betty upstairs to the minister's study to retrieve the mystery item in question. When the young girl descended the stairs, she held up a slim volume and brought it to Freya.

"Neither of us knows how to read," said Abby. "Would you read to us a little, Sister Beauchamp? We would like that very much!"

"Father will only read the Bible to us. He says this pamphlet's content is not for little girls," added Betty plaintively. "But it *was* written by a minister, so we do not see how it could be harmful. These *are* religious writings. And a very nice man came to drop it off. A friend of Uncle's, a tall man with a white hat."

Abby straightened her cap. "I overheard the reverend say to Mrs. Parris that the pamphlet is all the rage in Boston. Everyone has read it there. Why can't we?"

"All right," said Freya, staring at the pamphlet before her on the table. She ran a hand over the fine, swirling black-and-gold lettering on the cover and read it aloud: *"An Essay on Remarkable, Illustrious, and Invisible Occurrences Relating to Bewitchments and Possessions,* by Reverend Continence Hooker."

chapter twenty-two

Whish Witch

"That very same year, as providence would have it," Freya read aloud. "I had been summoned to the home of a most sober and pious man, a tailor by trade, and his wife, Robert and Sarah Barker, who lived in the north part of Boston. The couple had four offspring and, save for the youngest, an infant still feeding and mewling at its mother's breast, the children had been recently seized by odd fits, and it was believed they were under the dreadful influence and astonishing effects of witch-crafts."

The girls sitting around the table gasped, the younger ones clapping hands over their opened mouths. Freya continued.

"The three children (the oldest being thirteen and youngest eight) had always been remarkably pious and obedient, having received a strong and stringent religious education. These good God-fearing children and model Christians until then had possessed such docile temperaments and excellent carriage (several godly neighbors testified as to the virtues of their persons), it would have been impossible to believe they had any design to dissemble the strange fits with which they had been seized. So amazed were the scores of spectators by the children's contortions, they, too, could only conclude the fits preternatural and not simulated.

"Here, let us pause, whilst I return a few steps back in time to tell how it all began, the very cacodemonic incident giving rise to these innocent children's direful afflictions.

"Tailor Barker had sent his eldest, Helen, to purchase fabric from a local weaver, a Goodwife Mary Hopkins. No sooner had Helen stepped away from Hopkins's door with the newly acquired cloth did she see that it possessed an unsightly large brown stain. Immediately, Helen returned to the home of weaver Goody Hopkins to show her the stain and trade it for a new clean piece of fabric for her father. Upon these actions, weaver woman Hopkins, a most scandalous and loathsome old Irish hag (whose own husband had brought her to court for placing a curse on him and turning his favorite cat into a dog), proceeded to give the young, prepossessing Helen a tongue lashing so vile the girl at once fell ill."

The girls laughed, but Freya only blinked and went on reading.

"Upon the young Helen Barker's return home, with not a stitch of fabric nor the money her father had given her to purchase it, for the snarl-toothed Irish hag had kept both, the girl was seized by fits so severe they resembled the quaking that accompanies a catalepsy. Within a couple of weeks, one after the other, the Barker children were fell into fits, tortured in so grievous a manner as to break the most immovable heart.

"These fits would not cease and only grew progressively worse, no matter how much parents and neighbors fasted and prayed. By then I, Reverend Continence Hooker, had been called upon to visit and see for myself. Perhaps I could offer a sage word or efficacious reading and prayer. What I saw in the house of the Barkers was most unusual and unnatural, and it moved me to my very core. There, I witnessed the children in fits at their most extreme and exquisite: trembling, shaking, contorting, babbling incoherently. They hid beneath furniture; they stretched out and writhed on the floor, twisting their heads and pulling their tongues to an unnatural degree; they went deaf, dumb, and blind; they crawled whilst barking like dogs or purring like cats. Once did Helen take to running to and fro about the hall, flapping her arms and crying out, 'Whish, whish, whish!' The two smaller ones followed behind her, behaving like chicks, then Helen threw a hot firebrand from the hearth across the hall, nearly striking a neighbor. Finally, the oldest attempted to dash into the fire and up the chimney.

"It wasn't until the evening when I visited that the children calmed—as it happened, right before dinnertime. They ate most tranquilly and heartily, and at night they appeared to sleep peacefully. In fact, one might have thought them angels in their slumber, never possessed by such demonic contrivances as would seize them again upon awaking at dawn."

The girls listened, eyes glazed over and mouths agape. They were transfixed by the story, and Freya could see they enjoyed— even needed—this break from their humdrum and difficult little lives. She stopped worrying about whether it was right or wrong to read them this tale and immersed herself in the story.

Eventually, word of the strange happenings in the Barker home fell upon the ears of Boston magistrates, who with "great promptness looked into the matter." As soon as Goodwife Mary Hopkins was placed in the jailer's custody, the children were given some relief from their agonies. Then Goodwife Hopkins, along with the afflicted children, was brought before a tribunal.

At the trial, Goody Hopkins oftentimes refused to speak in English, answering the magistrates in Gaelic instead, which no one understood. Every time she bit her lip, the children fell into the most pitiful fits before the whole assembly, crying out that they were being bitten. If the goodwife so much as touched her

135

arm or scratched her head, the children cried out they were being "most grievously tormented," struck, pinched, or pricked on
those very same parts of their bodies.

The weaver's house was searched, and they found several
poppets made of cloth and goat hair. In court, "the hag admitted
she used these images to torture the objects of her ill will by wet-
ting a finger with her spittle, then rubbing the poppets." Further,
at one point during the trial, Helen cried out that she saw a
"small yellow bird suckle betwixt the fingers" of the accused,
which her siblings then saw, too, and the magistrates concluded
that the weaver had summoned her invisible familiar.

There had been enough damning evidence. Goody Hopkins
was charged with being a witch, then hanged. With her death,
the children's fits ceased.

FREYA SHUDDERED, slamming the pamphlet closed. She could
read no longer. What exaggerations and untruths! Goodwife
Hopkins must have been ridiculing the court because the trial
was, in fact, a mockery. Did the poppets even belong to Goody
Hopkins or had they been produced to prove a point? From the
start of his essay, Hooker had seemed to have a bone to pick with
the old Irish weaver, whom he lost no opportunity to call names
such as *loathsome*, *scandalous*, and *vile*.

The girls were silent, still absorbing Freya's reading. Abby
stood to walk to the center of the hall, where she faced the girls
at the table. She smiled and bowed her head. She had their full
attention. She reached for her cap, removed it, and placed it in
her apron's pocket. She pulled the pins out of her bun, and her
shiny dark hair fell down her shoulders. She shook her head
softly. The girls watched her wordlessly, hypnotized by her lan-
guorous movements. She was indeed ravishing.

Abigail's body began to tremble and shake, and she fell to the floor. Her head turned, her arms stretched out, her back arched, and her eyes rolled back. She flopped about. She went still. She was on all fours, swinging her head so that her hair flew up and down. She hopped up and ran about the room, pretending to be a bird, crying, "Whish, whish, whish!"

Struck dumb, the girls looked on in horror. Abby stopped in her tracks and stared at them, then burst into delighted laughter.

"Why the long faces, girls?" She smirked. "Come! Do try it!" She threw her arms up in the air and spun, then shook again.

The girls save for Freya ran to the center of the hall and began pretending to have fits, barking like dogs, meowing like cats, crying out about their agonies. So passionately did they carry on that their caps fell off their heads.

Mercy stopped and looked at Freya, still sitting at the table. "Join us!"

Freya shook her head no, feeling a sudden chill. This was all wrong . . . there was something here . . . something very wrong . . . *What had she done?*

"What a wet rag, you are!" Mercy made a face, fell to the ground, lay on her back, and shook her entire body.

Tituba came through the door into the parsonage, carrying two plucked chickens by their necks. The girls had been so lost in their fits that they hadn't heard her enter. The Caribbean servant, not knowing what had transpired, stared at the girls in horror. "What is going on here?"

The girls immediately stopped. Sitting on the floor, Mercy let out a little yelp of fear as she spied the servant.

"We were playing," said Abby, walking over to Tituba, patting her on the arm. "That was all we were doing, Tituba. It was nothing."

Tituba shook her head at Abby. "You girls let yourselves be

melissa de la cruz

tempted! Oh, I saw it, Abby, and I will not have it! Not in the reverend's house!" She looked about the hall. The girls were gathering their caps from the floor. "You put on your caps and go!" she said, addressing Mercy and Annie. "Abby, Betty, fix your hair and skirts and return to your godly endeavors." She carried the chickens to the table, where Freya had stood to take her leave.

Tituba gave Freya a look of such disapproval that she felt as if her heart had withered. She really shouldn't have succumbed to Abigail's demands as she had. In hindsight she saw just how manipulative the girl had been.

chapter twenty-three

Loose Lips

Freya had time on her hands now that she was practicing magic more frequently. She loved to be alone, rambling through the woods with her basket, gathering herbs for poultices and tinctures. It was good to get away from the Putnam farm and daydream about her upcoming nuptials with Nate. She was impatient to wed; she had not run into him lately, nor seen him at church, and she missed him. She found solace in the woods with the birds twittering, the insects' song swelling, and tiny animal feet scampering over dried leaves. Once when she had walked to the river, she spied a baby fawn taking a dip. Just its head bobbed on the surface, moving downstream, until the small graceful creature reached the bank and strolled out of the water with a little shake. Freya had mistaken it for a dog until that moment. She thought it the sweetest thing, with its white spots.

She arrived in the clearing where the wild rosebush grew. The rose's white-pink petals had fallen, but the rosehips they had left behind weren't big or red enough to pick yet. Someone coughed, and she turned around and saw her friend James standing by the large stone outcropping.

"Good day!" He gave a quick bow, removing his hat. "I am very glad to have found you," he said.

"You always seem to know where I am," she returned.

"Funny, that!" he replied with trepidation.

"What is it, James?" she asked. His expression had made her anxious.

He bit a knuckle, then let the hand fall to his side. "It's just that I felt I should warn you. I care very much about you, Freya . . ."

She peered inquiringly at him, nodding her head to encourage him to continue.

"You and your cunning ways . . ." He cleared his throat, appearing uncomfortable.

"Yes?" she said, batting her eyelashes.

He shifted on his feet. "Well, not everyone understands you . . . the way I do."

She thought he meant there was an implicit understanding between them because of their friendship, but he seemed to be suggesting more.

"What do you mean?"

James took a step closer. "It is terribly dangerous, what you are doing, Freya."

"What am I doing?"

"One hears things . . ."

"Things?"

"The other night . . . I happened to look up at the stars . . . and . . ."

"And?" she challenged.

He shook his head. "I cannot speak of it. It is too dangerous. Freya, you must promise me you will take better care. Do not . . ."

"Do not what?" she said impudently. She did take care. Mercy was her dearest friend and promised not to breathe a word about her talents. Those she helped in the village were appreciative. Added to which, she wasn't the only one who made physics. A few goodwives did as well; the only difference was that her physics always worked. So why not offer help when she could? Some people made such a silly fuss about it all, like the reverend or Thomas Putnam, who took everything so seriously.

"Do not do anything that will cause people to notice. People are always watching in Salem. There are eyes everywhere."

Freya softened. "Do not worry about me, my friend. I am safe."

"For now," James said. "Mind you listen to my advice," he said softly. "It would grieve me to see you come to harm."

With that warning, James bade his leave.

ONCE AGAIN, MR. PUTNAM sent the girls to Reverend Parris's with provisions the little man had hinted needing in his sermon. *What would be next? A horse and carriage?* Freya wondered. This time only she and Mercy made the trip on foot.

Annie stayed behind to sit with her mother, who had lately taken to talking to her dead sister and nieces and had somehow managed to set her Bible on fire. Most providentially, Mr. Putnam had been in his study at the time. He had run into the room at the scent of smoke and stomped on Mrs. Putnam's Bible. It was on the floor by the bed, and a candle had fallen on top of it. The whole event, which Freya had learned about through Annie, seemed strange. Ann Putnam Senior needed to be closely watched when she behaved like this. Poor Annie had been very frightened. She saw the burning Bible as a portent presaging some kind of doom.

As the girls walked to the parsonage, Freya was quiet while Mercy was her loquacious self. Freya nodded her head in agreement as the maid chattered, but she was miles away. She was thinking about what James had said, about being more prudent. As if on cue, Mercy asked about the very same subject.

"I saw you with James earlier," she said. "Was he asking about me?"

"Yes—no. I mean, yes, I was with James."

"What did he want?"

Freya told her about his warning. "He is right. I have been brazen with my . . . abilities lately, and it *is* dangerous."

Mercy was the silent one now. They walked along a narrow road lined with poplars. Freya gave the maid a sidelong glance, and as they moved in and out of sunlight and shadow, she saw that Mercy still looked troubled.

"How does James know about your magic?" Mercy asked finally. "Do you converse with him often?"

"How do you mean? I see him as often as you," Freya said. "Anyway, he did not say, but I think he might have seen us— flying the other night." She twisted her apron worriedly.

"Do not worry about James," Mercy said coldly. "He knows nothing." The pale-haired girl stared at her. "But I do wonder sometimes, Freya, if you know what it means to be a friend."

THE PASTOR WAS OUT—as usual, making his religious rounds. If anything, Reverend Parris was devout. A seat awaited him in heaven. Mrs. Parris, weak of health, lay in bed upstairs. Only Abby, Betty, and Lizzie Griggs, a seventeen-year-old girl who lived with her uncle, the physician William Griggs, were in the house. Lizzie had stopped by with supplies for the minister as well.

All three girls now ran to greet Freya and Mercy. No sooner had they stepped into the dark interior of the parsonage, the girls, full of awe, gathered around Freya with a barrage of breath-less, whispered questions.

"We hear you can make objects move!" said Lizzie.

"We hear you can fly!" followed Betty.

Abigail grabbed Freya by the arm, pulling her aside. She placed a hand on Freya's shoulder. "Will you show me how to fly, Freya? I would most love to fly with you!"

In a panic Freya looked over at Mercy, who stood off by herself. It was apparent she had given away the secret she had promised to keep.

"You told them!" Freya accused.

"They are but children," Mercy protested. "No one will believe them if they say anything."

Right then, Freya felt she would suffocate in Abby's clutch. She peered into the young girl's glinting dark eyes that bored into hers. "Do it!" Abby whispered.

"I cannot do these things you say! I know nothing about any of this!" Freya looked at Mercy for support, but Mercy only shrugged.

"We know what you are," Abby said. "Mercy told us." She narrowed her eyes and looked at Freya with contempt. "It doesn't matter if you show us or not—we know the truth about you. Show us your magic, or you will be sorry you didn't."

Freya felt herself grow cold with fear. James was right. She had been reckless. Henceforth, she would take care to ensure there would be no more magic.

143

chapter twenty-four

Love and Marriage

It was lecture day, a Thursday afternoon in June. The meeting-house had grown hot and rank. Reverend Samuel Parris finished one of his indefatigable windy sermons about heeding the devil and his minions. The congregation sighed in relief, seeing the end was near. But the diminutive Parris continued to speak. He realized everyone was eager to get back to their busy lives but he had something more to say. The parishioners in the pews and galleries perked up, or rather made a semblance of doing so. Freya straightened her cap, peering at Parris. *What now?*

The reverend nodded solemnly. "One of our noble and pious brothers has an announcement. A man of tremendous stature and standing, a leader of men, a prosperous farmer, a great man I am exceedingly grateful to, not a day goes by that I—" Stymied, Parris cleared his throat.

This appeared to be Thomas Putnam's cue as he had risen from the front row. Parris ceded the pulpit with a reverential bow. Befuddled, Freya and Mercy glanced at each other. As the barrel-chested Thomas made his way to the front, the impression was of watching a great storm cloud billow across the heavens. The man inspired fear and awe in the community, and all whispers ceased. Mr. Putnam faced the congregation. His face broke into an unexpected smile.

"Good day, parishioners. I will make this brief. I would like to bring to your attention the engagement of two individuals in our community. The young woman in question is a devout and devoted maidservant, an orphan my wife, Ann, and I took in not so long ago. Her name is Freya Beauchamp. I have agreed to give her hand in marriage one year from now when she is of proper age to marry." Mr. Putnam looked up, searching the gallery for Freya.

The parishioners craned their necks. They laughed when they saw Freya stumble forward. Mercy had given her a little push, and she caught the banister, turning bright red. Thomas hadn't forewarned her of this. She didn't think it would happen in quite this way.

Thomas's eyes settled on hers. He motioned for her to come down. She bowed her head. Mercy grabbed her hand and squeezed it, and in that auspicious moment, as will happen with friends who have been close but quarreled, all was instantly forgiven between them. The crowd parted to make way for her.

"Good tidings," servants and children whispered as she passed. She descended the stairs, which seemed to creak too loudly with the silence that had come over the meetinghouse.

As Freya walked down the aisle between the pews, all eyes were on her: the mysterious maid with green eyes and rosebud lips, her cheeks a similar hue to her apricot-colored hair tucked in her white cap, visible at the nape. She couldn't help but smile. Why shouldn't she make a show of her happiness? She stood before the congregation, lacing her hands. She had looked for Nate earlier but hadn't spotted him from the gallery. Perhaps he was waiting in the wings.

Mr. Putnam spoke again. "Let us wish the newly betrothed well and say a prayer for them this eve. I now call forth the gentleman who has promised to wed this poor, young orphaned girl. Mr. Nathaniel Brooks!"

The room became very still as the parishioners waited for him to step out from the crowd. Freya looked eagerly for Nate's handsome face. The members of the congregation began to clap, but her own face drained of color.

Nathaniel Brooks was walking toward her, but it was not the right Mr. Brooks at all. It was Nate's uncle, that tall, ridiculous, solicitous fellow she had met in the woods: goatee, black cape, bony legs peeking out from beneath in tight ocher socks. The buckles on his gigantic shoes clinked and clanked as he marched forward.

Nathaniel Brooks . . . Nate's namesake. Of course!

That was why Nate had been avoiding her at the barn raising the other day—he must have believed she had given her consent! The clapping became louder, deafening, and Freya's vision dimmed. She gripped the pew next to her lest she fall in a heap on the floor. She searched for Nate—her Nate—but when at last she found him he would not meet her gaze.

146

THAT EVENING FREYA pounded the door to the master's study with her fist so that it rattled in its frame. She was beyond following the rules of decorum. She pressed her face against the wood and spied through the crack, seeing Mr. Putnam at his desk.

"Come in," he said.

She bustled into the study and strode nearly all the way to the desk. She did not curtsy this time. "Mr. Putnam!" Her face was red.

Thomas glanced up. "Why, good evening, future Mrs. Brooks. We can discuss wedding plans. Dates . . ." Some of Freya's hair had come out of her cap, and Mr. Putnam cocked his head, his eyes traveling to those curls that fell upon her breast.

"There has been a terrible mistake!" said Freya. "I cannot marry this man . . . the elder Mr. Brooks. I do not love him, nor could I ever. He is repugnant to me!"

Mr. Putnam frowned. "When has it ever been about love? Especially not in your predicament, an orphan blown in on the wind. This is merely a means to an end, my dear. You will be delivered from your station. Does that not please you? Is that not enough?" he said calmly.

Freya glowered. "No, it is not, Mr. Putnam!" She squared her shoulders and stood firm.

Some air escaped from Mr. Putnam's nose, making a sound—*pfff.* He made a notation in his ledger. Freya believed she might say anything to him, and it would barely make a ripple. The man was immovable. Ponderously, he pressed his lips toward one cheek, then the other. He did this back and forth for a bit. "When I first informed you of Mr. Brooks's proposal, you had appeared so very delighted. Did I not say, the *venerable* Mr. Brooks?" He knit his brow questioningly.

Freya sought to remember. In fact, she recalled the conversation well. Mr. Putnam had called him Mr. Nathaniel Brooks and also Mr. Brooks but had said nothing with the word *venerable.* "You used no such adjective, sir," she stated flatly.

He gave one of his rare little laughs. "My mistake. You know, the younger Brooks—if that is whom you thought I meant—is known as Nate." He shrugged.

Freya thought she masked her emotions well, but apparently not. She didn't know how, but Mr. Putnam appeared to know she was in love with Nate. Mercy was the only one who knew. The maidservant had thought nothing of betraying Freya, sharing their secret with all the village girls, a secret that could ultimately lead to her death. Had Mercy been acting as Mr. Putnam's spy? It would never have seemed fathomable to her in the past, but in the light of Mercy's recent betrayal, she wondered if she could trust the girl at all anymore. Thomas appeared to be toying with her, mocking her love. Or perhaps it was all too evident . . . she would have, of course, assumed he had meant the young, good-looking Mr. Brooks and not the older, unattractive uncle. Mr. Putnam had purposely deceived her. How foolish and heedless she had been.

"Well, at the time, I know I did not say *Nate* Brooks," Thomas continued, pouring salt into the wound. "I would have said Nate, not Nathaniel, had I meant that particular gentleman. Besides, Freya, you are most fortunate. You would be nothing but a disreputable wench, a beggar, a ragamuffin had we not taken you in. And now you are to marry Mr. Nathaniel Brooks. You will be a wealthy woman, and one of high standing. The *venerable* Mr. Brooks has offered a substantial dowry, and I will receive a large parcel of land adjoining mine so that my land goes all the way to Salem Town." He smiled at her with what feigned to be gratitude. "You will marry Nathaniel Brooks, and that is that. I will hear nothing more." He grabbed his plume and resumed writing in the ledger.

Freya's arms stiffened at her sides. She would hear nothing more either, and so she spun on her heel and left the room as fast as she could.

"Where are you going?" called Mercy to her back. "I swear I had nothing to do with any of this! Freya! Wait!"

Freya strode across the hall and did not answer, only slammed the door on the way out of the Putnam house. It was almost seven according to the sundial attached to the wall of the farm, still light outside. She knew many of the men in the village went to Ingersoll's Tavern on Thursdays around this time, once they had finished with militia practice. Surely she would find Nate there. She would beg him to take her away—he could not let this happen—they were in love and they needed to run away together.

She took a shortcut, but she was so distressed, she lost the way and had to climb a wall that rose before her out of nowhere, it seemed. Briars caught on her skirt as she made her way down the other side, and she felt it tear as she jumped, but she kept running, frantically. She was in a wild, overgrown field, and she tripped on a sudden pile of stones, fell, fumbling for a moment in the tall grass, then she scrambled back to her feet. She would have flown on a pole had it not been broad daylight. She cursed this village. Her cap slipped from her head as she ran, so she pulled it off, tucking it into her apron's pocket. Her hair cascaded down, lighting up like fire.

She saw the village proper ahead, leaned over and placed her hands on her thighs, and panted. She found pins in her pocket, fixed her hair, then pulled her cap over it. Her pulse thrummed at her temples. Her petticoat had been torn on the thorns, but it was nothing too conspicuous. She glimpsed a deep scratch on her calf, where the blood had already dried. She was in such a state, she hadn't even felt it when it had happened.

She set a calm expression to her face and walked the rest of the road that led into the village's center. She passed a house on the way. The woman outside feeding chickens gave her a pained smile. Everyone recognized her now after that show in the meetinghouse. She was the young, comely maidservant who was to wed the old, homely, and wealthy widower.

A man on his horse came down the road. She recognized James Brewster and waved to him, relieved. James smiled, dismounting the chestnut stallion. He held the reins close to the bit as they stood together on the grassy shoulder of the road.

149

He squeezed her arm and let it go. "I was there," he said. "Do not worry." His green-gold eyes burned with compassion.

"It can't happen!" she said. "Where is Nate? Do you know?"

"Nate? No. I haven't seen him since Mr. Putnam made the announcement at the meetinghouse," he said.

"I cannot marry Mr. Brooks," Freya said. "I will not."

"Of course not. I would never let that happen."

His kindness overwhelmed her, even as it was Nate she wanted.

"Listen, I will help you, but we mustn't remain here lest we are seen. People will talk. Meet me at the dog rose bush." He was already mounting his horse, whose coat shone in the lowering sun. James looked quite glorious up there. He tipped his hat.

"Yes," said Freya. "I will. Thank you, James, thank you!"

James nodded and tugged on the reins, so his horse stretched its neck. He gave a little kick, and they were off at a trot, then canter.

Freya walked in the opposite direction in case anyone had seen. There was always someone watching in Salem Village, she knew now.

chapter twenty-five

The Immortals

When Freya arrived in the meadow, she spotted James's horse, but the stallion was alone. He grazed peacefully in the grass, the reins loose. Sensing Freya, the horse blinked in her direction, shook his mane, and returned his black nose to the ground to continue grazing. James's horse but no James. Where was he? Whatever he planned to do to help, it had to happen posthaste. But what about Nate? She had to let him know that she had left the Putnams, without a good-bye or any of her belongings, but she had to make him understand they would have to run away together immediately. She was a girl alone, with no family and no home. She was vulnerable, and somehow she knew instinctively her magic would not be able to help her out of this situation. She could make the butter churn by itself and plow a field of potatoes without lifting a finger, but she could not reverse Mr. Putnam's decision on her fate if he had already made up his mind.

Looking for James, she walked along the edge of the meadow, peering into the woods toward the west where the sun had begun to drop. The boughs of pines and leaves of oaks and beeches appeared backlit. Shafts of light poured through, resembling smoke as they lit the dust motes in the air. As she trudged along, the sun slipped between the bare spaces of trees, blinding her, and she brought a hand to her face to shield her eyes from the glare.

Then a shadow fell upon her face, and for a moment she thought it was Nate, but it was not. James stood before her.

"Where is Nate?"

"Why do you keep asking?" James asked impatiently. He carried a couple of blankets and a knapsack on his shoulder.

"Because . . ." She took a deep breath.

"Because?" he prompted, his face turning darker. "Why do you always ask about Nate? What is he to you?" James strapped the bags to the horse and turned to Freya. "Forget about Nate."

"I can't," she said. "I won't. Nate is . . . Nate is my . . ."

"Your what, Freya?" James said.

"Nate is my love," she whispered. "I cannot leave without him," and when she saw the hurt look on his face it dawned on her that this was yet another misunderstanding. Her life seemed to be so full of them lately. She had done this. It was all her fault. That morning when James was returning from night-watch duty at the tower, when she had kissed him on the cheek. She had been overflowing with feelings that day, because she was in love—*in love with Nate*. But now it dawned on her that James had come to believe he was the object of her affections.

She turned away from him, but he reached for her hand and pulled her toward him. His breath was warm on her face. "What . . . what did you say?"

"I love him . . . I love Nate," she choked. "James, I'm so sorry . . ."

He gaped at her, shaking his head. "No. No!"

She moved backward, away from him, and tripped on something that rose from the ground, a stone or a root. James tried to protect her fall but instead he fell on her, so that they were both lying on the ground. He was nearly on top of her, and they both were breathing heavily but for different reasons.

"You don't love him . . . you *can't* love him . . ." He pushed himself up slightly to look her better in the eye. He had one hand on her shoulder, his leg swung over hers, pinning her to the moist grass. His body was long, sinewy, the muscles heavy. The sun cast an orange-pink glow on her face. "Freya, listen to me. You love me . . . you've always loved me and only me."

"I don't know what you're talking about! Please let me go." She stared up into the dimming sky as she looked at him. "James . . . please . . ."

"My name isn't James Brewster." His eyes were hooded, and he looked so unhappy Freya could cry. "At least, it's not my only name. Some of us are not as lucky as you, Freya, to be able to keep our name over the centuries."

As James spoke, it was as if doors upon doors were opening in her mind, in her memories, her consciousness, her identity, trickling from behind a hidden and locked passage. She saw images that she did not understand, faces she did not recognize—an older, gracious woman with silver hair, formidable, with a softness around her eyes, and a younger one, blond and brittle looking until she smiled—and Freya felt an overwhelming sensation of love for them. They were part of her. "I am a witch," she said. "I have always been a witch."

"You are more than that," he murmured. James's lashes were wet with tears, and Freya put a hand on his face, to feel his pain and to try to understand what was happening here.

"Who are you, James? Who are you really? And who am I? What are we to each other?" She felt warm in his arms and no longer afraid.

He held her tighter and breathed into her ear. "You really don't remember me, my dearest love?"

His voice and his touch sent a shiver through her body, and in her mind's eye she saw a flicker of light, a memory, an image, of a beautiful dark-haired man, looming over her just like this,

153

the two of them entangled in each other, his body hot against hers, and there was no wicked shame, no guilt, none of the Puritan restrictions, for they were not Puritans, they were in love, and in lust, and he was so strong, his hands above hers, holding her down, and her body alive, open, needing, and she was screaming his name, his name . . .

"Killian?" she asked.

"Freya," he whispered. "It's me."

Then it came back to her, and suddenly it was as if all the doors had opened in a burst of light and understanding. The past, the future, the present. Killian at her engagement party, the two of them against the sink of the bathroom counter, without even a word to each other, overcome by desire, and the intense need to feel his lips on hers, her body on his. Their last night on board the *Dragon*, rocking against him, as if holding on for dear life, because she had sensed it was so close to the end . . . their end. The trident shadow on his back that had marked him as the thief who had stolen Freddie's trident. And finally, the Valkyries, surrounding him, ripping him away from her arms.

"But the Valkyries—they took you . . ."

"Here."

"Not Limbo?"

"No. I had no memory either, until I saw you in the meetinghouse, and then it all came back to me, but I did not want to frighten you. I thought you would remember on your own."

She shook her head, ashamed. She had no idea how she had gotten here herself. It had to be some awful form of trickery. She had been swept back here through the passages of time, her memory lost, unable to remember who she was and why she was here. Was this yet another punishment of the gods? Or another of Loki's tricks? Loki . . . was that why she had been inexplicably, irrefutably drawn to Nate Brooks? He must be Loki, there was no other explanation. Was this still part of the spell he had

154

cast on her when he was Branford Gardiner and had first come to North Haven? When her dress had fallen, the strap broken, and he had touched her skin, had branded her as his. But it couldn't be—she was not enchanted this time, she was sure of it. What was happening? Why had she felt that way? She did not love Loki, did not love Nate; she only loved Balder. Killian Gardiner. James Brewster. In any incarnation, under any other name, she always loved him.

"Killian, my darling," she whispered, putting a hand on his cheek. Her love. Her true heart. Her dearest friend. She would put aside her worries over her conflicted emotions for the moment and try to understand them later. "I'm sorry. I don't know what I was thinking."

"You do remember . . ." He smiled, relieved. "But it is dangerous to use that name. I must remain James Brewster to you for now."

She nodded. "But what are we doing here? How are we going to get away?"

"Don't worry, my love," he said, and kissed her. When their lips met it was as if they both realized at that same moment how near their bodies were to each other, and when he kissed her, she opened her mouth to him, and then his hand was struggling with her bodice, as she struggled to unlace his breeches.

She wanted him so much, wanted to take away the hurt she had caused, wanted to forget for a moment where they were—she was just so very glad to see him again, and that they were together—and he was kissing her neck and her breasts, and she helped him out of his shirt, and he fell back on top of her, and he was pushing up her skirts, and they were laughing softly together, at how terribly difficult it was to remove their clothing—and then it was done, and they were lying in the grass, and he was holding down her hands above her head, and kissing her, biting her lips, ravenous, hungry, they had been separated for too long, and when he entered her she gritted her teeth at the pain and the pleasure of finding him again.

"What are you doing?" came a voice above them—a maid's voice. A quiet, horrified voice as if the speaker could not quite believe what she was seeing.

James startled and rolled away, while Freya sat upright, frantically reaching for her clothes and covering herself as they separated from their embrace.

"And here I was making excuses for you to Mr. Putnam!" said Mercy, her voice hot with anger. "I thought you were my friend, my sister. You are nothing but a harlot, a temptress! A common whore! Look at you! Naked on the grass! With him! You are a witch! You have bewitched Mr. Brewster!"

Freya rose to her feet, her arm outstretched, the other holding her clothing against her body, red with shock and shame. What had they done? In the woods? In the open? "No, Mercy—please!"

The maid was trembling and her eyes watering. "I shall tell everyone! I shall tell them all the truth!"

"No—please! Mercy, I love you—I would never hurt you!" Freya said, buttoning her blouse while James quickly got dressed behind her. "You must understand—this is . . . he is . . ."

The girl stepped back, lifting her chin challengingly. She took in a deep breath, her face flushed, and her lips quivered as she spoke. "You are a liar, Freya Beauchamp! A liar, you hear me! A liar and a witch! I will tell them all!" She swung around and ran off through the field, leaving Freya and James alone in the dusky meadow.

"What do we do now?" she asked. She had lived long enough in Salem Village to know what would happen next. "They will kill us."

"Run," James said, tugging on his boots and handing her hers. "Run away as fast as we can."

north hampton

the present valentine's day

chapter twenty-six

The Hammer Strikes

Hudson held up a tiny pink one-piece with a tulle tutu to
show Ingrid. There was a decal of a piglet doing a pirou-
ette in toe shoes on the chest.

"What do you think?" The light flashed against the lens of his
tortoiseshell glasses.

"Um, Tabitha is having a baby boy?" she said.

They had snuck out on their lunch break at the library to
shop for Tabitha's baby shower at the nearby boutique Tater
Tots.

"So?" Hudson looked at it sadly and put it away. "You're
right. Why isn't she having a girl? *This is so cute.*"

Hudson was impeccably dressed as usual; only he could
make a thick down jacket look slim and elegant, but something
was different. A few months ago, he had finally come out to his
mother, and while things had been frosty for a while, the grand
Mrs. Rafferty had finally come around to the reality of the situation and had even agreed to meet his boyfriend. It turned out
that as long as any discussion of politics was assiduously avoided,
Hudson's mother and Scott got along swimmingly—to such a
degree that Hudson felt a bit left out at times. He occasionally
brought up politics just to put a little wedge between them.

Ingrid grabbed the tutu. "Let's get it! Why not? I mean

babies are babies. Can't you just dress them up however you want? They're kind of like dolls, right?"

"Um, not really. Put it back, Ingrid," Hudson instructed, being the voice of reason now. "If he wants to wear pink tutus that should be his decision when he's ready to make it."

She exhaled a sigh, putting the tutu back on the rack, then continued to flip through the pint-size clothes.

"I don't know," Hudson said wistfully, "doesn't this make you feel like . . ."

She turned to him with a look of horror. "Like what? Like having a baby?"

"Yeah . . ."

She shrugged. She hadn't ever really thought about it.

"Yeah, me neither!" He went back to searching through the rack, his fingers moving fast and adeptly. "Just testing you." He held up what looked like miniature lederhosen but were made of soft green terry cloth. "You've got to admit these are extraordinarily cute, and it's just fun shopping for baby clothes."

She eyed him suspiciously but let it go. "I need to talk to you about something," she said.

Hudson made a tsk-tsk sound. "I knew something was up and you were keeping me in the dark. You've been distracted today—and not a good distracted. I know that look. What's up?"

"I ran into them at that new café, Matt, Maggie, and, um, Maggie's mom, Mariza. His ex-girlfriend? They looked so perfect together, and perfectly happy. Mariza's a knockout. She's built like an Italian screen goddess and—"

"I know where this is going—stop right there!" warned Hudson, holding up a hand. "First of all, the *M* names? Totally dorky! And second of all, Matt chose you, not Sophia Loren. He could have married her by now if he wanted to make it work. *He didn't.* The reason they appear intimate is that not only do they have a history, but they also have a child together, so they're friends—*friends* being the operative word here."

"Friends."

"You have to be if you're going to be good parents, and from what you've told me, the kid is awesome, right? Well, that takes a lot of maturity on her parents' part."

"I suppose."

"You have nothing to worry about."

"Okay," she agreed morosely. Though Hudson's advice was always sound, she still had her doubts.

By the time they made it to the cashier, their arms were full. They couldn't help but get the tutu and also the terry lederhosen, a hooded hippo robe, and a trendy stuffed toy that was supposed to put babies in a good mood—and various other items that seemed absolutely necessary.

OUTSIDE, A CHILLY BREEZE blew against their cheeks, and there was a dusting of new snow on the sidewalks. She and Hudson strolled along the sunny side of the street. He proposed a round of cocktails after the frenzied bout of shopping, which had left him thirsty. Ingrid reminded him they had jobs to get back to and weren't rich housewives. Besides, they had a baby shower to plan.

"Speaking of hausfraus and marriage and babies," said Hudson as he walked jauntily along, "I forgot to tell you: Scott and I are thinking about tying the knot!"

Ingrid stopped mid-sidewalk. "Now you tell me? As if I'm the one withholding all the information!"

"Well, we're just considering it. Now that it's legal in New York and all. We thought we'd do a weekend in New York City at Hotel Gansevoort in the Meatpacking District—after City

Hall, of course. Although I've heard that doing it in Brooklyn is better, less busy than in downtown Manhattan. So—"

"No!" said Ingrid irately.

"Excuse me!" said a tall man standing behind Ingrid, whom neither she nor Hudson appeared to hear.

Hudson glared incredulously at his friend. "What do you mean, *no*?"

They had created a jam on the narrow sidewalk, and the young man in front of them cleared his throat to get their attention. "Excuse me!" he repeated. Politely. He was attempting to get past them on the skinny sidewalk with all of their Tater Tot shopping bags. But Ingrid and Hudson did not budge.

She had a fist planted on one hip and was scowling. "If you and Scott are going to get married, I want a *real* wedding! Think of the *Times* announcement at least!"

The young man had grown impatient. *"Excuse me!"* he boomed, his voice a deep, operatic bass, like rolling thunder.

Ingrid huffed and swung around to confront him. Hudson craned his neck to peer up at the man, who was easily six feet five inches, dressed in a smart pin-stripe suit under a lush black cashmere overcoat, the jacket hanging unbuttoned on his large frame. She stared into the square-jawed face: large pale green eyes beneath light copper lashes and brows, a strong nose. A bolt of lightning struck her, and she nearly dropped her shopping bags.

"Erda?" he asked.

"Thor?" she said, knitting her brow.

"What's going on?" said Hudson. "And am I hearing things or did you just call him Thor?"

Ingrid stared at the towering redhead before her. Freya had told her a while back that when she'd been living on the Lower East Side in New York City and running the Holiday Lounge on St. Mark's, their old friend had set up shop nearly next door. Freya had made a few trips to spy on her competition, reporting to Ingrid that he had opened up a small, dusky, hole-in-the-wall after-hours club across the corner, the kind of place you might miss if you blinked. Known only to an elite set of mismatched night owls—the Fallen and the *Waelcyrgean* among them—with a new password circulated each week, the Red Door had a small stage featuring burlesque dancers, aerial artists, starry-eyed Hula-Hoop performers, and the occasional red-nosed clown. "Hottest thing in the city right now and I don't mean the club," Freya had said with a smirk. "You should see the ladies go wild for him!" To which Ingrid had replied, "I'd rather not!"

Thor, the god of thunder.

Her old flame.

163

He had carried a torch for Erda for centuries: she was different from all the goddesses who threw themselves at him, and the more she rejected him, the more he sought her out. But Erda knew Thor's reputation for breaking many an immortal heart and had kept him at bay.

"My darling Erda," he said, taking her hand and kissing it.

"It's Ingrid now," Ingrid said sharply.

"Will someone please explain to me what's going on?" said Hudson. "Is someone going to introduce me to the Hunk—I mean the Hulk—or is it Thor? Or do I have to do it myself?"

Ingrid finally remembered to breathe. She turned to Hudson, flustered. "I'm sorry! This is—" She made a helpless gesture with her hands.

"Troy Overbrook," the giant redhead said with an affable smile that made a dimple in his cheek. He held out a hand.

Hudson beamed as he shook it. It was obvious that he had already fallen under the handsome god's spell. "Hudson Rafferty. Any friend of Ingrid's is a friend of mine," he said.

Troy tilted his head at her. "We have a lot of catching up to do, *Ingrid*!" He winked at the name. "You look amazing."

Ingrid coughed. "Well, Hudson and I need to get back to work. We're running late."

"When can I see you again? I'm here in North Hampton for the winter. Coffee sometime?" Troy said, leaning seductively against the wall, playing shy for a moment as he looked down at his sneakers. "You know, it's Valentine's Day soon."

"I'm at the local library," she said flatly. "Come get some books."

Hudson nudged her sharply in the ribs. "Don't be silly, Ingrid. Give your old friend your phone number."

Ingrid hesitated for a moment before riffling through her shoulder bag and fishing out a slightly shopworn business card to hand to Troy.

He slipped the card into his pocket and winked at her. "I'll call you," he promised before they parted ways.

Once he was out of earshot, Hudson spoke. "I can't believe you were just going to walk away from *that*!"

"You have no idea what you're talking about, Hudson!"

He glared at her. "Oh, really!"

Ingrid frowned. "Troy and I have a history."

"Pray tell!"

"It's a long and boring story. Besides, I have a boyfriend, remember?" They crossed the street toward the library. *"One cup of coffee.* Jesus!"

Hudson laughed. "I didn't say, 'Sleep with him!' Although if you don't, I will!"

chapter twenty-seven

The Family Three

"I'll do it," Norman said simply, turning to his wife. They were on the train headed back to North Hampton. "I'll do what the Oracle said would get Freya back."

Startled, Joanna looked at her husband. She shook her head and frowned. "Absolutely not!" she said, letting her head fall on his shoulder. "There must be something else we can do."

"There isn't," Norman said softly as he held her close. But he let the subject drop for the moment.

They had passed Patchogue, the midway point between New York City and Montauk, where Ingrid would pick them up. Norman's car had broken down in the city. The trip had been more than the dinosaur Oldsmobile could handle.

He gazed out at the hills covered in frost, the weathered barns. The view gave hints of seascape, his beloved ocean. He lowered his Ray-Ban Clubmasters from the crown of his head over his eyes. He felt the pull of the water, but it was weakening, fading like a slowing pulse. His wife was now fast asleep, her head on his chest, and he dared not move an inch, even as his muscles cramped. Instead he sat awake, listening to the rhythmic thrum of the train. Small moments like this made him happy—he was here with Jo.

He thought of Freya trapped in Salem Village and recalled

those horrific days. Before the witch hunts he and Joanna had lived happily as *Waelcyrgean* among mortals. They observed the rules of the White Council, interfering as little as possible in human affairs, keeping their powers secret and contained. He worked as a fisherman, Joanna as a midwife. Eventually, his girls got carried away, Ingrid with her healing ways, Freya with her potions.

When the witch hunts reached a fever pitch, and the ring of accusing girls ran out of names to name in their own village, they called out new ones, ones they had heard their parents speak of bitterly as they gossiped. Soon the marshal came and took Ingrid and Freya away. There was nothing Norman could do to stop any of it, no matter how much Joanna pleaded with him. The White Council forbade any interference. Ingrid and Freya would eventually be returned to them—they were immortal, after all. If they would let things be, Joanna would give birth to them again.

Freya and Ingrid Beauchamp were brought to stand trial in the ad hoc court of oyer and terminer in Salem Village, where they were charged with witchcraft. He and Joanna had watched their daughters hang at Gallows Hill. Joanna could not forgive him for being unwilling to save them, for following the rules of the Council, and had cast him out of her life. His wife had finally forgiven him and had taken him back. Now they were reliving the pain of Salem all over again, but this time, he would not fail her. He would show her just how much he had always loved her. He would be the one to do as the Oracle instructed. He would get it right. He wouldn't screw it up this time. He owed it to Joanna after everything that had happened between them.

The train stopped, and his wife shifted. Norman placed a hand on her head protectively, running a palm down the length of her hair, as he watched passengers disembark. He observed a few bundled-up New Yorkers looking for a quiet, romantic winter weekend in the Hamptons. The train doors closed. He turned to the window and watched another beachside town roll away beneath the blue sky.

"Dad?" came a voice.

Norman looked up. His gorgeous golden son stood over him, flaxen hair tousled, a knapsack slung over a shoulder. "Freddie! What are you doing here? What a great surprise!" he whispered. "Your mother's asleep. I can't move."

Joanna's head lolled. "No, I'm not," she said. She lifted her head, yawning, turning toward the aisle as she pulled her hair off her face. "My baby!"

"Mother!" he said.

Joanna stared at her son with a sleepy smile. "Now this is a happy surprise!" She and Norman laughed as they rose from their seats. Joanna embraced her son. Norman came into the aisle, grabbing the strap of Freddie's knapsack. "Come sit with us! Let me help you with your bag." He lifted it, placing it in the overhead carriage, and hugged his boy.

"Can I be in the middle?" Freddie asked.

"Where else?" Joanna sat down, moving over to the window, patting the spot next to her. Freddie scooted in beside her. "Oh, my sweet, it's so good to see you!" She kissed and hugged him some more, making a fuss. For once Freddie didn't seem to mind. "What are you doing here? Where's Gert?"

Norman knew Joanna had come to really like Gert, and they had believed the two of them were happily ensconced in New Haven. But now Freddie was staring into his lap. Puzzled, Norman asked, "What's the matter?"

Freddie tilted his head, glancing at his father.

"You can tell us," said Joanna.

"Yeah, I know," he said. "It's just . . . it's not easy." He sighed. "Gert left." He put his hands over his face.

"What?" said Joanna, suddenly livid. "Why?"

"She needed to study, she said."

"Well, students do need to concentrate . . ." Norman said, but his wife shut him up with a look.

"Not now, Norm," Joanna warned. She patted Freddie's shoulder and frowned at her husband.

Norman hugged his son. "It's going to be okay. We're going to get through this, kiddo."

Freddie's hands dropped into his lap. He sniffled. "But I guess the good news is the pixies picked up the scent again. They're on their way to the trident. Or so they say. Who knows with them." He looked at his father, then mother, then back and forth, studying them. "What's wrong with you? You both look awful . . . I mean . . . really tired . . ."

"We're okay, Freddie." Norm peered at Jo, giving her a look. They simultaneously shook their heads, exchanging a tacit agreement not to share what they had learned on their trip to the city. They mustn't tell him what the Oracle said would save Freya. Freddie already had plenty on his plate. And they had also decided to keep the Oracle's suggestion secret from Ingrid, lest she fret more than she was prone to.

Freddie yawned loudly. "I'm exhausted!" His head fell onto Joanna's shoulder.

Norm squeezed his knee. "You just rest, son. You probably need it."

"I do," said Freddie, closing his eyes.

All three sat silently for a while, and soon Freddie was fast asleep, lulled by the hypnotic sound of the train, comforted by the safe feeling of sitting between his parents. Norman and Joanna smiled at each other, watching over their boy sleeping peacefully between them.

"We did good, didn't we?" Norman whispered.

"Yes, we did," returned Joanna.

Still, the danger Freya was in and the knowledge imparted by the Oracle weighed on them. There was no ignoring it. Norman recalled what Jo had said at the meeting. Her words had haunted him: "I wouldn't wish eternity in the underworld to anyone, least of all to our Freya. I would rather die myself."

So would he.

chapter twenty-eight

The Manny Diaries

ae ⚱ ⚋

L ight poured through the gauzy curtains billowing over the open sliding glass doors inside the little beachfront shack. Freddie felt the sun against his face and the cool, soft morning breeze floating in from the ocean. At first he thought he was home, back at Mother's, as it had been a few weeks since he had returned to North Hampton. Then he remembered where he had spent the night. He grinned, keeping his eyes shut. Soon the sounds of the ocean lulled him back to sleep, the sheet only half covering him, exposing his tawny back and legs.

The little weathered hut was all the way at the end of town, way past the Beauchamp house and Gardiners Island, on a small ragged stretch overgrown with sea grass, the sand more pebbly and putty colored than fine and golden.

A sudden thump beside him woke him merely seconds after he had turned his head.

"Crap!" exclaimed a voice, followed by more bed thumping.

He reached out his arm and felt the empty spot. He opened his eyes and rolled onto his side, stretching.

Kristy smiled at him.

"Why are you cursing so early in the morning, babe?" He sat up to watch her, rubbing his eyes, blinking at the light. The bartender from the North Inn was still naked, riffling through a dresser drawer. The tan lines from her bikini emphasized her round bottom, a tattoo of a passionflower above it, slightly off to the side near her hip. She yanked on her underwear, then snapped on her bra.

"Hi, babe," she said. She twisted her silky brown hair and tied it into a topknot. The light played in her hazel eyes as she batted her thick lashes. Like Freya, and now Freddie, Kristy was a bartender at the North Inn. With Freya gone, Sal had needed an extra hand, and Freddie had stepped in to fill it. His first day at work was also the first day he had started pursuing the hot single mom.

After all, Gert had left him, then rebuffed his many attempts to work it out. After two weeks of frantic calls, e-mails, and texts, Gert still refused to answer, and Freddie began to feel like a stalker. She had even sent him a text that read <<Stop it. U & I r over 4 now>>. Rover? They were rover? Then he realized she meant "you and I are over." He had refused to believe it and had texted a <3 back.

Radio silence from Gert again.

<<B that way!>> he punched in his phone after three days of self-control, deciding it would be his very last text to her. He couldn't quite believe how immature they were being. He was "rover" it as well.

He wasn't the type to cheat—okay, okay—he did have a bit of a wandering eye, but he had tried, hadn't he? He had tried to make the marriage work—but Gert had left him. What was he supposed to do? Be alone? He had been alone for five thousand years!

Kristy had a pretty face and was fond of showing off her cleavage squeezed inside a low-cut tank—which had immediately caught Freddie's attention. She had resisted his charms at first, which only made Freddie want her more desperately. She was thirty-six, she told him, while he was barely drinking age, let alone prepared to be with a woman who had two kids. "I'm, like, fifteen years older than you, Freddie." He hadn't the heart to tell her he was actually thousands of years older.

Plus, he was definitely not her type, she added emphatically.

"But I'm everyone's type," he had argued. He tried to settle for their playful, friendly banter as they slung drinks behind the bar. Most of the time she humored him. She was steadfast in her rejection, which made her even more appealing.

One evening in the basement ice room, he slipped his arms around her slim waist. She said, "Listen, you're cute and all, Freddie, but I can't. I have kids. Maxim and Hannah. I don't do one-nighters, and we work together, love." He let her go and apologized for being so forward.

Then they began making out. It was Valentine's Day, after all.

"Love?" he teased when their lips parted.

So here he was, dating a single mom with two kids. He tried not to think of Gert and he liked Kristy. She was beautiful, cool, and no-nonsense. She had a heart-shaped face, bee-stung lips that felt plush and tasted sweet when he kissed her. Their lovemaking was good but hurried and frantic, which he supposed was to be expected when there were two kids lurking about.

He swung an arm out toward her, wiggling his fingers, beckoning for her to get back in bed.

She walked to the closet, then glimpsed over a shoulder, grinning. "I can't! I'm running late." She took a dress off its hanger and threw it on. It clung nicely to her frame, not too tightly, just right.

Freddie rubbed his eyes, sitting up. "What time is it?" He grabbed his phone by the bed to answer his own question just as Kristy's cell gave a little catcall whistle. It was six A.M.

172

"Well, that's a monkey wrench!" Kristy said, glancing at her cell's screen.

"What do you mean, you've got to get out of here?"

She tilted her head, appearing distracted. "You know, my daytime job. The place I usually go most days. But listen, I need a favor."

Freddie lifted his eyebrows and scooted over on the bed, glancing down at the empty spot. He wasn't giving up.

Kristy ignored the signal. "The babysitter called in sick last night, and now their dad, who had promised to take them for the day, just texted that he can't. I need you to take care of them. You know, just for the day. Max has Little League practice and Hannah ballet." She threw his clothes at him and smiled sweetly. "Come on, babe? They're good kids, right? And you have nothing to do all day until you have to work tonight."

Freddie sighed. They were good kids.

She kissed him. "Thanks, love!"

He rose and began to dress.

"Don't worry, it's easy. I'll write down instructions, and you can use my car. I'll take the Vespa. You just have to drop them off and pick them up on time. Make sure they eat. Good food, not junk." She stopped talking and smiled, then came over and leaned in to give him another appreciative kiss. "They really like you, Freddie. Oh, and Max is a vegetarian. But Hannah isn't. Try to remember."

"Okay," said Freddie.

Just then, on cue, Kristy's seven-year-old, Hannah, began wailing in the house.

"Quick!" said Kristy, motioning to the sliding glass doors. "Go! Come back and say you're their babysitter for today. You are officially the new manny."

"Manny?" Freddie echoed, grabbing his Chuck Taylors and

slipping out. Outside in the cold, he put on his shoes, shivering. The kids normally knew him as "Mommy's friend." He would pretend to leave when he came over, only to sneak back in through the sliding glass doors.

He heard Kristy's little girl come into the bedroom. "Mommy, Mommy, Max hid Floppy. I can't find him! He says Floppy is stinky and that I'm too old for him."

Freddie knocked on the glass.

"Oh, look at that!" said Kristy. "Freddie is already here! He's your new babysitter. He must have come up from the beach. He'll help you find Floppy." She slid the door open, and Freddie entered, smiling sheepishly.

Hannah clung to her mother's leg, looking up at Freddie with huge, wet pleading eyes.

Kristy ran a hand over the little girl's fine, scraggly light brown hair. She was a tiny slip of a thing. "Floppy," she echoed. The little girl stared at Freddie as she cried and hiccupped, and her little chin trembled before she let out another whimper and hiccupped again.

Kristy's son, Max, tore into the room, canonballing onto the bed. "Hey, tiger," Freddie said. Wasn't that what you were supposed to call little boys? Either that or "champ." "Tiger" suited him better—Max was a terror.

"What's he doing here already?" Max was kneeling, fists on the mattress, his shiny brown hair, like his mother's, going every which way. His face was tan, cheeks rosy, and his button of a nose sunburned at the tip. He wore round blue-framed glasses that made his brown eyes look even larger.

Freddie mussed his hair. "You're stuck with me for the day, tiger."

"Don't call him that, his name is Max," said Hannah, still clinging to her mother's leg as she walked about the room, both of her feet balanced on one of her mom's. Kristy gathered her purse and keys. "Kids, please be nice to Freddie today, okay?"

They made faces at him before they ran out of the room.

Just when Freddie had gotten rid of the pixies, he found himself saddled with two new wards. He wondered which were better—delinquent pixies or little mortals who cried and hiccupped and asked prying questions? Ah well. He had wanted to be a dad, hadn't he? You get what you wish for.

When he walked into the living room, Hannah was waiting, and together they went to find Floppy.

175

chapter twenty-nine

My Boyfriend's Back

A wheel on the book cart wobbled. *I need to fix that,* thought Ingrid as she pushed it along an aisle in the library. She could ask Hudson, but he was even less mechanically inclined than she was. Tabitha, her belly resembling a dirigible, could barely bend over. The squeaky wheel echoed throughout the empty, quiet library.

Troy Overbrook had called the very same day Ingrid and Hudson had run into him. Then he had called the next, and the next, until she finally acquiesced, agreeing to meet for that one cup of coffee. Troy had even insisted on picking her up at the library today.

She came around a bend, rolling the broken cart into the nook by the window that faced the sea. It was past five o'clock and the sun would be setting soon. She was glad to be inside the quiet library, with the constant, soothing whir of the heater.

She placed *The Great Gatsby* in its rightful spot in the *F* section and felt a hand gently scoop around her waist. She jumped from the sudden unexpected touch.

Matt stood there in his civilian attire, a collared shirt and dark trousers, giving her a slow, sexy grin.

"What are you doing here?" she asked, immediately regretting her words.

He stared at her silently, cocking his head. "What do you mean? I dropped by. I do that sometimes, don't I? Is something wrong?"

She adjusted her glasses, pushing them up farther on her nose with an index finger. "No, *no*, nothing's wrong." She shook her head in an exaggerated way. "It's good to see you!" She smiled and moved forward, tripping over her own feet, giving him a hug.

Matt stood there a bit stiffly, holding out his arms, as if not knowing what to do with his hands for a moment before he hugged her back. "Are you sure nothing's wrong?"

She felt immediately guilty, thinking about Troy, even if it was just a casual coffee thing. To make up for it she lifted up onto her toes and kissed him on the lips.

177

"Get a room, you two!" Hudson teased from the front desk, where he and Tabitha were sitting. Tabitha yawned hello and Hudson yawned, too. The lack of work, along with the hum of the heater, seemed to be making everyone drowsy.

Matt nuzzled her neck. "Mmm, that's better," he said.

Hudson coughed. "Um, Ingrid, Troy's here."

Matt released her from his embrace and gave Ingrid a puzzled look. *Who's Troy?* he mouthed, just as Troy strolled into view. The strapping redhead seemed to suck all the air in the room—even Tabitha looked enamored.

Ingrid looked between the two men standing in front of her. "Hey, Troy, this is Matt, Matthew Noble. He's a detective for the NHPD. *The* detective, that is, of our little town," she said, fumbling with her words a little. "And Matt, this is Troy Overbrook, an old friend from way back. We knew each other when we were, uh . . . kids . . . Troy and I ran into each other—"

Matt nodded. "Hey, Troy, how's it going, man?" he said, offering a hand to shake.

"Hey, Matt," Troy said.

They released hands, and Matt swung an arm over Ingrid's shoulders. "So you're visiting? You in town for a while?" he asked, seeming genuinely curious, friendly even.

Troy hesitated. "Um, yeah . . . I guess you could say that." He nodded.

"We should all go out for drinks sometime. North Inn's always a blast," said Matt.

Ingrid put a hand on his shoulder, her heart pounding hard. "Actually, honey, Troy and I had plans to go out for coffee now . . . to catch up on old times."

Matt's grin looked painful. "Fantastic!" he said. "You have fun, babe." He gave Ingrid a smack on the butt, which made her stand to attention.

Babe? Matt had never called her that before.

"Cool," said Troy, bobbing his head.

Matt kissed her good-bye, a kiss that seemed to go on forever and left her a little dizzy. When he let her go, he gave her a salacious once-over, and Ingrid worried he would slap her behind once more. "Later," he said.

Matt left, and Ingrid and Troy were alone with the wobbly cart. She pushed it toward the nearest bookshelf.

"You need help with that?" Troy asked, kneeling down to fix the wheel. He looked up at her. "So that's the new boyfriend." He whistled.

"Shut it," Ingrid warned. "Not a word!"

Troy twirled the wheel expertly into its rightful place. "Just one. Mortal?"

"Uh-huh," said Ingrid, sighing. "Look, he knows about me, okay?"

"I'm not worried about him, I'm worried about you. You know what mortal means . . ."

It meant she would outlive Matt, it meant she would get her

heart broken. Yes, she knew exactly what it meant. Perhaps Troy was right to question her choice of mate.

OUTSIDE THE COFFEE SHOP window, the sky tinted pink and orange as the sun sank into the waves. Out on the beach, a lone couple watched the sunset, while a few people strolled along the shore, walking their dogs.

She told Troy what had happened to Freya, her voice shaking. Across from her, Troy peered at her from behind his cappuccino and torn sugar packets. His eyes shone, as if he were tearing up, too. The muscle at his jaw twitched, and he reached out a hand, enfolding hers.

She'd forgotten what a steadying presence Thor possessed. She didn't have to explain or make excuses for any of the details. He understood because he was like her.

179

"It seems the passages have closed," she continued. "We can't get through. Our powers . . ."

"Are ineffective," he completed the sentence.

"More like gone," she said wistfully.

"It has crossed my mind that I might be turning into a mortal," he said with a grin.

"Oh dear!" Ingrid said, and they both laughed.

She talked about what she had discovered in her research on Salem, the similarities between the accusers' actions to those in the pamphlet she had found. "You don't think I'm crazy, do you? To think that maybe the girls did this . . . to get out of their chores? I mean their lives were rough—and here was a chance for them to be treated like . . . well, like celebrities."

Troy nodded. "People have done a lot more for a lot less," he said. "It's not implausible that their hard lot was a factor. Why not?"

Ingrid nodded, glad he agreed. "And there's the Putnams,

too. Thomas Putnam filed most of the complaints for witchcraft during the trials. He hated his half brother so much, according to Putnam family lore, that Joseph Putnam kept his horse continually saddled during the witch hunts so he could be ready to skip town once the finger pointed at him. Joseph was actually one of the few townspeople to speak out against the trials."

"What are you saying?"

She frowned. "That maybe once the girls started having fits and calling people witches, Thomas Putnam saw it as a convenient opportunity to knock off some of his enemies. He probably would have gotten to Joseph except it sort of got out of hand before he could get to him."

chapter thirty

The Price of Admission

Tyler Alvarez sat on a stool at Joanna's kitchen counter, concentrating on the pastry before him. He stared at the little fruit tart: one strawberry, a slice of kiwi, an apricot half, and a scattering of blueberries in a clear glaze inside a perfect round crust.

"You made this, Jo?" The six-year-old son of Joanna's housekeeper, Gracella, stared at her with his big, curious brown eyes, his face tan and cheeks pink.

Joanna glanced at him from the kitchen table. "Actually, I bought that at the new bakery." She'd been out to the market and was now putting a bouquet of roses together, cutting the stems and removing the leaves and thorns before placing them in a cylindrical vase. She loved when Gracella and Tyler were there. It made the house feel especially homey and tranquil.

Gracella was at the kitchen sink, doing the dishes. "You stopped baking, Jo! We really miss that."

"I know," Joanna said wistfully. "I just haven't had the time." It was a lie. Well, not entirely, but really she had stopped baking because she had lost her touch. How sad to discover that with her magic gone, she had no real natural talent at baking, only the ability to fix burned crusts and sweeten tasteless cakes.

Tyler's fork hovered. "This looks yummy!" he said.

Joanna laughed, snipping at stems.

Gracella turned around and leaned against the sink, her forehead beaded with sweat. She lifted a rubber-gloved hand to wipe at her brow with her wrist. "There is something I need to talk to you about, Jo."

"You know you can talk to me about anything, Gracella," she said.

"It's about *you know who*." Gracella gave a little nod in Tyler's direction as he dug into the tart, which made him wince, then lick his lips.

"It's about me," said Tyler, jamming another forkful into his mouth.

Gracella rolled her eyes.

Joanna laughed lightheartedly, but then she saw that Gracella was suddenly on the verge of tears. "Oh, Gracella!" She rushed over. "Let's you and I have a little chat while Tyler eats that. Can you give us a moment, sweetie?"

He dropped his fork onto the plate with a clank. "Can I play with Oscar when I'm done?"

"Of course," said Joanna. "He's upstairs in Ingrid's room. Don't let him out."

"Promise," said Tyler. He was a smart child. He had never told a soul about Ingrid's griffin, nor anything about Joanna being able to bring his toy soldiers to life. Well, she couldn't do anything like that now, but she could console Gracella.

Gracella removed her rubber gloves and apron, and Joanna took her by the hand, guiding her to the living room, where they sat on the couch.

"You see, Miss Joanna, you have been so kind to me and my family. I really don't want to seem like I am asking for anything. It's j-just . . ." she stammered.

"Come, come, Gracella, let it all out," encouraged Joanna, patting her on the knee.

Gracella nodded and forged on. She reiterated that Joanna had been so generous putting Tyler in preschool. "But now he is kindergarten age, and the public school is terrible. My friend Cecilia said that there is a lot of bullying going on there—and as you know, Tyler is not like most kids. He's too smart, for one, and takes everything too literally. I am very worried the children will pick on him . . ."

"Ugh!" said Joanna. "When is all that bullying going to end? You read about it in the papers all the time." She realized that in all this distress over Freya she had forgotten that she had meant to do something about Tyler's schooling in September. There was no way she would let him be subjected to bullying. He needed to be with children who were as special as he was and teachers who would nurture such uncanny intelligence.

"Of course we are going to do something about it. Tyler will not enroll there in the fall, don't worry."

Gracella wiped at her nose and cheeks, sniffling a little as they hugged.

Joanna wasn't rich, but she had some money socked away for emergencies such as this. She was going to go upstairs and give Norm a ring, tell him to hold off on looking for that new car today—did they really need a second one?—and ask if he had any pull at some of those fancy private schools in the Hamptons.

THE NEXT DAY Joanna and Tyler were on their way to their first appointment at one of the most prestigious elementary schools in the area. It had been recommended by a certain Hamptons creative set. Norman had a painter friend who was on the board, a successful artist whose shows often got rave reviews in the *New York Times* and was written about in the *New Yorker*. Norman had pulled some strings to secure the appointment for Joanna and Tyler.

183

She parked the car in the lot, which was surrounded by a neatly trimmed boxwood hedge. "This looks nice," she remarked to Tyler as she squeezed into a spot.

She took Tyler's hand, and they made their way across what appeared to be a large soccer field. It was cold out, but in the field sat a circle of little girls and boys wearing wings over their heavy coats. At the center of the circle, a woman with long pink hair, wearing much larger wings over a long violet coat, held a book in one hand. She was gesticulating as the children attentively watched her.

"This looks fun!" she said to Tyler, somewhat skeptically.

The pink-haired woman and little children waved as they strode past them toward the schoolhouse. A man with a shag and scraggly beard, dressed in white, waited out front. Joanna wondered if she had stepped into the seventies, if the passages of time had in fact reopened.

"Mr. Rainbow?" she asked.

"Just Rainbow." He smiled. "There are no such formalities around here," he said as they shook hands.

"Well, I'm Joanna Beauchamp, and this is Tyler, the boy in question."

Rainbow kneeled down to be at Tyler's eye level. "Hello there, Tyler." He winked, tousling the boy's curls.

"Hey," responded Tyler, then he looked down at his feet and kicked at the cement, intimidated by the man's overfriendliness.

"Come on inside and see one of the classes in session."

Joanna and Tyler followed Rainbow into the school. Children's paintings decorated the walls. The school was bright with sunlight, airy, and smelled of Elmer's Glue. They pushed through doors into a hallway and made their way down it. She could hear fun, happy Spanish-sounding music.

"What's that?" she asked.

"The class is in 'movement' right now." Rainbow swung a

door open onto a huge room with blond wood floors, where boys and girls shifted desultorily about, some spinning in circles, some wandering off into far corners, all appearing to have no real sense of direction.

"Movement?"

"Other schools call it 'physical education,'" he explained with a look of distaste. "You want to dance, Tyler?"

Tyler shook his head no, then looked at the floor.

"That's okay. In time. But if the mood strikes you . . ."

"Can you tell me about the curriculum?" asked Joanna.

Rainbow smiled in his affable way. "This is an experimental school. For movement, we might take the children out to the gym and have them invent their own ball game. We like our students to feel free to express themselves in order to reach their full potential."

"Even when it's freezing outside?"

"What is weather anyway?" Rainbow smiled.

Joanna attempted a serious expression while Tyler did a little break-dance move beside her.

"That's fantastic!" said Rainbow. "Keep going, Tyler!"

Tyler stopped immediately and watched the dancing children.

Joanna expressed her concerns about bullying, and Rainbow reassured her that there was none of that here. The school was a breeding ground for pacifism, if anything. Classes were given in an impromptu, unstructured fashion, often letting the children themselves dictate the tone. There were no textbooks or homework or lesson plans. The staff believed they were in the middle of creating something new, revolutionary, creative, and were inventing it as they went along. The mission statement: "Freedom in learning. Learning in freedom."

The cafeteria was vegan, using local organic produce only, which added to the already prohibitive tuition, of course, but who would want their kids to eat anything else? Rainbow happily rattled off the illustrious names of all the rich and powerful and famous parents who had donated time and money (a lot of money) to make the place what it was today.

The more she learned about the school, the more Joanna grew wary that Tyler would learn anything here. She imagined the classes as utter chaos. Children needed—even wanted—discipline and structure. They needed *books*.

The music changed; this time it was a man singing in an angelic, operatic voice. The children drifted about, waving their arms as if they were flying, mimicking the movements of the young woman who began to lead them.

"So if there are no books, how do the children learn to read?" she asked. "Or do they not?"

"Oh, they do! They do!" said Rainbow. "Somehow they do," he added with a serene smile.

"What about when they go to high school? Won't making the transition be a bit like culture shock? This is so different."

Rainbow gave her another big, happy grin. "I'm not saying there aren't going to be challenges later."

Joanna sighed. Oh well. At least there wouldn't be any bullies. And Rainbow did say the kids learned to read . . . *somehow.* "When are applications due?" she asked.

The serene smile left his face. "You have not applied?"

"No?"

Rainbow shook his head sorrowfully. "I am so sorry. Applications were due a year ago. We only have sixteen spaces, and we had hundreds of families apply. I am so sorry."

And that was when Joanna realized that the little school with no textbooks, no lesson plans, and no physical education did have one thing: a surfeit of prestige—which was the one thing that mattered in the Hamptons.

chapter thirty-one

Tequila Sunset

L eaning against the cash register in a plaid shirt and jeans, Freddie crossed his arms as he ran an eye down the bar of the North Inn. The lone bleached blonde at the end, with oversize pearls and coral lipstick, was tilting off her seat, and he thought he better cut her off soon and call her a cab. Overall, he was getting good at this mortal thing, being unable to avail himself of his powers. His customers had drinks and ramekins of peanuts. It was midweek, early in the evening. Sal was in the back, playing poker with his septuagenarian buddies, and Kristy was home with Max and Hannah.

AC/DC's "Hell's Bells" began to play on the jukebox, the tolling of bells followed by a guitar's opening riff. Freddie dug a beer out of the ice bin and popped it open. He took a long, hard swig, exhaled a satisfied sigh, and looked up at the hockey game on the old-school TV above the bar. His team was in the midst of scoring a beautiful goal and they were winning. *Small pleasures,* he told himself.

He always sensed the shift in atmosphere when a customer entered the bar. This time he felt it before the door opened. One second he flicked his eyes at the door and it was closed, the next the door swung open and someone was walking through it. He still had a little magic in him after all. The man striding toward him was nearly as tall and wide as the doorframe itself—football-player size, at least the breadth of his shoulders. *Wait a second*, thought Freddie, *I know this guy* . . .

"Odin's beard!" Freddie said.

"Wha?" Troy laughed, swinging a hand out at him. Freddie grabbed it and his old friend tugged him forward to give him a bear hug over the bar top. The young men patted each other hard on the back as they laughed.

Troy took a seat. "Hey, man!"

"Wow! Look at you!" Freddie shook his head and whistled. "Thor, how have you been, my friend?"

"Good, good, everything's great. Good to see you, man. I saw Ingrid the other day. She told me you were here. So . . . here I am!"

"That right?" said Freddie with a grin. "Wow! Ingrid, huh? Erda and Thor." He laughed.

"Yep! Except I go by Troy Overbrook now." He swung his bangs out of his face.

Freddie shook his head with a smile. "Troy Overbrook, Freddie Beauchamp at your service. What can I get you?"

Troy eyed the bottles on the shelves behind the bar. "How about we have ourselves a little reunion celebration?" He squinted at Freddie and gave a nod. "Tequila?"

"Perfecto!" Freddie got an unopened bottle of Sauza Gold along with shot glasses and dewy cold Coronas. He had already finished his own beer. He set the tequila and beers down between them. They licked salt off their fists, slammed down their shots, bit into limes, and took deep swigs of the chasers.

Troy flashed his glowing white teeth.

Freddie saluted Troy with his beer bottle. "What the hell have you been up to?" He didn't usually drink on the job, but this reunion was a special occasion.

As they downed more tequila shots and beers, Troy proceeded to tell Freddie about his life in Midgard. He told him about his more recent fiasco: the after-hours club he had owned in the city, and how he finally had to give up the ghost. He had sold it and made a modest but decent chunk of change. He believed the club's lack of success was somehow related to their magic waning. Then, on a last minute whim, Troy had decided to spend the winter in North Hampton and enjoy the quiet. He had some business here.

Freddie lifted his eyebrows inquisitively at Troy as he poured two more shots that spilled over the glasses.

"Well, I kind of just wanted to see Erda, to tell you the truth." Troy shook his head. "I mean Ingrid. You know, give it the old college try." The Sauza had loosened his tongue.

"Oh," said Freddie. "Right, well, good luck with that!" He grinned.

"Help me out here, Freddie! A guy needs all the help he can get. Can't you do something? I mean, she's your sister! She really serious about that mortal?"

Freddie hiccupped. He took a long swig of beer, which seemed to help. "Sure looks like it. Sorry, bud."

They laughed good-naturedly. Freddie replenished their beers, and they drained two more shots and bit into lime quarters, making puckered-up faces. Freddie quickly served the new customers who had wandered in, disappointed to find Freya and her pop-up drinks were gone, but Freddie made them forget his sister soon enough with his own brand of magic: being an energetic, good-looking guy at the bar. He refilled a few drinks, and returned to Troy, all ears, but not before pouring himself and Troy two additional shots.

Troy regaled him with tales from his immortal life—in Roman times, he had been a senator (tons of gold, bacchanalia, and debauchery); in sixteenth-century France, he had lived in the courts of kings (more gold and oh-so-many lovely breasts heaving up from tight corsets); then in the nineteenth century, he was with Jefferson in Paris (excellent cash flow and not stodgy at all—in fact, the libertines were total babes). And on it went with raves about gold and women, then eventually cars and motorcycles.

Freddie had started to feel a little edgy—or, rather, envious of Troy. His friend had lived all these amazing lives. What had Freddie done since he'd arrived in Midgard? Since he had made his way back from Limbo, he had fallen for this chick, Hilly, who had totally bamboozled him and he ended up forced to marry her sister, and just when he had completely fallen for Gert, she had left him. Most of his time in mid-world had, in fact, been spent playing video games, if he really thought about it. He had put out a few little house fires, but big deal.

He felt miserable, unaccomplished, drowsy, and punchy. A total loser. Tequila had a way of doing that. At first you felt wickedly on top of the world, then you were ready to sock the first person who looked at you askew. Vodka would have been better. And where was that bleached blonde at the end of the bar? It was looking a little blurry down there. Had she fallen off her stool? He had forgotten to call her a cab. He'd take care of it later. It was her own damn fault if she'd gotten too wasted. Someone came over and asked him for a drink, and he mixed it hastily, making a mess on the bar, which he didn't bother to wipe, then he slapped the cash in the register.

"So what's been going on with you? Tell me all about your lives!" Troy said enthusiastically, giving Freddie his big, dimpled grin.

Freddie stared blankly back. Why had Troy just asked him that? Of course Troy knew what had gone down, that Freddie had spent the last five thousand years whiling his time away in friggin' Limbo because he had been wrongfully accused of destroying the Bofrir. WTF?

Troy's smile went slack, and his broad shoulders deflated. He realized the faux pas. "Oh, I'm so sorry, dude . . . yeah . . . about that . . . At least you're out, right? I heard the Valkyries found the real guy who did it."

Freddie didn't answer. It was his fault, what had happened to Killian. There were so many things he wished he could have done differently. Freya back in the past, Killian in Limbo, and here he was, stuck in this little town, getting drunk on tequila. He was useless. His life had been a waste.

"Hey!" said Troy, reaching over the bar to grab Freddie's arm. "Did I say something wrong?"

Freddie smiled. "It's cool, man. It's totally cool! We're good!" Freddie poured the rest of the Sauza into their shot glasses.

He couldn't do anything for anyone. Not for his sister or his best friend. There was nothing to do but drink. Might as well finish the bottle.

chapter thirty-two

Shower the People

ஸே⚓ஸ

G uests sat on the carpet in a half circle around Tabitha. It was reminiscent of her reading hour at the library, only she was unwrapping baby-shower gifts in her living room. Hudson gathered the ribbons from the discarded wrappings and stuck them onto a paper plate, which then would be turned into a hat to place on Tabitha's head. "A delightful and hilarious tradition," he had remarked.

Ingrid was making a list of the gifts for thank-you notes. She had to admit there *was* something adorable about tiny, tiny socks and shoes and ever-so-soft miniature T-shirts and swaddling cloths, something that gave her a vague stirring. A baby. None of her siblings had ever had children. They were stuck, somehow; Freya and Freddie were perpetual adolescents, while Ingrid had been a spinster all her life, an unripened fruit, withering on the vine. But love had changed her, and she could finally understand what all the fuss was about.

"A tutu!" exclaimed Tabitha.

"Um, that's from Ingrid!" Hudson quickly shot back.

Tabitha and her friends laughed.

"It's a boy, right?" asked Betty Lazar, who had recently shacked up with her boyfriend, Seth Holding, the junior detective.

"Well, you never know!" said Ingrid, scribbling down *tutu* and her name beside it. She giggled.

"I love it!" said Tabitha. "It's perfect. Every child should have a tutu. Thanks, Ingrid."

"No trouble at all," retorted Ingrid.

"I thought it was genius," said Hudson, grabbing a pink ribbon to stick onto the belle-of-the-ball hat.

Ingrid glanced at the many shelves in Tabitha's home library, which was so like Matt's. Thinking of him made her wistful. She had been avoiding him lately, and he was starting to notice. She knew she was being silly, but she couldn't stop feeling like a home wrecker even if Matt and Mariza had never shared a home.

"I've decided I'm going to practice attachment parenting," Tabitha announced as she balanced a gift on her knees.

"What's that?" asked Hudson. "Is that the thing where you see parents walking around with a child on a leash? Those little harness things? I always wondered about that."

Even Ingrid had to laugh. Although she had always been puzzled by those leashes, but usually chalked them up to parents having watched too many true-crime shows.

"Silly!" replied Tabitha. "It's a type of parenting method created by a pediatrician and has to do with developmental psychology. There are eight principles."

"Like what?" asked Hudson.

"Like 'Feed with respect and love.'"

"Oh, Scott does that with me," he retorted.

Tabitha giggled. "It's about nurturing a healthy dependency so that the child becomes a confident person."

"I think my mom got the other handbook," Hudson quipped. "Detachment parenting. The hands-off method!"

Ingrid laughed but her mind was still on Matt. Over coffee, Troy had told her that he thought she was making a big mistake, letting herself fall for a mortal. "I've done what you are doing. Trust me. I don't recommend it. The pain . . ." he had said. "To be honest, it's agonizing . . ."

Yes, the pain, thought Ingrid. Matt would be a fleeting moment in an endless life. Matt would die and she would be left with the pain of his loss for all eternity. Was it worth it? Was loving him worth the pain of losing him?

"Oh, my God!" squealed Tabitha, holding up the mini lederhosen.

"I hope your child yodels!" said Hudson.

"Oh, he will!" said Betty Lazar. "I hear they keep you up all night long yodeling!" At that she let out a yodel.

On the notepad, Ingrid inscribed the word *lederhosen* after *Hudson.*

chapter thirty-three

The Price of Admission, Part Two

In front of the low-slung main building—made of wood and blue glass—stood a white marble reproduction of the Greek statue *Winged Victory of Samothrace.* The goddess Nike of peace, efficiency, speed, and victory splayed her wings as she pressed her chest forward, facing the sea, as had her original counterpart in the port of Samothrace, to welcome incoming ships from their conquests. Every morning the statue greeted the five hundred or so kindergarteners through twelfth graders and the staff of the Carlyle School.

On the orientation tour, Joanna and Norman had visited the quaint little green schoolhouses, connected by wooden walkways at the back of the campus. They admired the lovely little playgrounds, gardens, greenhouses, and small farm with two pigs, five goats, and six sheep, which the smaller students were taught to care for. The barn doubled as the "art studio."

Now Joanna and Norman sat in the principal's office for the interview. Charlie Woodruff was a disarming, good-looking fellow in his early fifties with white hair and sincere blue eyes. He explained the school's mission as one that encouraged their students to adopt a global outlook, embrace technology, pursue the arts and sciences as much as competitive sports. "We're traditional but forward thinking, at least we hope to be so," he explained. "So what do you think?"

"Where do we sign?" Joanna joked. Truly, it seemed like a dream school. She could already imagine Tyler in one of those little blazers with the school crest and gray flannel pants they wore as uniforms.

The principal smiled. "Of course, we will need to meet with his parents as well, but ultimately everything will hinge on how Tyler tests."

"Of course!" echoed Joanna and Norman.

196

"So who is your patron?" asked Dorothy.

Joanna stared blankly back from across the luncheon table at Dorothy De Forrest. What was her dear but self-important heiress friend asking her now? Joanna had grown weary of Dorothy's chronicles of finishing schools and debutante balls but had agreed to the lunch, because if one did not see one's annoying old friends, one might not have any old friends at all. "Excuse me?" She blinked.

Dorothy blinked back. "My dear, who do you have on the inside? At Carlyle?"

Joanna was from an old, well-known family. She was a Beauchamp. But she never understood why certain people gained a sense of entitlement from a name. Gentle birth. Landed gentry. Old money. It was all dumb luck. Who cared? "What do you mean?"

"I mean who is backing your application. Surely you have someone on the board? Surely Norman . . . ?" Dorothy asked.

"The Carlyle School is extremely selective. Admission is practically a miracle," she said with a small laugh. "Surely you know somebody who can help."

Joanna shook her head, feeling a bit sick to her stomach. "No, we don't know anyone at Carlyle." She took a sip of her wine. "Besides, we were told it all depends on how Tyler tests and I'm certain he'll do very well." She returned to slicing her duck.

"Of course, of course," said her friend, cutting up the quail on her plate, which sat in a tiny basket made of potato strings on a bed of baby greens. "Sorry to mention it. Please pass the salt, darling."

chapter thirty-four

Where Things
Come Back

Sunday morning. Sort of. It was noon when Freddie awoke in his own bed for once. He would have slept longer had it not been for his cell persistently ringing on the bedside table. It had been a long week caring for Max and Hannah after evenings slinging drinks, and he had told Kristy he needed time to recover in his own space. The previous night had been a doozy, the North Inn remaining packed until four in the morning. He'd had to get ironfisted about last call, eventually kicking out the last lively hangers-on. "It's not the Fourth of July yet. No need for fireworks," he told them. "Just go home!"

He wished he had turned off his ringer, but remembered he had a brunch date with Kristy at one. *That must be her.* Good thing she had called—he might have slept through the date. Her ex had the kids for the weekend. After brunch, they had planned to go antiquing (her choice) and after that spend time lazing around in bed (his). He grabbed the phone with her name on his lips, but just as he was about to say it, the person at the other end gave a chipper "Hi, love!"

Love? But the voice wasn't Kristy.

"Who is this?" he asked suspiciously.

"Babe, it's me."

Freddie sat up, glancing at the room. Everything was much cleaner and more organized than he had last left it. *Gracella*, he thought. *Mother really shouldn't subject the poor woman to my messes.* After a lengthy pause, he came back to the uncomfortable moment.

"Gert," he said, his voice flat.

"Hi, sweetie!" she replied cheerfully.

This was not a good way to wake up. "What do you want?"

"I finished my thesis early!"

"Great!" he said. Did she expect them to pick up where they had left off after she had abandoned him out of the blue? Wasn't that actually considered grounds for divorce? Abandonment. Wouldn't that be a way out of Mr. Liman's contract he had signed with his blood? Although it said nothing about abandonment by one of the parties.

Freddie had made a decent life for himself since he had moved back to North Hampton. He made a living at the bar and enjoyed working there. Kristy appreciated him. He was becoming attached to her kids—imaginative Hannah and her quirky and quick-witted bespectacled vegetarian brother. He liked when Hannah told him crazy stories about fairies, and he was teaching Max how to ice-skate. Kids . . . he liked kids, but Gert had never even wanted to talk about them.

She exhaled into the phone, and he had to pull the cell away from his ear for a second. "Freddie, I'm sorry I left like I did. I know it was a little cold."

"Cold?" he said. He remembered his various attempts to fix the marriage and how they all had failed. He glanced at the clock. He had to shower and get ready to meet Kristy. "Listen, Gert, it's a bit early for me to talk about all this."

"Early?" she said.

"I was up late. I mean, I work at a bar."

"Oh," she replied. "Can we talk later today? I really need to." It was always on her terms, wasn't it? "Freddie, there wasn't anyone else, if that's what you're thinking. It *was* totally about school. I . . . I . . ."

It wasn't what he had been thinking. He didn't care anymore, or at least he tried to convince himself he didn't care. It hadn't been easy to forget her—no matter how much he liked Kristy, he had to admit he missed Gert, he missed his wife. But she had left him with a note, and now she just expected them to pick up where they had left off? Amazing. He couldn't be more furious, but when he heard a tremor in her voice, he relented. "Look, let's talk later."

"Okay," she said. "I miss you . . ."

"Uh-huh." Freddie exhaled. "Look, I really have to run." It came out curtly, which hadn't been his intention. Gert had a way of getting to him. "I'll call you later," he said, and hung up the phone.

WHEN HE RETURNED home after his date, the house was empty. Joanna had left a note saying she and Norman had gone out for clam chowder. You had to love the specificity. Well, at least that was one relationship that appeared to be working.

Freddie climbed the stairs, done in. He glanced in Ingrid's room to see if she was around but only saw Oscar, Buster, and Siegfried curled up on the bed. Buster blinked at him. His eyes appeared heavy, and he quickly closed them as he pressed his snout against Oscar's fur. Since the Beauchamps had lost their powers, it was as if the familiars had gone into hibernation. *Poor kids*, Freddie thought. He closed the door.

Freddie felt sorry for himself, too. He had been late to his date with Kristy, and they'd had their first fight. Afterward, they had gone back to the shack on the beach and made up in bed. But after their lovemaking, Kristy got teary eyed. She complained about being so much older than Freddie and that eventually he would leave her. Max and Hannah were getting attached. It wasn't good. It had all been a huge mistake. As much as he tried to assuage her—he planned to stick around and he really, really cared so much about her—she seemed dead set on being negative. "Is that really enough?" she asked. She had never been like that before.

Perhaps Kristy had a point. He was reluctant to say those three little words that might seal the deal. It felt so right with Kristy, but . . . he was still *married*. He just wasn't ready to say it. Perhaps Gert had ruined him. Then Kristy said it was best if Freddie went home. They needed space. The whole thing had made him feel shitty.

And here he was. He emptied out his pockets onto the dresser—cell, change, crumpled bills—pulled off his T-shirt, and stumbled out of his jeans, whipping them onto an armchair. He just wanted to be in bed and resume what he hadn't finished earlier that morning: sleep.

He closed the windows, pulled the curtains, and turned down the heater. He liked getting the room chilly as he snuggled up in the duvet; it made for the best kind of sleep. It was only about seven, and he was glad to be getting an early start. He crawled into bed and stretched himself out luxuriously. His leg hit something. "Ack!" he said, jolting up.

"Kelda!" Freddie's arms fell protectively to his sides, shielding himself with the duvet. "What are you doing here?"

The pixie widened her almond eyes, pushing strands of messy white hair behind an ear. "I was waiting for you. I have some crappy news."

"Nice! Do you mind? Hand me my shirt, will you?" he said.

Like the pixies, he was comfortable with nudity, but if his mother strolled in, it might be awkward. Joanna made unexpected check-ins, needing to reassure herself that Freddie was still home from Limbo.

"Good news, bad news kind of thing." Kelda rolled off the bed to hand him his shirt. She was filthy, in a rumpled T-shirt, dusty black jeans, stained tube socks.

Freddie grimaced, thinking about his clean sheets.

Kelda did a yoga stretch, coming up in a reverse swan dive, her hands forming a prayer at her chest. "Good news: we found the trident. Bad news: Jörmungandr has it."

chapter thirty-five

Put a Ring On It

They had barely sat down at the table in the French restaurant when Ingrid noticed a platinum band on Hudson's ring finger. "Hudson! You didn't tell me!"

"We wanted to keep it a surprise!" Hudson laughed, holding Scott's hand.

Scott and Hudson liked to joke that they did not look so much like a couple as a pair of gay twins, even if Scott was half Korean. Like Hudson, Scott was meticulously dressed and boyishly handsome. "We wanted to wait till dessert to make the announcement. Really, we don't want to spend the entire dinner talking about us." Although of course now that they had announced it so early they would have to spend the entire dinner talking about them, but Ingrid didn't really mind.

She and Matt were on a double date with the couple. Matt had reserved the table in the nook by the window facing the sea at La Plage.

"Wait!" said Ingrid, flustered. "You didn't get married without telling me, did you? You couldn't have—"

"Of course not. Scott just popped the question. The wedding bands are gold. They fit on top of these. Cool, right?"

"Congratulations!" said Matt. He stood and held out his arms to Scott, who was sitting beside him.

Scott gave a wry smile and rose to receive the hug, while Ingrid embraced Hudson. Matt flagged the waiter to order a bottle of bubbly. The champagne was brought to the table with an ice bucket, and Ingrid and Matt raised their flutes.

"To the happy couple," Matt said.

"To our friends," Ingrid said, her eyes sparkling.

While Hudson and Scott clinked glasses, Ingrid turned to Matt, squeezing his knee beneath the table. He slipped a hand on her thigh underneath her skirt. The slinky touch sent a warm shiver through her. She felt the crimson flush rise to her cheeks and took a sip of champagne to steady her nerves. "So . . . any plans yet?"

"We're thinking May," piped Hudson.

"Wow, so soon! That's great!" said Ingrid, adjusting herself in her chair.

"And of course I would be honored if you were my maid of honor," Hudson said with a tentative smile.

"Me?"

Hudson nodded with a grin and they hugged again.

"We have a lot of planning to do, then!" Ingrid gushed.

"Wait a second," said Scott. "This is what I mean. *Let's not.* Let's just relax."

Ingrid winked. "Hudson and I will talk."

"Absolutely!" said Scott.

"That we will. And guess what?" Hudson widened his eyes.

"What?" Ingrid leaned in.

Again, Scott cut in. "His mom is coming. After all that fuss!" He folded his napkin on his lap. "I really don't know why Hudson hemmed and hawed for so long. My mom's Korean—she wasn't even born in the States, and when I came out to her at thirteen she barely batted an eye."

"Your mom was not a debutante from Charleston," said Hudson. "Your mom is cool."

"Not really," returned Scott.

Hudson lifted his fork. "Anyhow, it's all behind us now. Mom says she's looking forward to the wedding. That's *huge!*" He dug in to his coquille Saint Jacques with a smile.

"Next thing you know, she'll be asking about kids," said Scott. "Mark my words."

"And?" Matt nudged with a grin.

Hudson and Scott exchanged a knowing look. "We already found an egg donor," confessed Hudson with a cheeky grin. "Now all we need is a womb!"

OUTSIDE IN THE parking lot after Hudson and Scott had driven off, Ingrid and Matt watched the taillights disappear in the mist. The air was chilly and she huddled close to him. She could have stood there forever with Matt.

He twined his fingers in hers. "Ingrid, what's going on with us?" he asked. "You're avoiding me and not just because of your work. I feel you drifting away." He had asked her why she had left so abruptly during that lunch a few weeks ago, but she had lied and told him she hadn't been feeling well. Since then, they had hardly spent any time together.

Ingrid took a deep breath. It was time to come clean and tell him what was bothering her. "Do you wish you and Mariza had stayed together?" she asked finally. It wasn't quite how she had planned to say it, but there it was. She wanted to do the right thing by Maggie, but she also wanted to protect her own heart. It was both selfless and selfish of her. She lifted his hands that were holding hers and let them drop against her as she waited for his answer.

"Sometimes," he admitted. "We tried once. For Maggie's sake. But that was a long time ago. Maggie was in diapers." He ran his cheek along her hair, breathing in its fragrance, then let go of her hands and leaned on the car so they were both facing the beach. "Is this what's been bothering you?"

She shook her head. "Yes . . ." she whispered. It felt good to no longer skirt around it. She looked up at the deep black blue of the night and sighed. A din rose from the nearby North Inn. The crowd seemed to be getting rowdy. Someone whistled. A woman squealed. Clapping.

Matt stared out at the ocean. "I met Mariza when I was sixteen. I was a kid, an irresponsible kid. Not that I regret it, not at all. I wouldn't change anything because it meant we got to have Maggie. But Mariza and I, it was a lifetime ago. We're friends, Ingrid, we have to be, for our daughter. But as that song Maggie keeps playing says, 'we're never, ever, ever getting back together,'" he said with a grin.

He turned to Ingrid and flipped around to hover over her, his hands pressing against the car's roof, one at each side of her shoulders. He had her locked in so she couldn't go anywhere but here, which was exactly where she wanted to be.

chapter thirty-six

The Price of Admission,
Part Three

❧ ⚶ ☙

Her stomach lurched. Joanna wasn't the one about to be tested, but it felt as if she might as well be as she strolled past the goddess Nike into the Carlyle School, holding Tyler's hand. The little boy wore a crisp pale blue shirt and red paisley tie, his big curls slightly wet and brushed flat, appearing pasted to his large forehead. They took the flight of stairs to Principal Woodruff's office. He had sent Joanna a personal e-mail, saying he would accompany her to the office of the admissions director, a Mrs. Henderson, for Tyler's interview and test. He was looking forward to seeing her and Tyler.

"Where are we going?" asked Tyler.

"It's going to be fine, sweetie," said Joanna, her voice almost shrill, as they ascended the black marble steps. She squeezed his hand to reassure him.

"Ouch, you're hurting me! Your hand is clammy, and my shoes are too tight!" Tyler pulled his hand away and stomped on the step with the polished black leather shoes in question. He leaned against the banister and refused to take another step.

Joanna attempted to pull herself together. She should have asked Norman to do this. It was too nerve-racking, but she had wanted to do it because she needed to ensure it went smoothly. "You came here with your mother and father, remember? Didn't you see Principal Woodruff? Mr. Charlie? He told me you were a very intelligent little boy. You made an excellent impression on him."

"Oh!" Tyler looked down and ran the side of his shoe along the step. "I can walk up the stairs myself. I'm a big boy."

"Yes, you are, Tyler. You do that. That's very good." She loved Tyler, but he was making her jitters worse.

"WELL, HELLO!" said Principal Woodruff, rising to greet Joanna and Tyler as they entered his office. "You are looking extremely dapper, young man!"

Tyler looked down at his shiny shoes and shrugged.

"Say hello to Principal Woodruff." Joanna patted his head, and he immediately pushed her hand away. Since when had Tyler begun behaving this way? Joanna forced a smile. "Tyler?"

Tyler glanced up. "Hi," he said to the principal, then quickly looked away to gaze out the window at the front yard.

"It's very cold today," said Mr. Woodruff. "I understand. We're all a bit cranky when it gets like this."

"I do apologize, Principal Woodruff," said Joanna in a rush. "I think his shoes are bothering him. You know how fast they grow at this age. It's hard to keep up, really!" She reached out to shake his hand.

"Call me Charlie. Please don't apologize." He smiled amicably, but he seemed a little frayed around the edges, as if he were trudging through these formalities. "Let's go," he said. He accompanied them to the admissions director's office, where he introduced them to Mrs. Henderson, wished them good luck, and said good-bye.

Joanna felt that sudden dropping sensation in her stomach again.

SHE AND TYLER sat facing the gleaming desk, where manila folders, a glass paperweight with a tarantula trapped inside it, a pen carrier, and photos were neatly arranged. Mrs. Henderson appeared to be a fastidious woman. She was British, attractive, with fine, light blond hair up in a French twist and big turquoise blues with a left lazy eye that roamed to the inner corner. When the eye righted itself, Mrs. Henderson smiled with her bright scarlet lips.

Joanna could only see the backs of the photo frames on the desk. Perhaps, she mused, if she could see these photographs—Mrs. Henderson's family or dog or cat—she might feel less intimidated by this gatekeeper to her top-choice school. Dorothy De Forrest's questions rang in her head. *Who is your patron? Who do you have on the inside?* She glanced at the large black-and-white print on the wall, a pretty freckle-faced Amelia Earhart in an aviator's cap and goggles, and quickly recited an incantation in her head to little effect.

Tyler studied the room and, with watchful eyes, stared at Mrs. Henderson as she went on about the scholarships the school offered.

Joanna could feel vast rings of sweat forming at the armpits of her silk blouse. She kept her arms pinned to her sides and collected herself, a witch without magic. To her dismay, Tyler appeared to be moping. She noticed the bright yellow room adjacent to the office, which could be spied via a connecting glass window. Inside, she saw a play area with colorful toys, desks, and chairs. This was most likely where the kindergarten consultant would administer her test.

"Yes, that's where Tyler will go and *play* in a little while," the admissions director said, and nodded. She turned to the boy. "First off, why don't you go ahead and take off your shoes, Tyler. And while we are at it, you are welcome to loosen that nice tie of yours. I want you to be as comfortable as possible."

Tyler shook his head no, then looked down. Joanna immediately leaned over to help him, and his little hands fluttered at hers as if she were an irritating fly. He was being so very uncooperative today of all days. Usually, he was such a good kid. What had gotten into him? "I don't understand. He's never like this," said Joanna.

"It's okay, I want Tyler do it by himself," Mrs. Henderson said. "Tyler, please remove your shoes." Her voice remained polite but firm.

Joanna realized the testing had begun, even if the director hadn't taken him into the adjoining room. She watched Tyler's lack of response, panic rising.

Tyler slumped in his chair and wouldn't budge.

"Tyler, is there something troubling you?" asked Mrs. Henderson.

He looked up at her and stared. This was going to be a defining moment, Joanna knew. Her pulse rang in her ears and her stomach flip-flopped once again. She begged Tyler in her head to be a good little boy. He pouted.

"Tyler?" urged the admissions director.

He glared up at her. "Leave me alone!" he shot, his black lashes blinking out a tear that rolled down his cheek. He glared at the admissions director. "Leave me alone! I don't want to be here!"

JOANNA WAS SILENT as she drove Tyler back to his home. She combed through what had happened at the school from beginning to end, trying to pinpoint where she had gone wrong. Perhaps her nerves had rubbed off on the sensitive child. They had completely flubbed the interview, and while she had been successful at finally coercing Tyler to go "play with the nice lady," the rest of the meeting was just as awkward as the beginning. If she could just get Tyler into a decent kindergarten, then she would be a good mother, not one whose children were being threatened all over the nine worlds of the universe.

Mrs. Henderson had remained unflustered, responding graciously to Tyler's awful little temper tantrum. "We all have our off days," she had said cheerfully. "Don't worry about it. He's six years old, after all!"

But Joanna knew she had flubbed it. There wasn't going to be a second chance at Carlyle. She glanced at Tyler in the passenger seat.

"Did you have fun with the nice lady?" she asked. "What did she want you to do?"

Tyler shrugged. "Nothing."

She sighed.

He turned to look out the window and ran his pudgy little index finger over the glass.

She mussed his hair and watched the road. "It's okay, Tyler. Everything's going to be okay," she promised.

WHEN SHE PULLED into the driveway, Norman was waiting outside for her, shoveling snow, waving and smiling. She was relieved to see him. He opened the driver's-side door for her.

"How'd it go?" He saw her face. "That bad, huh?"

Joanna laughed—she had to. At least it was over. Perhaps

she had grown too serious about this whole kindergarten thing. You never got anywhere if you came off desperate. "I'd rather not talk about it, but needless to say I'm back to the drawing board."

"Ouch!" Norman said, hugging her. "I have some news. I'm packing a bag upstairs. I heard from Arthur, and I'm on my way to meet him."

She released herself from Norman's grasp, feeling a thousand new worries as she remembered the conditions explained by the Oracle. That certainly put the private school admissions race into perspective.

"Wish me luck," said Norman with a brave smile.

They had very little time left, and if Arthur, as the keeper of the passages, couldn't provide a better solution than that of the Oracle . . . well, there was no reason for Joanna to think of that now.

"He'll think of something, I know he will," Norman said. "Everything's going to be okay," he said, echoing the words she had just said to Tyler and with just as much conviction.

chapter thirty-seven

The Monster at the End of the World

Jörmungandr was the sea serpent whose head rested near the bottom of Midgard. He wrapped himself around mid-world, long enough to bite his own tail and form a circle. He did the latter while he slept, much like a child sucking on his thumb for comfort. His fangs dripped blood and black poison that killed in an instant. He was fond of ridiculous riddles.

And now he had Freddie's trident.

"You've got to be kidding me!" Freddie said to Kelda. "How the hell did *he* get it? *Whatever*. Don't explain. I'm exhausted. So what? What do we do now?"

She blinked at him as if he were slow. "Duh! It's an emergency?" She looked at him sideways. "You've got to come down with us to get it back unless you're, like, not in the mood to save the world."

Just when Freddie had thought he was going to get a good twelve hours. He covered his face with his palms, took a deep breath, and flicked a hand at Kelda. "Can you just . . . um . . ." He gestured, making a circle with his index finger. "Turn around!"

Kelda grabbed her combat boots and faced a wall.

Freddie got out of bed and found a pair of pants neatly folded on a chair, which appeared to have been freshly laundered, thanks to their industrious housekeeper. "Save the world, but how? I'm tapped out. No magic. We all are. You guys might not have thought this through. How are we even going to get there?"

"Nyph and the guys are waiting for us on Gardiners Island." Kelda stepped into her boots and kneeled to tie them. "Just get ready. You'll see."

"All right," Freddie said, distracted. The clothes Gracella had washed smelled like flowery fabric softener, which somehow made him remember he needed to call Gert back although he didn't know what he wanted to say to her. He had no clue what he was going to do with any of his women. Women! There were always so many of them around him. He slipped on the clean clothes and grabbed a hooded sweatshirt. It would be cold at the bottom of the world. He knew; he'd lived there before.

"You can turn now," he told Kelda.

She swung around. Freddie jumped back, clutching his heart and gasping. Kelda had donned a large, terrifying mask of an ox's head with two large horns. Though the mask was dirty and made of rubber, its verisimilitude was striking. She tilted the large ox head toward him.

Freddie studied her. "Where'd you get that?"

"Dumpster," came her muffled voice. "Like it?"

He nodded. "Bring it. We're going to need it."

Freddie walked to the dresser and grabbed his cell phone. This was exactly what he needed. It made him feel like he was in Asgard again, when the world was young and he was ready for adventure. He decided he would ring Kristy on the way to Gardiners Island to let her know he had business out of town.

EVER SINCE FREYA and Ingrid had stepped through the hidden
door in the ballroom almost a year ago now, Fair Haven had
vanished beneath a tangle of green, even in the dead of winter.
The trees and grass were overgrown. Ivy, kudzu, passionflower,
and other vines swallowed the property—only the greenhouse
on the southeast side of the house, which Killian had fixed up for
Freya before he had disappeared, looked tidy. Vines as well as
moss crept along the ground, down the dock, and onto the
Dragon, Killian's sixty-foot sport-fishing yacht, which was raised
on blocks and covered in canvas for the winter, looking sadly
funereal. The overall impression of Gardiners Island was that of
a jungle engulfing the remains of an earlier civilization.

Kelda, still in the ox mask, led the way up the front steps. A
path had been cut through the growth to the front door of the
mansion, which the pixies had unlatched with a skeleton key.
Inside, everything had remained intact, preserved by the blanket of foliage.

Freddie followed Kelda through an empty room with an enormous nineteenth-century painting entitled *Ragnarok: The Death of
Balder*. An arrow pierced Balder's heart as he lay on the ground,
one arm outstretched, surrounded by Valkyries with pale skin,
blond tresses, and eyes as cold as the steel of their helmets. He
recognized Brünnhilde. Hilly. What a deceptive vixen she had
been. There she was holding a spear. *Valkyries!* Feh.

They entered the ballroom where the pixies waited, sprawled
on velvet divans and damask armchairs. The burgundy drapes
had been drawn, the windows opened, and the moonlight cast a
silver glow inside the room.

"Don't all get up at once!" said Freddie.

Nyph, on a dusty-rose loveseat, looked up from her magazine
and tossed it to the floor to pounce on Freddie. She wore a green
satin gown, white gloves to the elbows, her hair up, and a boa

twirled around her shoulders. The other pixies ambled over to greet him as well.

"Something's different," said Freddie, knitting his brow.

"We're clean," said Nyph, smiling up at him, her face shiny.

Freddie did an about-face. At one end of the ballroom, the wall had been crudely demolished, revealing a wooden door carved with the image of a tree. A pile of Sheetrock and rubble, along with a crowbar—the very same Ingrid had once used to uncover the ghost door—lay on the floor.

"The way to *Yggdrasil*," said Val. "And Jörmungandr." He pulled a gold watch from his pocket, glanced at the time, and straightened his ascot.

Sven, decked out in a three-piece suit, exhaled a stream of smoke from a pipe that smelled of apple tobacco. "*And* the trident," he added gruffly.

"I gathered," said Freddie. He studied the pixies, the costumes and props, and grinned. He had missed them.

They followed him to the door, where he ran a hand over the intricate design of flowers, birds, and twining branches, the tree an island in the sky.

Irdick crouched, a cigarette clenched in his lips. He pointed to a bottom section of the panel. "You walk to the end here, then you jump. Pretty self-explanatory." He winked from beneath the brim of a 1940s felt hat.

"Who's coming with?" asked Freddie.

The pixies stared at him. Sven made a show of yawning. "I'm beat!" he said.

"I need to change for dinner," Kelda muttered from inside the ox mask.

Val shuddered. "I can't st-st-stand Jörmungandr. He gives me the jitters."

"The kid's got serious halitosis," added Irdick, studying his fingernails.

Nyph snorted with disgust. "You're all a bunch of cowards! I'll go, Freddie."

Freddie patted her on the head. "Okay, but don't bring the boa." He glanced at Kelda. "And let me have the mask."

Kelda pulled it off and tossed it at Freddie.

He took Nyph's hand in his and together they walked toward the portal.

chapter thirty-eight

Sliding Dates

I ngrid climbed the stairs to her room. The familiars leaped off the bed and clambered at her feet to say their hellos. Siegfried rubbed hairs off on her leg. Oscar stared up at her with mournful eyes while Buster snorted at her feet. "Hello, pumpkins!"

She tossed the books in her arms onto the bed so she could play with the familiars before she took a shower. One of the books fell open, and something on the page caught her eye. She stared, then picked it up and ran to her mother's study.

"Mother!" Ingrid held up the book as if she were about to swat someone with it. She shook her head, unable to speak, her color drained.

"Darling, what is it?"

She handed Joanna the book held opened to the offending page.

It was a list entitled PERSONS HANGED IN SALEM FOR WITCH-CRAFT DURING 1692. A date she had never seen in the list before had been added. In this new list, the death toll began on June 10—as it always had—the date the first of the accused, Bridget Bishop, had hanged. But between June 10 and the date that usually followed it, July 19, when five more hanged at Gallows Hill, was an entirely new date: June 13.

"See what it says—right there—two new names . . . I've never heard of them before—but look at the third . . ."

"Freya Beauchamp," Joanna whispered.

"Freya's been hanged!"

"No—look!" Joanna said.

Mother and daughter watched as the names faded from view and the list returned to the original one she knew with no anomalies. Nineteen hanged and one person pressed to death. No Freya. Before their eyes, the list became evanescent, changing, names vanishing and reappearing, then going back once again to the original. Freya Beauchamp, hanged, June 19.

Ingrid thought she had glimpsed June 13 originally instead of June 19 for Freya's death. It had faded so quickly, she wasn't certain what she had seen.

"What's happening?" Ingrid whispered. "Why is it changing?"

Joanna took the book from Ingrid and set it down on her desk. Her hands were shaking. She turned to her oldest daughter. "Remember when we saw the Oracle in the city?"

"Yes. You said he was unhelpful."

"That wasn't quite truthful. There was nothing he could do to help us, but . . ."

"But?"

Joanna told her what the Oracle had told them, about how time was fluctuating, undulating, and if Freya were to die while the passages were closed, how she would be doomed to remain in the underworld forever.

Ingrid sank to the couch. "No," she whispered. "No."

"But it's all right, her death hasn't been set yet. See? That's why the ink keeps changing. It means it hasn't happened yet— only that there's the possibility that she could die. She's still alive, Ingrid. There's still some hope. Father has gone to . . . to see Uncle Art . . . He can help us. He *will* help us."

"And if not?"

"If not . . ." Joanna clenched the book's edges tightly. "Well, we will come to *that* bridge when we cross it."

chapter thirty-nine

Trickster's Son

N yph placed a hand on the door, whispering the ancient password that would open it. The door gave way, swinging open onto a silent, enveloping darkness. Freddie stuffed the rubber mask into the front pocket of his hoodie, Nyph lifted the hem of the green satin gown, and together they stepped through to the other side.

Once they had crossed they found themselves standing in a dense green thicket. Beads of dew clung to the grass and leaves, glistening like jewels in the soft moonlight. "This way," Nyph said, leading them down a path toward the void.

Freddie explained his plan for retrieving the trident as they trudged ahead. "I know it's not much, and we'll probably have to wing it in the end," he added. "You know how Jörmungandr is. You never know what to expect."

They heard crickets, cicadas, and katydids, but also the croaking of toads and the occasional startling screech of a barn owl. The air was thick, moist with the perfume of rich soil, mushrooms, and the grass that crushed underfoot. Enormous roots rose around them and snaked along the ground. Eventually, they arrived at the heart of the tree that held the path between the worlds.

Freddie held on to a root and swung out into the void. He peered down. Beneath, he saw something resembling stars, floating white lights, some stagnant, some shooting in sprays across the darkness.

"Here we go!" he said, swinging back. "You remember the plan?" Nyph nervously nodded yes.

Freddie took the ox mask out of his hoodie pocket and pulled it over his head, hoping his plan would work. He took the pixie's little hand, and they jumped.

They fell sideways, floated upward, spun fast then slow. The air held them like a net. This went on for some time—turning and turning until neither knew what direction they had gone altogether. The end of mid-world was somewhere in the middle of the glom, the twilight space, right before Limbo, before Helheim, before the abyss.

221

THROUGH THE SLITS for eyes in the ox-head mask, Freddie peered into the wide-open jaws of Jörmungandr. The black poison coating the snake's fangs dripped into the void as it hissed. Irdick had been right about the halitosis. A fetid wind wafted at Freddie, smelling of onions and sour, rotting meat.

Behind Jörmungandr's head, a little ways off, Freddie spied his golden trident floating in a nest of white lights. Nyph poked her head out from behind one of Jörmungandr's scales, where she hid, keeping an eye on Freddie.

Jörmungandr yawned. "Nice try, Fryr!" He had a lethargic way of speaking, carefully enunciating his words, and his *S*'s rasped with extra sibilance. "Thor tried the ox-head-as-bait trick on me once before. Fool me once, shame on you. Fool me twice—"

"Shame on me," said Freddie. The Midgard serpent spoke so slowly, it was difficult not to complete his sentences.

Jörmungandr smiled.

Freddie hadn't forgotten the story and was depending on it to help. Once upon a time, back when the world was young and

Asgard whole, Thor and the giant Hymir went fishing for Jör-mungandr, using an ox's head as bait. Thor caught the sea serpent with the bovine lure, but terrified of the monster, Hymir cut the line, setting Jörmungandr free. Freddie hoped Jörmungandr would feel pleased not to have been trapped by the same bait this second time around. He was counting on Jörmungandr's vanity to lull the snake into a false sense of confidence so that the monster could be coaxed into offering a riddle in exchange for the trident. The serpent's riddles were easy enough to solve, but even if things went awry Nyph would snatch the trident while Freddie kept Jörmungandr distracted. She was his backup plan.

Freddie pulled the mask off his head, which was the signal for Nyph to stay hidden but also that they were moving on to phase two. "So how did you know it was me under the mask?" Freddie examined his fingernails.

Jörmungandr gave a grin. "Well, I figured you would come sooner or later. I do have your trident, after all." The sea serpent turned his head to glance at it just as the pixie ducked. He turned back to Freddie. "It's not like I get many visitors down here." His large reptilian eyes blinked. *"You want it, don't you?"*

Freddie shrugged sheepishly. "I kind of do . . ."

"I could offer a riddle? If you answer it correctly, I'll give you back your trident. It's not like I need it. I was just holding it hostage, because I'm bored."

"I don't know," said Freddie. "Your riddles are much too clever, my friend. What about I fight you for it?" Freddie ran a hand through his hair, examined his arm, flexing the muscles.

"No, no, no, I'm not in the mood," said Jörmungandr. "I have a good riddle. Please?"

Freddie pulled his eyes away from his arm. "All right," he relented. "I'll give it a try."

Jörmungandr blinked happily. "So . . . my dad . . ."

"You mean Loki," said Freddie.

"Yes, Loki, my dad," replied the serpent. He loved to weave Loki into the conversation whenever he could, as Jörmungandr was very proud of his Asgardian heritage. "But that's not the complete riddle. I'm not done yet."

Freddie smiled. "Oh! I'm sorry, Jörmungandr. Go on, then . . ."

"So my dad says, 'I have no brothers and sisters,'" he continued.

"But he does!" said Freddie. "He has one brother at least."

"Just pretend for the sake of the riddle that he doesn't," said Jörmungandr, a little frustrated. "And while you are at it, also pretend I don't have siblings either. I hate mine. I have forgotten all about them myself. They don't exist." He grinned broadly.

"Okay," said Freddie. "Loki has no siblings, nor do you. Done."

"Great!" said Jörmungandr. "So Loki says, 'I have no brothers and sisters, but this *god*'s father is my father's son. Who is the *god*?'"

Freddie narrowed his eyes at Jörmungandr. "So I'm answering Loki's riddle?"

"Yes." The snake smiled dumbly.

"Aren't you overcomplicating things?"

Jörmungandr sneered. "Maybe."

"Jeez, that's really tough. How long do I have to figure this out?" Freddie glimpsed Nyph peeping out, and he scratched his head to signal she should stay hidden.

Jörmungandr laughed. "Like five seconds ago."

"Hmm," said Freddie, appearing flummoxed. "I really do get my trident if I answer correctly?"

Jörmungandr nodded his head. "Yes."

Freddie smiled. "Okay, well, I *think* I know the answer. But I'm not really sure . . ."

The snake licked his fangs.

Freddie bit a finger as if still pondering. He realized the snake was actually very lonely and trying to extend the rare

223

company he had. It was sad. The riddle itself was so narcissistic and obvious that Freddie had instantly figured it out: Loki says, "This *god*'s father is my father's son. Who is the *god*?" A riddle that went in circles, from god to son. Jörmungandr and Loki and Odin. Jörmungandr's father was Loki who was Odin's son. The *god* then was Jörmungandr.

"The answer is you, Jörmungandr."

The serpent blinked at Freddie. "Is that your answer?"

"Because it is the correct one. Now, the trident, please."

The serpent hissed. He was not at all pleased to have lost his favorite game.

Freddie began to back away. He tugged his ear to give Nyph the signal to grab the trident while he kept Jörmungandr focused on him.

But the pixie had trouble navigating the void, and the ballroom gown didn't help, with all that fabric floating around her. She kept missing the mark.

"The trident please, I won't ask again," Freddie threatened.

"Take your trident." Jörmungandr laughed and, with a sudden shake, whipped his tail to the skies, sending Nyph tumbling into the void. He turned to Freddie, opening his jaws wide.

Freddie pushed off the snake and grabbed his trident—it fit into his palm perfectly—and the trident sizzled with power as it returned to its rightful owner, and Freddie Beauchamp was no longer. Only the mighty god Fryr of the sun and sky stood before them, Fryr, golden and powerful and glorious, returned to himself, whole, complete. With a roar he lunged at the serpent, his trident blazing with white fire as it pierced the heart of the snake.

There was a deafening explosion, a blinding light, before everything went black.

chapter forty

Mother Goddess

ᴄᴇ 𝚿 ᴇꜱ

She had lied to her daughter. She had lied to her husband. She couldn't bear the good-byes and she hoped they would understand. It was better this way. The morning was still cool as the sun rose in the east, dissipating the fog enshrouding North Hampton. She gazed beyond the tall grasses, rocks, and sand below the deck, out at the yellow light that slinked on the water. To the left, Gardiners Island was covered in a blanket of mist.

Joanna knew she had to act now, before they discovered what she had in mind. Norman's brother would not be able to help them, she knew. There was no way to repair time once it had been set. The only solution was the one that the Oracle had proposed.

"There is a way to stop this and save your daughter from certain death. But it requires a sacrifice. Are you willing?" the Oracle had asked.

A life for a life. A death for a death.

Of course, they were willing to do anything to save their daughter. On the train ride back to North Hampton, Norman had declared he would be the one: he would sacrifice himself so that Freya could live. "I'll do it," he had said. Joanna knew there was no arguing him out of it, so she had encouraged him to find an alternative solution—had sent him off to find his brother once more.

Because there was only one sacrifice needed here. Hers.

It was why she had been dead set on getting Tyler into a good school. She wanted to leave her home at peace. Ingrid would be happy with her detective. Freddie—he would fumble but ultimately find his place in the world. So there was only Freya whose future was uncertain.

Joanna was their mother. She would make everything all right. That was what mothers were for, to kiss away wounds, to soothe heartaches, to provide a soft cushion for hard landings, for failures. But this was her failure. She had been unable to protect her daughter from harm, but perhaps she could reverse the course of fate—her magic was one of resurrection, after all, of fixing that which could not be fixed. No mother should outlive her daughter, and Joanna would see to it that she was not the first of her kind to do so.

She would be the first to admit that she was not perfect, nor the perfect mother, far from it. Her daughters loved her, but they kept her at a distance that she could not cross, no matter how hard she tried. The girls were unknowable to the end. Freya especially—her spark plug, her wandering saint, who had so much love to give that she lost it all.

With a sigh, Joanna reread the letters she had written the other evening. She arranged them on her desk where Ingrid could find them. They contained instructions for how to handle the estate; whatever legacy she had left, she had left to them, to do with as they wished. She hoped Ingrid would keep the house; perhaps she and Matt could move in at some point and raise a family. Freya had little use for money, and Freddie even less, but it was always nice to have a little inheritance. All these long years on earth and so little to show for it, and if she was being

honest, even her children had been something of a disappointment. None of them settled, all of them a little lost. Even Ingrid
had chosen a mortal to love, which could only bring her pain.

She looked at the photographs arranged on the wall for the
last time. Her beautiful girls, a new one of Freddie and Gert
from their Vegas wedding, Tyler holding a baby chick, and finally Norman, with his glasses pushed up on his forehead, looking handsome and scholarly. He would always be Nord, her
North Star, the wave that had crashed on her shore. Joanna
remembered the first time they had met. She had been sunbath-
ing on the shores of Asgard and fallen asleep on the sand in the
shade of a rock that cut jaggedly into the sky. Cold droplets fell
onto her skin, waking her suddenly. When she opened her eyes,
she stared into Norman's face. He stood looming over her, dripping seawater. He held something in his hand. "Is this yours? It
was blowing across the beach," he said, holding a star in his
palm.

She smiled. It was hers. She'd worn stars in her hair then, a
gift from another suitor. But the starlight faded as she looked
into his eyes—as green and warm as the sea itself—and she knew
then that she had found her immortal mate.

Their children came soon after—Ingrid, her firstborn, the
hearth to her home, the twins: sun and sky, Freddie and Freya.

She was doing this for them.

She walked out the back door, closing the sliding glass doors
behind her and catching a rare whiff of honeysuckle from the
breeze. Maybe it was her garden's way of saying good-bye. She
made her way barefoot across the cold sand to the water. There
was no one around. She walked into the freezing depths and felt
strangely warm. Her magic? Or something else?

Her red dress floated around her so that she resembled a giant poppy as she trudged ahead until the water reached her

waist. She dove headlong into its warm welcome. The sun on the waves flashed in her eyes, and she kept swimming farther and farther out. Her muscles grew weary and she was panting.

She turned around and saw her home, the stately colonial, one last look before the end. She floated on her back, letting the waves lift her, transport her, the sun on her face, a soothing sensation of water and foam.

The sound of the waves lulled her. Even if she had a sudden impulse to turn back to the shore, she had swum too far.

She was tired.

Joanna felt the sudden weight of all the lives she had lived.

She felt the water fill her lungs.

She did not fight.

So this was death.

The years did not flash before her as they say they do.

She felt the sunlight on her face one last time, the cool water above, and her eyes closed for the last time as Joanna Beauchamp passed from this world to the next.

time in a bottle

salem
north hampton
past
present

chapter forty-one

Friend of the Family

W hile Freya was always on her mind, there was nothing Ingrid could do to help her sister at the moment. It was Maggie's thirteenth birthday and she and Matt made plans to take the precocious child to the city to see *Somnambulists* that afternoon. The play wasn't theater exactly but more like an experience—the set occupied five floors of a building overlooking the Hudson, and the action took place simultaneously on all five floors while the audience walked through it to piece together the narrative. The *Times* had called it "a stormy, vertiginous amalgam of Shakespeare's *The Tempest* and Hitchcock's *Spellbound*." Ingrid was touched that she was now included in Maggie's birthday festivities.

Matt had already arrived to pick her up and was waiting for her in the foyer. Ingrid slipped on her black pumps and walked down the stairs just as the doorbell rang again.

"I'll get it," he said, unlatching the lock. "Oh, hey, man." He opened the door but leaned against the doorframe, barring the way inside.

Troy Overbrook stood at the entrance, a worried look on his face. "Can I come in?" he asked.

"We're running late. Ingrid and I were just about to leave," Matt said flatly. "We're not going to make the train . . ."

"Ingrid?" Troy asked. "I'm sorry—but it's important."

"Matt, could you—" Ingrid asked, motioning for him to move away. Matt reluctantly moved to the side so that Troy could come inside.

"Can I talk to you . . . in private?" asked Troy, appealing to Ingrid.

"Whatever you say to her, you can say to me," said Matt. He affected a possessive stance and for a moment Ingrid was worried that he would slap her on the behind again, although to be honest she had rather enjoyed that.

Ingrid nodded. "It's okay."

"It's about your family," Troy said.

"What do you know about Ingrid's family?" Matt interrupted.

232

"Matt, see, Troy's one of us—"

"One of you!" Matt said, his tone mocking. "He doesn't look like a witch to me," he mumbled.

Troy crossed his arms, which made his muscles appear more pronounced, biceps and pecs bulging beneath the snug navy sweater. "Well, I personally prefer the term warlock," Troy said.

Matt snorted.

"What's going on, Troy?" she asked.

"You know Val?"

"Yeah—he's one of the pixies," Ingrid said, turning to Matt so he could keep up. Matt nodded wearily. He knew all about the pixies and had booked and released them for many a minor crime. Like the Beauchamps, Matt was grudgingly fond of the little guys.

"Well, Val came over to my place this morning and he told me they'd found it, Freddie's trident, they found it somewhere on the yellow brick road but they couldn't bring it back, so Freddie went after it, with only Nyph with him . . ."

"So we've got to go and rescue Freddie?"

"No. Freya."

"Freya?" Ingrid asked.

"The passages are open again. Val thinks the trident fixed it maybe—there was some huge explosion at the end of the world, which means Freddie must have gotten it back somehow. Freddie's the only one who can wield its power."

Ingrid sat down to absorb the news. "Where's Freddie now?"

"He's down in the abyss somewhere. Val said they were all going after him, make sure he's all right. Sounded like the rest of them felt pretty guilty that they didn't go with him, but with the passages open, he should be okay. He should be able to make his way back here."

She nodded.

"Look, we don't have much time—we don't know how long they'll remain open—but we have to go."

"Go?" Matt asked. "Go where?"

"Back in time . . . to save Freya, of course, and bring her back here," said Troy as if it were the most obvious thing in the world.

"You're leaving?" Matt said, turning to Ingrid.

Ingrid stood up and tightened the belt on her trench coat. "I have to go. This can't wait. The passages might close again, and then we could lose Freya—forever," she said, thinking of what her mother had finally confessed to her.

"You're going with him?" Matt lifted his chin at Troy.

Troy tried to make himself as small as possible. He slumped his shoulders and fiddled with his hands.

Ingrid pulled Matt aside. "I told you, Troy and I are just friends," she whispered emphatically. She couldn't believe they were quarreling right in front of Troy. She was mortified, but she did realize she was putting Matt in an awful position. She hated doing this to him, today of all days.

Matt's shoulders slumped.

Troy looked at Matt, then Ingrid. "I'll wait outside. Let me know what you decide, Erda."

They watched Troy exit the room, and they both waited until they heard the front door close behind him.

"What did he call you?" asked Matt.

"Erda . . . it's my real name," she said.

"And you never told me?"

"I didn't think it was important."

"It is to me," said Matt, looking hurt. "I want to know everything about you, Ingrid."

"You will," she said. "I promise. But right now I have to help my sister, Matt. I want to see her again. I don't want her to die." Her voice cracked. "You have to understand. This isn't about Troy. It's about getting Freya back."

"Of course—I know. I just—it's not about Maggie's birthday. It's that—I want to help you. I want to go with you, through these passages, or whatever. And I know you won't let me. I've let you into my life, but you won't let me into yours."

They stared silently at each other. Ingrid realized what he was saying was true. She had shut him out of that side of her life.

"I wish you could," she whispered. "But . . ."

"I might not be magic, or a warlock, or whatever *he* is, but I am a trained officer of the law," he said, a hint of a smile playing on his lips.

"But then who would take Maggie to the Four Seasons and the theater?" she said as she hugged him tightly.

chapter forty-two

Black Widow

In her sleep, Freya wiped the ant crawling across her cheek, its tickling of her face like the tendrils of the wind upon her hair. She felt Killian—or James, as she must call him here in this lifetime—stir beside her. They had left Salem the night before and had hidden in the woods when no one would offer them shelter for fear that they were carrying the pox. After what happened with Mercy, they could not bear to be together again. It was too dangerous, too risky. She was far from home, far from safety, and was lying on the forest floor next to a man who was her true love, but they were in danger. She snuggled closer to James as she dreamed of her home by the sea. In her dream, she saw her mother floating in the ocean. Joanna seemed to be sinking into the water—and Freya felt a twinge of fear. She grimaced and heard the sound of water breaking on the shore.

The waves crashing on the rocks.

No—a different noise . . .

Branches crackling underfoot . . .

Footsteps!

She opened her eyes to scream but it was too late.

They had been found!

She was yanked by her wrists to her feet, woke to an ambush. They were surrounded by men carrying guns, constables and marshals sent by Thomas Putnam to retrieve his property. She was glad that this time she was fully clothed, although with the way the men were looking at her, she might as well have been naked.

"James!" she screamed, fighting against the men who held her too closely, the better to feel her body against theirs.

It took the whole group of them to subdue him; James put up an incredible fight, but like her, his magic was useless in this instance, and in the end there were too many of them and he was handcuffed and bruised, half of his face swollen from the fight. She would not cry, she would not show them how scared she was, how defeated. James glowered silently as a marshal read their arrest warrants.

"Freya Beauchamp, you are hereby accused of adultery and witchcraft, tormenting in spectral form Ann Putnam Senior, Ann Putnam Junior, and Mercy Lewis in the house of Thomas Putnam Junior, and also bewitching to death your husband Nathaniel Brooks. James Brewster, you are hereby accused of the theft of a horse, adultery, and the demise of Nathaniel Brooks by conspiracy with a witch."

"Adultery!" Freya said. "How could we commit adultery when I never married him? And what is this you say? Nathaniel Brooks is dead?"

"You were married in proxy," the marshal explained. "Shortly before Mr. Brooks was found in his deathbed."

"So I am a widow."

"A rich one," James said grimly.

"Too bad you won't live long enough to enjoy it," said one of the constables, laughing.

"What happens when I die?" she asked. "Who gets the land?"

"Your former patron, of course," the marshal said. Through Freya's marriage, her husband's death, and her subsequent arrest, Thomas Putnam would soon become the richest landowner in Salem Town.

chapter forty-three

Fork in the Road

"Leave me alone!" Someone was shaking Freddie when all he wanted was to sleep. His head pounded as if it had been struck on the side with a steel bat, and he heard a faint, annoying buzzing sound, like fluorescent lights. A glare pressed against his eyelids. He covered his head with his arms and tried to shut it all out. What had happened last night? Had he tied one on with Troy at the North Inn again? He rolled onto his side and curled into a ball. He would retrace his steps later when he could think.

"Rise and shine, sunshine god!" came a rumbling voice.

"Get up!" Hands pushed at him from all sides.

"What time is it?" He groggily opened his eyes and made out a blur of pixies around him. "What are you doing here? Go away!"

He turned back onto his side and glanced around. He was in bed in a hospital wing. The room appeared as still and colorless as a black-and-white photograph. It was certainly not the twenty-first century but another era entirely. What was going on? Where was he? This sure didn't look like anywhere in North Hampton.

Begrudgingly, he pushed himself into an upright position. Rows of black metal-framed beds—each with two plump pillows, crisp white sheets that illustrated the term *hospital corners*, and a folded gray blanket—ran along the length of the room, separated by tall windows that flooded the room with a glaring white light.

Globe lights dangled from the high ceiling, serving no purpose whatsoever, filled with dead moths. The gray marble floors gleamed, reflecting the harsh light. Then there was that grating low hum in the background, coming from nowhere in particular.

"Whew!" said Idrick, twirling his gray felt hat. "We were worried there for a second. Do you need anything, Freddie?" His voice had an unpleasant echo.

Nyph came over and placed a hand on Freddie's shoulder. Her hair looked electrified. She had black smudges all over her face, one white glove, which was blackened, and her green satin gown was tattered and torn, revealing her combat boots.

"What happened to you?" he asked before realizing he looked just as bad—his jeans dirty, his sweatshirt torn. He lifted a sleeve to his nose: it smelled of flowery fabric softener.

238

Everything came back to him in that instant. Going through the portal at Fair Haven down the yellow brick road to the bottom of the world. Meeting the serpent. Playing riddles. Getting his trident back. Killing the serpent. The explosion. "Where are we?"

Irdick sat down beside him. "A waiting station on the yellow brick road. Sort of a nonplace, hence the colorless atmosphere. Neither here nor there, if you get what I mean."

Kelda sat on Freddie's other side as she attempted to open an overly complicated plastic red cap on a bottle of water. "You and Nyph were taking way too long, so we came searching for you. We went down to Jörmungandr's lair but there was nothing but a pile of snake bones, scales, and ashes. Then we started digging a little and found you two buried underneath all that rubbish. Good riddance, by the way. He was a pest."

"So we brought you here to recover," Sven said smugly. "You're welcome."

"You all right, Nyph?" Freddie asked.

"Yeah," the little pixie said wanly. "I'm okay."

Freddie smiled. "What about the trident?"

"It wasn't there," Irdick replied, shrugging. "We looked."

"But I had it—I used it—"

"Yeah, we know, but it wasn't there, man."

Freddie cursed. He needed fresh air—the hospital was stuffy and smelled of formaldehyde. He pushed at the pixies, trying to stretch out. "Open a window, please."

"Don't!" said Sven. "For one, you might go into a perpetual slumber. The air is filled with the serpent's poison—his dying breath. But we do bring some good news. Whatever you did down there reopened the passages of time somehow. Either that or the Fallen, those Blue Blood vampires, are getting their act together finally. As they say, that's another story, but something's definitely going on in the passages of time."

"Oh, and we got our powers back," added Irdick. "Can't you feel it?"

Freddie stretched. "Yeah, I felt it when I held my trident again. But right now I just feel like crap." He brought a hand to his temple and rubbed. "Ouch!"

Kelda handed him the water bottle. "Drink!"

Freddie sighed, trying to think beyond the excruciating thumping in his head. He drank the water, which was ice cold and delicious. He blinked. His headache had miraculously vanished. A little hydration went a long way. Hangovers and the murder of serpents seemed to require the same remedy.

"So the passages are open—what are we waiting for? Let's go get Freya back," he said.

"Not so fast," Sven said. "Freya's fine. Val went to get Thor and Erda to fetch her."

Freddie raised an eyebrow. He wondered what Ingrid's cop boyfriend thought of that.

239

"While you're still missing your trident," Kelda reminded. "We need to find it! That thing's too dangerous to leave around."

"Destroyed a bridge, killed Jörmungandr, who knows what else it will do next," piped in Irdick, who couldn't stop fussing with his hat—twirling it with a flourish, then tossing it upward, where it hung in midair. He grabbed the hat suspended above him and placed it back on his head.

"It can't have gone far," Kelda said. "Probably just went deeper into, you know . . ." Down below . . .

The abyss.

Limbo.

Freddie remembered the painting of Balder at Fair Haven and realized here was a chance to save Killian as well. "Okay then, let's—"

Kelda cut him off, placing a finger to his lips. A noise reminiscent of a sneaker skidding on a basketball court came from the adjacent room, then heels, two resounding sets, clacked along the marble floor. "Nurses Fenja and Menja," she whispered, eyes wide. "The twins make the rounds every hundred or so years. Don't make eye contact, or they'll see you. Hide!"

The pixies scrambled under the bed, and Freddie hid under the sheet, pulling the blanket over him as the clicking heels approached. He had heard of Fenja and Menja, who were *jötnar*, snow giants. So now the twins roamed the halls of the hospital waiting station. He wondered what would happen if he did make eye contact.

After the destruction of the Bofrir bridge, the gods had been scattered, displaced hither and thither in all the corners of the nine worlds of the universe, some like his family, the Vanir, had been trapped in Midgard. These two seemed to think working as nurses was far better than being slaves chained to a king's grindstone, which was pretty much all he knew of the sisters'

history. Although they had cleverly eluded King Fróði by grinding out the stone that produced his happiness and wealth until
there was nothing left of it and their shackles fell loose.

The door to the hospital room swung open, and two giant
nurses in white uniforms and caps strode in with clipboards.
The sisters looked left and right, strutting down the aisle between the rows of beds, heads held high.

Freddie peeked out from under the blankets, but he was too
distracted by the sisters' formidable cleavage to make eye contact. He pulled the sheet over his eyes as they clipped past.
When Fenja and Menja reached the end of the room, one of them
flipped a switch. The room went pitch-black and the maddening
hum from nowhere abruptly stopped.

There was the sound of the door opening and closing, and
Freddie and the pixies came up for air. "All clear?" he asked.

"Yeah, they're gone. And they seem to have taken everything
else with them," Nyph said, annoyed.

They were standing in nothing—the hospital was gone, as
were the beds and the floor. Freddie looked around. It was familiar. After all, he had once been imprisoned here for five thousand
years. *This* was the abyss.

"Well, what are we waiting for? Let's go get my stuff back,"
he said.

chapter forty-four

Crucible

"Oh dear! I believe we've arrived." Ingrid pulled her silk cape and petticoat from the muck, hopping to a drier spot in her brown leather lace-up boots. She was relieved to see Troy standing by a stone trough, looking about, his dark leather suitcase in hand. Along with his hammer, he had packed two ingots of gold for the trip. As pious and pure as Puritans portended to be, they were not above receiving a bribe.

A horse nudged her with his nose, and she patted his neck. "What's the date, Mr. Horse?" Needless to say, the horse did not reply.

Troy turned to Ingrid. "Here, give me your bag." He took Ingrid's luggage and hid it with his beneath some bales of hay. "I don't think the Salem witch hunts qualify as pleasurable, but traveling with you, my dear 'Mrs. Overbrook,' certainly is!" He followed this with a wink and that fetching dimple of his.

She narrowed her eyes at him as she straightened Freya's gold pendant at her neck, then pulled the large hood of her cape over her head. Had it been too much to hope that Troy would not read into her choosing to go with him as a sign of affection? She felt a pang when she thought of Matt back there, alone, unable to help.

The jarring, headachy feeling one experienced coming out of the passages was not dissimilar to jet lag, and it did take a few days to adjust. Time traveling could sometimes be more approximate than accurate, especially while journeying backward. Ingrid hoped they hadn't landed too far off their mark.

Troy dusted the hay off his cape, adjusted his high-crowned hat, and they stepped into the pale light of a small cobblestone alleyway. It was early morning and a fishy, rotten scent laced the cool, salty air. Ingrid immediately recognized that smell on the breeze—*and* the alleyway.

They had landed in the right place. This was Salem Town, and Ingrid had lived here once before, even had some very fond memories of the small port.

That is until . . .

She felt her knees give way as they strolled along the cobblestones.

"You all right, Mrs. Overbrook?" Troy asked. He placed a hand at her waist to steady her as she walked.

She nodded her thanks.

She had loved the town until the marshals came for her and Freya, wrenching her and her sister from Joanna's grasp. Ingrid brought her trembling fingers to her temple and sought to shut the memories out as they strained to push their way back. Now it was a matter of finding out if they had arrived at the proper time, before the date of Freya's hanging.

They heard noises somewhere down the way and walked out onto Essex Street, where a crowd waited, restlessly peering in one direction. A craggy-faced woman slammed into Ingrid. "Come and buy your witch poppet! Hang her from a noose!" she sang, carrying a basket of little rag dolls in scarlet bodices with embroidery thread tied around their necks. *Like the red paragon bodice Bridget Bishop wore when she allegedly came to men as a specter in the night, smothering and choking them,* Ingrid remembered with a start.

Ingrid knew exactly what day it was now. These early risers had eschewed their morning labors for some entertainment.

It was Friday, June 10, 1692.

The day the first witch would hang.

"Bridget Bishop!" Ingrid whispered.

"The cart!" Troy said gravely. "It should be coming up Prison Lane. What can we do to stop this, Ingrid?"

She shook her head. "Nothing!" Her heart sank. "It's too late!"

"Bring the witch bitch!" someone cried.

"Witch bitch!" people echoed.

"Teach the whore witch a lesson!"

"Come and buy your Bridget Bishop poppet and hang her from the noose! Hang her right here!" sang the street peddler, twirling a Bridget doll on her finger from the string at its neck. A mother bought one for her child.

Ingrid tried to quell the panic rising in her throat. Freya was here somewhere—but where? Freya could hang any day now. All they could do was find her as quickly as they could.

The crowd cheered and hooted. Feeling faint, Ingrid grabbed Troy's arm, and he tugged her protectively against him. The crowd shoved them against a wall. Bridget Bishop was to hang at eight A.M. at the top of Gallows Hill.

Bridget was a proud, intelligent woman with what one of her accusers described in his deposition as a "smooth, flattering manner." The poor, doomed woman had been carefully selected as the first to stand trial because she had the most damning evidence against her with a tainted past and history with the courts. The judges had wanted this first win.

This was what Ingrid knew: Twelve years ago, Bridget had been summoned to court on suspicion of bewitching some horses and turning into a cat. Though she had been cleared of these

charges, it didn't matter. The stain on her reputation had remained. Plus, she had been to court for marital quarreling (her
face was bruised), considered a criminal offense, and another
time for calling her second husband an "old devil" on the Sabbath. She and the husband had paid for the offenses by standing
gagged back to back for an hour in the market square with no-
tices of their crimes posted on their foreheads.

At what was to be Bridget's very last trial, the afflicted
girls—the Salem foursome: Abigail Williams, Betty Parris,
Mercy Lewis, and Ann Putnam Jr.—had provided all the drama
the judges had needed to seal the deal. They fell into fits as soon
as they were brought into the meetinghouse and saw Bridget.
They cried out all the usual: how Bridget's specter did pinch,
bite, and choke them, and insisted they sign her book.

Ann, who had begun to emerge as one of the most quick-
witted, claimed Bridget had wrenched her from her spinning
wheel and carried her on a pole to the river, where she threatened to drown her if she did not sign the book. Abigail said that
she saw ghosts appear inside the meetinghouse. "You murdered
us!" they cried at Bridget. Mercy Lewis confirmed she saw the
ghosts, too.

The girls had been ruthless, unrelenting. They mirrored
Bridget's gestures in an exaggerated way, confounding the
woman as the judges badgered her with circuitous questioning.

But Bridget held her own quite well. She said she had never
seen these girls prior to her examination. She was from Salem
Town and had never even set foot in the village before. Why
would she wish harm to complete strangers?

Poor Bridget had not one friend to attest to her character, let
alone a defense lawyer. Neighbors testified she was a witch. A
man claimed she had struck his child with a deadly illness that
killed him. Men said her form had come to them at night in a red

bodice. A strip search by jury members yielded a "preternatural teat" between Bridget's "vagina and anus." Finally, there was also hard evidence: poppets found in Bridget's cellar walls. Ingrid had often wondered if those rag dolls had not been planted to solidify the case.

"HERE SHE COMES! Here she comes!"

Ingrid craned her neck. All she could see were caps, hats, dirty clothes, and capes. Troy pushed forward, and the crowd ceded enough for them to move to the front. It all unraveled like the very worst kind of dream, but there was no waking from it.

"There she is!"

"It's the witch!"

"Witch bitch!" the chant took up again. "Hang the witch!"

The procession moved westward on Essex: men on horses, magistrates, judges, marshals, constables.

Inside the cart Bridget stood upright in chains, holding up her shaved head, arms crossed over her soiled and torn shift. Her piercing brown eyes with dark circles beneath them stared out above the crowd, her full lips, parched and scabby, moving faintly. Ingrid could tell Bridget had been an attractive, sensual woman, but all of that had been beaten out of her now. She looked gaunt, dirty, tired. She glared down at the crowd jeering at her.

Ingrid recognized two key players from her past. There they were again: the burly, somber, and formidable Mr. Thomas Putnam, dressed in black upon his horse, and the sniveling Reverend Parris in his minister's collar and frock, walking behind the cart, Bible in hand.

Then the afflicted girls appeared. They were anywhere from twelve to seventeen and, apparently, well enough to be here despite the "witchcrafts" inflicted "in and upon" their bodies, as Bridget's death warrant stated. They worked the crowd, whisking them into a furious frothing frenzy, striding close to the cart, mocking the poor, bereft Bridget. They sneered. They smiled in ecstasy. Ingrid remembered them from her own trial in Salem Village, when she and Freya had used the same futile defense as Bridget. Why would they wish any kind of harm to girls they had never met nor seen prior to court?

"She's praying," Ingrid remarked, observing Bridget's moving lips. "Praying for us to see her innocence." She tugged at her hood to conceal her tears. Troy stared stoically. The sun flooded the street. The crowd smelled dirty and sweaty. If it weren't for Troy to hold on to, Ingrid would have crumpled.

The cart approached, and Ingrid heard the girls' words. It was all theatrics.

"Getting yours now, aren't you?" said one very prepossessing girl, whom Ingrid gathered was Abigail Williams, one of the ringleaders.

An older girl with a fair complexion—Mercy Lewis, it had to be—cried out, "You look so very proud now, but when you see the noose, we'll see if you look proud then, Goody Bishop! Oh, how you did taunt and torture me!"

"You won't be torturing us anymore!" added a third young girl. *Ann Putnam?*

Ingrid felt a chill.

They were untouchable. Monsters.

INGRID AND TROY fell wordlessly into step with the procession following the cart down Essex. What was there to do or say? This was their history, a history of blood and madness. Little girls telling lies and spreading evil.

They walked in a daze, in shock, like victims emerging from a violent accident.

"We need to turn back," Troy said. "I've seen enough!"

Ingrid appeared hypnotized. She stumbled ahead. She was hoping that she could help Bridget somehow, that she could change the course of events, but it was futile.

"It's useless," Troy insisted, but he couldn't very well leave her here, so he continued by her side.

On Essex the dark wooden houses stood near one another, but the crowd turned north on Boston Road, where the houses grew farther apart and sparse, giving way to larger estates. They continued walking for about half a mile. Ahead, in the watery morning light, Bridget gazed out, to the right at the fields and orchards and then North River, to the left at the marshland and South River. She avoided looking straight ahead, where towering Gallows Hill came into view. Without noticing, Ingrid grabbed Troy's arm.

As they made their way up the hill, the cart halted. The ascent was too steep and rocky to go any farther. Bridget was carried off the cart in her chains, then shoved forward and made to walk the rest of the way to the top. The girls and the crowd mocked her as she struggled up the hill.

"I am clear! You are the guilty ones, and you will suffer for this!" Bridget said before she was made to climb the ladder tipped against the oak tree.

The people only jeered and shouted back. The executioner climbed up behind her, then placed the thin white cotton hood over her face. Reverend Parris read aloud about fire and brimstone. There was no pity here.

Ingrid buried her face against Troy, barely able to watch, recalling how the rope had felt around her neck. She recited a calming spell for Bridget. That was all she could do. The girls and the crowd grew incensed and wild. There were cries of triumph and jubilation, but also screams of fear. At the back of the crowd couples kissed and groped at each other when they thought no one was looking. Hysteria. Sex. Death.

The executioner pushed Bridget off the ladder, and she swung forward. She gave a faint yelp, stopped short by the noose, and a dead silence fell over the crowd. The crowd froze as if startled by the horror of the culmination of their actions, as if suddenly aware of the brutal reality.

The only sounds were of Bridget gargling as she dangled, her arms and hands fluttering up and down her body. Beneath the diaphanous hood, Ingrid saw her face contort, her lips swell, her eyes bulge and redden. A trickle of blood seeped through the cloth at her mouth, and she went stiff.

Ingrid turned her head away.

249

chapter forty-five

The Man in White

It had been a week since their capture. Freya and James had been taken to the Boston prison and placed in separate cells. Freya huddled against a wall, pressing her skirt over her nose and mouth. The overwhelming scent of human waste made it nearly impossible to breathe. She was placed in the cell with women who admitted to covenanting with the devil. By now, many had confessed, having been told that doing so as well as naming other witches would spare them from a hanging.

She hadn't been there a day and yet it felt like an eternity already. The women who had confessed, unlike those who had clung to their innocence, had not been shaved from head to foot to be searched for witch's teats. Nor did they wear manacles meant to tether their specters. But like all the prisoners, they had wasted away to skin and bones. Most had bartered their clothes for additional food from the gaoler. They shuffled about in their dirty thin shifts and sat apathetically on the rushes scattered on the stone floor, their eyes large and vacant. Some stood, clasping at the bars, calling out to a husband, child, or friend in another nearby cell.

Freya called to James but there was no answer. She tried again and was ordered to be silent, but regardless of the harsh stares of her companions, Freya kept calling until her voice had turned too hoarse to continue and now she had no energy left.

There were whimpers and whispered prayers all around. The ill cried out in agony. The dying moaned. She closed her eyes, turning her head to the wall. She had been whimpering as well, although she was unaware of it until now. She hushed herself, slowed her breath, and sought to find a silence within.

Someone placed a hand on her shoulder. She jumped. Through a blur of tears, she stared at the woman in the dimness. It took time to parse out her features and recognize them; the woman's skin, once lovely and creamy brown, was now sallow, dry, ashy. She looked years older, her black hair peppered with gray, her plump pretty face thinned, the spark in her eye extinguished. Dressed in rags, she stared at Freya with crusty, watering eyes.

"Tituba!" Freya whispered. "Why are you here?"

Then she remembered—the girls, the accusations, the trials . . . it was all happening again. Tituba was one of the first victims.

"I am most sorry!" Tituba rasped. "He came to me! The tall man with the white hat. He gave me a pin to let my blood, and I signed the book. He made me do it . . . I am most sorry!" There was something crazed in her eye. "The demon had come! He appeared to me—he made me do it!"

The poor woman was terrified of something or someone. Who? Was it Mr. Putnam or the reverend? Who was the tall man in the white hat? Perhaps Tituba had lost her mind.

"Shh! Shh!" said Freya, rocking the woman gently to sleep. She left Tituba lying on the floor.

A feeble light poured into the corridor beyond the bars: the gaoler was coming down with rations of rancid biscuits and water. Freya's belly grumbled.

Someone called her name, and when she looked through the bars, there was a man standing there. He was in shackles.

"Nate!" she said. "What are you doing here?"

"I helped James get you away, so they've charged me with

conspiring with a witch." He bowed his head. "I'm sorry about my uncle—I couldn't stop him . . . it was Putnam's idea from the beginning. He put it in his head. I lent James money and told him to take you as far away from here as possible. I'm sorry, I didn't know Mercy would find you . . ."

"You helped us? Why? After what I did to you—when I sent you away," she said, remembering their previous encounter in a different life.

She had fallen for him when he had called himself Bran Gardiner, but he had betrayed her. It was all a trick to get her to love him, to claim her for his own. But she loved Killian, had chosen him over Bran, as she had in their ancient past. In retaliation Bran had brought death and disease to North Hampton, releasing the doom of the gods, and she had banished him from her heart forever, or so she had believed.

"Isn't it obvious?" He looked up at her, and she could see him—truly see him—the mischief in his eyes, the affection in them, the wildness that had always drawn her to him . . . to Loki. "I love you, Freya. I always have and I always will."

His WORDS STIRRED the magic inside of her, and somehow, she was out of the ugly, filthy prison, and she was standing in the woods, in the forests of Asgard, at the beginning of time, and she was young and beautiful, and alone. She looked up at the stars, how bright they were, flashing in the darkness, and she was waiting for her love.

There he was, the beautiful boy she had given her heart to. His name was Balder, and this was before, before everything, before the poison, before the breaking of the worlds, before Salem, so long before, when they were just spirits, young, and alive, and immortal, and beautiful.

He kissed her then, and she was all joy, and love, and their clothing fell away, forgotten on the grass, and she wrapped her arms around his strong back, and his mouth was on her breasts, and her hands were on him, and his body was tense, and hot, and they were slippery and ecstatic . . . and then . . . in the middle of their lovemaking . . .

She could feel the eyes on her.

Another pair of eyes.

But they were not eyes of hate, not eyes of jealousy . . .

But of love.

She opened her eyes and there he was, Loki, standing in the shadows, watching them . . . as Killian would watch her one day, when Bran took her in his bed . . . one of them, always in the shadows, watching, while she was in his brother's arms . . .

One of them outside the circle . . .

While two were joined together . . .

When it had happened so long ago, during the dawn of the universe, Freya had stopped and screamed, and sent him away, and the poisonous jealousy in his heart had festered, and centuries later Loki would take his revenge . . . but perhaps . . . perhaps there was another way . . . perhaps it could save them even . . . from this . . .

She looked deep into Balder's eyes. "My love . . . we are not alone," she said.

Balder continued to kiss her—giving her his blessing, she did not know—but she knew he would not stop her from doing what she must, what she thought might save them all . . .

She motioned to Loki in the trees. She would take away the hurt in his eyes. She would replace jealousy and anger and centuries of ruin and revenge with love. She was love. She was love. She was love. She loved him. She had always loved him. She put out her hand and motioned to him. "My love," she called. "Join us . . ."

253

chapter forty-six

Down the
Rabbit Hole

T hey had left the way station a long time ago and had already passed several levels of Limbo, but Freddie could no longer recall how many, exactly. The geography of Helheim had eluded him even as a resident. All he knew was that they were way down below, and it was getting colder by the second. He shivered in the cold damp of the stairwell, tugging the hood of his gray sweatshirt over his head. The pixies followed him down the endless flights, grumbling all the way.

Lights buzzed, flickering off and on. Water trickled along the puckering orange-and-yellow trompe l'oeil print of the 1970s wallpaper. Between levels, the stairways changed decor, sometimes lavish but always with a faded kind of splendor—broken chandeliers, dusty candelabras, peeling velvet-flocked wallpaper—suggesting not only a prolonged period of neglect but hardship, even ruination. Most likely, Freddie guessed, this dilapidation had resulted from the destruction of the Bofrir bridge.

He stopped on a landing, turning to the pixies behind him. "Why did you say I wasn't supposed to make eye contact with Fenja and Menja when we were in the waiting station?"

Kelda grabbed the rusty chrome banister beaded with moisture. She took a breath. "You know what, Freddie, I really think we should go back. Maybe your trident isn't down there."

"Yeah," agreed Nyph. "Let's go back, you don't need it anyway." She hugged her tattered dress, her teeth clattering in an exaggerated way. "We aren't properly dressed. It's freezing. We really should go back."

Irdick swiftly slid down the banister while Sven hopped onto the landing. "Stop your kvetching! We're almost there. It's just a few more levels down," Sven said.

"We've come this far," said Freddie. "They're right." He looked at the girls empathetically and shrugged.

The girls glowered at Sven and Irdick, then turned to each other, sighing helplessly. Kelda took off her jacket, offering it to Nyph, who donned it.

"I still want to know why we aren't supposed to make eye contact," Freddie said.

Sven gave Freddie a little shove toward the steps. "Cui bono? It's nothing. Keep going."

"Excuse me?" Freddie was ready to smack Sven right then.

Irdick righted the hat on his head. "If Fenja and Menja made eye contact with you, they would have fallen in love. That's all. You'd have two sister snow giants at each other's throats, fighting for your attention."

"Not fun, not good," concluded Sven. "Now let's go!"

They continued downward, and it became even colder and darker.

chapter forty-seven

Appointment
with Death

So this was death. It wasn't terrible really, just sort of gray and dim, like she had stepped into an old black-and-white movie. She had died in mid-world and had awoken in the twilight of the glom. A fan whirred noisily, barely stirring the stagnant air. It had taken Joanna hours to get to this particular waiting room, one of many inside her sister Helda's byzantine offices, housed in an unremarkable gray skyscraper in Tartarus, the capital of Hell. Helda's trolls had ostensibly sent Joanna on a wild-goose chase throughout the building. But this time, having arrived on the top floor, Joanna glimpsed the plaque on the receptionist's desk and believed she had finally gotten much closer to finding her sister.

The plaque read MRS. DELILAH DELAY. Joanna was familiar with the name. She was looking at Helda's personal messenger of death, but scarcely had she begun addressing the woman, when she found herself in a heated argument. Mrs. Delay now glared at her from behind thick, bleary cat-eyed glasses with dull rhinestones. Joanna glared wordlessly back. A staring contest had

begun during which Joanna became all too aware of an unpleasant odor.

When she had first approached Mrs. Delay, she had gleaned
from her desk that the receptionist was on a strange mono-food
diet. Among the towers of folders and papers sat stacks of cans,
each with a plain white label that said all of two words in black:
TUNA FISH.

"Yes?" said Mrs. Delay, continuing to leer at her from above
her glasses.

"I said, 'I am Joanna Beauchamp!'"

Mrs. Delay harrumphed vociferously. "I know."

"Otherwise known as Skadi . . . Helda's sister?"

"Name-dropping isn't going to help you, ma'am." Mrs. Delay
ploddingly grabbed a folder, opened it, then began running a
pudgy finger along its lines.

"I want an appointment with my sister!"

It was clear Mrs. Delay was losing her patience because she
then spoke as slowly as one could: "I've already told you, I can
only give you an appointment with Helda's receptionist."

Now they were going in circles. "But *you* are Helda's receptionist!"

Mrs. Delay took a deep breath, then a long exhale. "I am the
receptionist to the receptionist of Helda."

"No, you're not!" said Joanna.

Here Mrs. Delay glared at her, but Joanna could tell the
woman was laughing on the inside. It wasn't funny. The receptionist searched for something on her cluttered desk. "Just have
a seat. Someone will be with you shortly."

Joanna knew what *shortly* meant in the eternal dwelling
place, and it certainly did not mean soon. She glowered at the
woman.

"We have a lot of work here, ma'am, and believe it or not,

we're understaffed." With her long, glossy black Goth nails, Mrs. Delay excavated a grimy can opener from beneath a pile of magazines.

Joanna thought it best to try another tack—perhaps some friendly conversation might loosen up this Mrs. Delay. "I just have one more question . . . well, a rather silly one if you don't mind?"

The matronly emissary of death peered up at her without expression. "Yes?" she droned.

Joanna playfully looked at her sideways with a smile. "On my way over, in the square, I couldn't help but notice that some festive preparations were under way. Could you possibly tell me about the upcoming fete?" She didn't want to insult this woman's city, but it would have been more apropos to say *gloomy* preparations, because everything in the glom, the twilight world, had a glum air. It would, however, be impolite to suggest this. In the square, trolls were stringing up garlands of desiccated flowers and dim twinkling lights in the black trees around the wading pond, where a lone black swan floated sullenly on the water. Pavilions as well as a fancy gazebo were also being erected.

Mrs. Delay gave another tuna-scented sigh. "This isn't the tourism office. For that, you'll have to go downstairs to the sixth floor, but then you'll have to go through whatever rigmarole you went through to get here again. And I'm being kind by even telling you that." She worked on opening a can of tuna, a challenge with her long nails.

"Yes, you are," Joanna acknowledged. "I certainly don't want to go through all that. Very nice of you!" She gave a languid smile. "Oh, come on, Mrs. Delay . . . Can't you tell me?"

She gave another sigh. "Will you leave me alone if I do?"

Joanna promised she would. She could tell the woman just wanted to eat her tuna fish lunch in peace.

Mrs. Delay swiveled around in her squeaky chair. Everyone in the cubicles behind her seemed to be minding their own business, clacking away on keyboards. She leaned forward, her large bosom pressing into the papers on her desk as she whispered, "Those preparations are for the arrival of the goddess of love."

It took a little while for this to sink in. Then Joanna could see it dawn on Mrs. Delay that she realized she had just made a gross blunder. No, Mrs. Delay shouldn't have told Joanna that the upcoming fete was for welcoming her daughter Freya to the underworld.

Joanna's face turned scarlet. "I want to speak with my sister *now*!"

chapter forty-eight

Alpha Girls

At the crack of dawn on the Monday following Bridget Bishop's hanging, a small horse-drawn carriage carried Ingrid and Troy from the port of Salem Town to Salem Village. They bumped along the road, Troy at the reins, their chestnut stallion, Courage, moving headlong at a gallop. Ingrid's cape flew in the wind. The light grew brighter, the sky bluer as the sun rose higher.

It had taken too long to get a fair price for Troy's gold and buy Courage and the carriage. The townspeople had sent them from one shady person to the next. Finally they had come across an honest man, a spice merchant with a gold tooth, who had warned them to stay as far away from the backward village as they could.

Ingrid glanced at Troy, who was still pale looking. Bridget's hanging had shaken them to the core, had brought back their recollections of this terrible time—and now Freya was cursed to endure the same fate at the noose's end unless they could find her. The horse unexpectedly drew to a halt.

Troy shook the reins but Courage let out a sigh, refusing to go any farther.

The noise of cicadas began to swell in the trees as it grew warmer. There were three types of mating calls, Ingrid knew.

One resembled the sound of a ghost, another a caterwaul, a third a death rattle. This was a strident death rattle. "Come on, boy," she said to the horse. "Let's not be scared of a few bugs."

Troy jumped down from the wagon and pulled the reins until he finally conceded to trudge along.

A few farms appeared along the way among the lush meadows and trees. Cows, sheep, goats, and horses grazed in the fields. When they saw houses clustered together, they knew they were closer to the village proper. There were girls everywhere—standing in the fields, grouped along the road, peeking out the windows—girls as young as five and as old as seventeen. Some stared at them blankly, while others hissed like angry monkeys. In the practice field by Ingersoll's Inn, a few girls crawled and flailed about in the grass. Girls walked desultorily in the square, their arms outstretched, their gaits contorted.

A few villagers tried to help, while others only watched. Ingrid saw three men wearing tall hats holding one girl down and caressing her chest and limbs to calm her. Ingrid shuddered and looked away.

Hysteria. Madness. Evil.

She remembered it all too well.

But Ingrid noticed most of the villagers carried on with their lives, paying little mind to the girls around them. They fed their chickens and corralled the hogs, inured to it all. They looked up to glimpse at Ingrid and Troy as they passed, but returned their attention back to their chores.

The hinterland folk had grown used to strangers arriving for the proceedings at the meetinghouse. The sessions had become increasingly crowded, the band of afflicted girls growing so large that only its most famous members—the stars of the show so to speak—the original accusers, Abby, Mercy, and Ann— were admitted inside to take part in the examinations and

261

eventually the oyer and terminer trials. Little Betty Parris had been sent away to stay with relatives in the hopes her fits might abate: her father believed she was too sensitive a child to remain in the mayhem. The other afflicted girls waited outside the meetinghouse during proceedings, mimicking the cries and laments of the girls allowed to testify inside.

Queen bees and wannabes, Ingrid thought as she observed the girls pulling their faces and spinning in circles. The witch hunt had become a craze, a fad, a teenage trend, and they were all hankering to be victims. Certainly having fits was easier than washing soiled laundry in the cold river.

A girl of about sixteen years of age, dressed in a vivid green bodice and yellow blouse, stepped in front of the carriage. Troy tugged hard on Courage's reins. The girl faced them, pulled off her cap, and flung her head to and fro. Her bun came loose and her hair whipped around her face. She stared at them, eyes glinting. "She tells me I must rip off my cap and twirl my head or the devil will cut my throat!" she screamed. After, she skipped away toward the field by the watch house, dangling her cap, looking perfectly merry.

"And welcome to Salem Village to you, too," said Troy.

"They're running rampant, aren't they?" Ingrid said, still incredulous. She had forgotten what it was like, for a moment had forgotten that she had lived through it already. She had been a young witch in Salem once and had been hanged for the crime, and here it was again—as terrible and banal as ever. A terrible prank that had started as a lie, a spark whose flames had taken many lives, and now had come for her sister's once and for all.

Two girls approached the wagon on Ingrid's side. Troy tapped her, nodding at them. When she turned, she recognized two of the girls who had been following Bridget Bishop's cart a few days ago. They seemed perfectly natural and normal, neat and well dressed, although they stared at her with a blatant curiosity. Ingrid noted Abigail Williams's arresting beauty, the dark brows and eyes, the swath of glossy hair tucked inside of her cap.

The older one, Mercy Lewis, moved in closer. "Who are you, missus?" she asked. This one was blond and fair, her lashes as pale as her skin. She ran a hand over her forehead, and Ingrid saw that it was scarred and mangled.

"What is happening here today?" Ingrid returned.

Mercy cocked her head and crossed her arms, giving Ingrid a thorough once-over. "I asked you first."

Ingrid returned a pleasant smile. "Why, if you answer me first, since I am your elder, I would be happy to reply."

"Nothing is happening here today," Mercy said. "Not one examination or trial. A judge has quit, and they are seeking a replacement." She sounded bored. "Pray tell us, who are you?"

Impudent girl. Ingrid hid her irritation and smiled. If it were a different century, this girl would be chewing gum or smoking a cigarette and blowing smoke in Ingrid's face. Abigail hedged in. She stared at Ingrid in a way that made her feel naked and uncomfortable.

"Thank you for that!" Ingrid acknowledged. "I am Mrs. Overbrook, and this is the great Admiral Overbrook, who fought in England." Troy smiled, raising his hat, which had obscured his face until now. The girls stared, caught off guard by Troy's good looks. Ingrid cleared her throat to get their attention.

"We have come all the way from Boston, where Admiral Overbrook, my husband, is a successful barrister and has his own firm." She smiled for effect. "We are presently here for my younger sister, who vanished several months ago. We have been terribly worried and searching the country far and wide whenever we can. We fear something terrible might have happened to our dear girl. We are, well . . . we are well-to-do . . ." Ingrid coughed, feeling uncomfortable adding this last bit, but she knew that in Puritan eyes if you were successful and rich, it meant God smiled favorably upon you—you were among the elected and a seat in heaven waited for you with your name on it. "And we're willing to spend whatever it takes to find her," Ingrid continued. *That* should spark their interest.

"What is the missing maid's name?" asked Abigail, widening her eyes.

"Why don't you tell me yours first," replied Ingrid.

"Why, I am Abigail Williams but you may call me Abby." Just as Ingrid had guessed. Abigail smiled nervously, then bit her raspberry lips.

"Delighted!" Ingrid reached a hand out of the carriage, which Abby shook.

The other girl, appearing envious, butted in. "I'm Mercy Lewis."

Ingrid shook Mercy's hand while Troy minded his own business, keeping a somber face. Ingrid was grateful to him for letting her handle this. "My sister's name is Freya Beauchamp."

The girls gasped at the name, and Ingrid gasped in response, bringing a hand to her mouth. "What is wrong? What do you know of Freya? Is she . . . ?"

"Oh, no, nothing bad has happened to Sister Beauchamp, Mrs. Overbrook!" said Abigail, blushing. "Not yet!"

"Not yet! What on earth do you mean?"

Mercy leaned against the side of the carriage. "Why, Freya is a rich little widow now!" She laughed. "She doesn't even know it because—well, it is *said*—she ran off with Mr. Brewster." She raised her eyebrows. "The old, ailing Mr. Brooks was so distraught upon learning of her flight, he died on the spot!"

Ingrid shook her head in wonder. This was confusing but hopeful. The girls explained more clearly, albeit in a rush. They glanced around distractedly and peered down the road as if they were expecting others to enter the village as well. Some of the girls in their fits wandered by, eavesdropping on their conversation, and when they did, they nodded at Mercy and Abigail with deference, or perhaps fear. Mercy and Abigail were clearly their leaders—and the ambassadors.

From the two, Ingrid learned that Freya had shown up in the village without memory save her name and age a year ago. She had been employed in the Putnam household where Mercy also worked, and Mr. Thomas Putnam had arranged Freya's marriage to the wealthy widower Mr. Brooks. Freya disappeared shortly after, and when Mr. Putnam apprised the older Brooks of his bride's absconding, he had died from shock.

Ingrid pressed the girls further as to her sister's whereabouts. But at that moment, a group of men solemnly exited the parsonage, and the girls turned mum. Ingrid recognized the pastor, Mr. Parris, in his collar, who nodded at the girls. She did not see Mr. Putnam among the group. The men, perhaps magistrates— they looked self-important—seemed anxious. They peered at Ingrid and Troy suspiciously, but they did not, surprisingly, summon the girls.

Ingrid continued. "We will be here for a little while. We would like to look into all you have told us and plan to stay at Ingersoll's Inn for a few days. We would very much like an interview with Mr. Putnam." She addressed Mercy. "Do you think you could arrange that?"

"Mr. Putnam is a busy man. Certainly not today," replied Mercy. "However, I do suppose I can tell him you would like to see him."

As the men talked outside the parsonage, they continued to

265

glance over at Ingrid and Troy conversing with the girls. The reverend then made a gesture to call the youngsters.

"We must go!" said Abigail, curtsying. "My uncle needs us. I believe it would be best if you were on your way. Sister Freya is not here. She is not in Salem Village."

Troy tilted his hat. "Oh, we plan to stay!"

"Do you know where she might be? Where she could have gone?"

Mercy smirked. "They say she is hiding in the woods with the young James Brewster—although some say she was also seen with his friend Nate Brooks. Or perhaps she is with the two of them, together." The girl sneered and Ingrid felt a chill. James Brewster. Nate Brooks. These were the other two new names from the book. They had been hanged with Freya.

Oh, Freya, Ingrid thought. *What happened here? Who were those boys?*

Abigail tugged at Mercy's sleeve, and they both lowered their heads and briskly walked off to join the pastor and the men.

Ingrid and Troy watched from the carriage as Parris and the men questioned the girls. They obviously hadn't been schooled in subtlety and kept staring outright. It was exactly what Ingrid wanted. The girls were probably repeating verbatim what she had told them. She wanted to instill a little fear in them—let them know that they must turn Freya over to her wealthy family.

"I think it worked," said Troy.

"Yes, we stirred the pot. Let's hope they take care before they think to lay a hand on her head."

"Shall we search the woods?"

Ingrid nodded. *Freya, where are you?*

chapter forty-nine

Nemesis

L imbo had an institutional look, like a boarding-school dorm or a vaguely stylish Swedish prison. Freddie and the pixies tiptoed down the brightly lit hallways that smelled of TV dinners. The blond wood floors gleamed. Identical Ikea closets—to store the obligatory white clothing worn on the level—lined the walls between each cell. The sameness of it all was what became so utterly mind-numbing over time, Freddie remembered.

They knocked softly at the closed cell doors to ask who might be inside and came upon the brave Sigurd, a gifted trumpet player whose father died in battle at Odin's hands, in one, then Brock, a mischievous long-nosed, crooked-bodied dwarf, in another. There wasn't time for conversation as much as these two wanted to chat, so they moved on.

No one had seen the trident.

The place resounded with silence, most of the cells vacant, the doors swung wide open. Inside each, furniture could be reconfigured to express individuality but only in limited variations: a single bed, a blond desk, a halogen lamp, and a modish white plastic chair.

On each landing, Freddie found the laundry nook and shower room—narrow stalls with no doors for privacy and a row of small steel sinks—empty. Even the quarters for the wardens appeared unoccupied.

They made their way to the remaining floor in the groaning elevator but found it deserted. Freddie's cell looked pretty much as he had left it: his deck of cards laid out in an unfinished game of solitaire on the desk, the bed unmade, a rabbit-ear television flickering with black-and-white static.

Nothing. No trident. No Killian either.

"Well, then I suppose we must go lower. All the way to the bottom of the universe, if we must," said Sven.

"Guess so!" returned Freddie.

"No!" yelped Nyph, but the other pixies shut her down with a look.

268

THEY HOPPED INTO the elevator and pressed *B* for *bottom*. The doors shut ominously, and Freddie immediately began to sweat, enclosed in what he couldn't help but think resembled a hermetically sealed steel coffin. He pushed off his hood and tugged at the neck of his sweatshirt to breathe better. When he tried pressing the buttons that corresponded to the floors before the bottom level, none worked, which was all the more disconcerting.

The elevator creaked downward and his ears popped. The ride went on forever, growing hot, claustrophobic, terrifying, especially when they came to a sudden dead halt and the lights went out, leaving them in complete darkness. This happened more than once, and even so it didn't make Freddie feel any more optimistic that they would continue descending. It seemed an eternity each time, during which Freddie mused about how they would suffocate and perish here. But he was too afraid to mention it for fear he might jinx the ride altogether. Then the lights would flicker back on, the suspended metal box groaning from above, and it would begin to move down again.

As they descended farther into the bowels of the universe, Nyph and Kelda, huddled together, fell asleep in a corner. Freddie, Sven, and Irdick solemnly stared up at the numbers above the door, waiting for the next to illuminate with a *ding*, which took forever given the great distance between each floor. Finally, the doors opened onto B.

As Freddie watched Sven and Irdick yank Nyph and Kelda, he thought the girls' reluctance to get out of the elevator odd given the nightmarish ride they had just endured. Once all were out, the doors shut, and the elevator traveled back upward, and Freddie pressed the return button, hoping Hell's handbasket would be back by the time they located Killian.

THE VERY BOTTOM of the universe was one long white room connected to another long white room. It was bare and smelled of disinfectant. Behind him, the pixies whispered, in the midst of an argument. He turned around, scowling at them.

"What's gotten into you two?" he said to Kelda and Nyph. They looked on the verge of tears.

"We're so sorry Freddie . . . he *made* us do it," said Nyph.

Irdick began trying to quiet her, a hand over her mouth as she squirmed and widened her eyes.

Freddie shook his head. "What are you talking about?" He had an awful feeling. There had been something nagging at him ever since they had entered the abyss, but he had been avoiding giving it credence. "Guys, leave them alone! What is wrong with you?" Still, Irdick continued holding a hand over Nyph's mouth.

"Hmmph!" she said, horror in her eyes.

Meanwhile, Kelda was struggling to wriggle out of Sven's grasp. "We're really sorry, Freddie! We didn't have a choice!" She finally succeeded in extracting her arm from Sven's hold and seemed to be pointing at something above Freddie's shoulder.

"Welcome home, Fryr," a velvety and sinister voice rumbled behind him.

chapter fifty

Freya's Diary

∽ ψ ∾

W hen Ingrid and Troy returned from the woods an hour later, the village had turned eerily silent. All the afflicted girls wandering outside had vanished, doors and windows shut tight. They checked into the inn. Mrs. Ingersoll was elusive and taciturn when Ingrid questioned the quiet. The woman said the village was observing a day of silence and prayer.

Troy gave Ingrid a look. "It wasn't silent before, an hour ago when we arrived!"

At that Mrs. Ingersoll decided to observe the silence. She frowned, left the room, and returned with the bread, fruit, and cheese they had requested, gesturing for them to bring it to their room.

"I VOTE FOR A NAP," said Troy from the bed, hands clasped behind his neck as he watched Ingrid pace the floor.

She was tired, but the bed was too small, and there was so much of Troy in the room.

"Mrs. Overbrook," he said. "You must rest." He patted the spot beside him.

She came over and sat down. She lay on her side, her back to his, careful not to touch him, awkward and uncomfortable in her tight and cumbersome clothes. The bed creaked as Troy turned toward her. "Aren't you going to take that heavy thing off?"

"No. It's a nap. Just loosen the laces for me, would you?"

When he finished pulling at the laces, he rested a hand on her back, an invitation, a question. "It's been a long time, Erda," he whispered. "I've missed you."

She inhaled and turned to him, and put a hand on his face, as if seeing her friend for the first time. They had a history, she had told Hudson, and so they did. The god of thunder had been her first suitor, and she had spurned him, but she had kissed him once before sending him away, and she remembered that kiss a little too well at the moment. "I can't," she said. "I love Matt."

"I knew if I didn't find you soon you would find a love of your own." Troy sighed. "You lied to me, you know, when you sent me away you said you would never marry."

"I am still unmarried," she said gently.

"You'll marry him, that mortal," Troy said, a petulant tone in his voice. "I know you will. I can see it. You'll marry him and make little half gods, and he will die and you will mourn him forever and still you will not have me." He looked up at the ceiling. "Are you sure you want that?" he said bluntly. "Mortals . . ."

She remained silent. Everything he was saying was right. Loving Matt would only lead to an immortal lifetime of pain. Was that what she wanted? To choose love and pain? She saw herself standing at Matt's funeral. He would be old and gray and she would be the same, only a few gray hairs to fool the mortals, when in truth she would be ageless and heartbroken forever.

When here was a friend, a friend from home, a friend who knew and understood everything about her and her family. They could be together for eternity. Thor and Erda. Thunder and hearth. She would tame the wrathful god, build him a home, a fire, bring him the immortal children he craved.

A future lay before her—she could see what could happen if she chose it—he would kiss her and she would kiss him back, and then he would pull her against him, slip his hand inside the bodice he had just loosened, his hand on her skin would make her shiver. It could be done. It was so easy. Perhaps this was what she was waiting for all her immortal life.

Then the vision faded as she remembered Matt's sweet smile and his bravery. He was flawed, mortal, weak in comparison to Troy . . . but he was hers.

"No," she said aloud. "I mean yes. It is what I want. I want Matt. I love him. I'm sorry, Troy, but you and I—we were never meant to be. You know that. You only chase me because you know I will say no." She smiled.

He smiled back and kissed her forehead. "Fine, have it your way. But I can hold a torch for a long time, just you wait and see."

Someone knocked, and they exchanged a startled look.

"A moment please," Troy called as he helped Ingrid back into her clothes. This was the visit they had been expecting: Mr. Putnam.

Ingrid fixed her lace cap and tucked her loose strands of hair inside it, and answered the door. "Abby!"

Abigail Williams rushed in, her cheeks flushed. She curtsied, then straightened her apron. "I'm sorry to bother you, ma'am. I would have come sooner, but I had to sneak out of the parsonage. My uncle has ordered silence and prayer for the remainder of the day. They believe I am still in my room."

"Why have you come? What do you have to tell us? Is it about Freya?"

Abby nodded. "Yes. I have injured her I am afraid, and I have come to make penance. I am so very fond of Freya. I did not

think it would come to this. But it has. My uncle is very angry—he found this—" She thrust a black book toward Ingrid.

"What is it?"

"Freya's diary."

Ingrid scanned the pages. It was all there, written in Freya's
recognizable and pretty handwriting. It was practically a confession, detailing her practice of magic and witchcraft, and meeting young men in the woods. As if they needed any more proof.
"Who has seen this?"

"Mr. Putnam, my uncle, a few magistrates . . ."

"And?"

"That's what I came to tell you. Freya and her friends James
Brewster and Nate Brooks are being held in prison in Boston.
Tomorrow a few of us are to travel to the city for the examina-
tions."

"Examinations?"

"To prove Freya is a witch." Abby told them that Mr. Putnam
and her uncle had arranged with the magistrates of the court of
oyer and terminer for a special tribunal to take care of the highly
dangerous triumvirate, who were believed to be the leaders of
the witches in Salem Village. After the examinations, the three
would be brought to the village for a special session of the court,
conducted à huis clos, without the public's knowledge. The next
witch trials weren't scheduled until June 29, but this one, of the
greatest urgency, was to take place before, on June 13.

Mr. Putnam had persuaded Governor Sir William Phips
that this would bring an end to the torments of the afflicted. The
sooner the three hanged, the safer the inhabitants of Salem Village and its surrounding regions would be.

"And the richer Mr. Putnam will be," Ingrid added, when
Abby explained that upon Freya's death her holdings from her
deceased husband would go to Mr. Putnam, her patron.

"Which is why you, too, are in danger here," Abby said. "You would jeopardize Mr. Putnam's plans. And it is said that Mr. Brooks died under suspicious circumstances. Mr. Putnam is very powerful, Mrs. Overbrook."

"I see." Ingrid placed a hand on the young girl's shoulder. "Do not worry," she said. "We will go to Boston. You have done the right thing coming to us, Abby. Best you run off before your uncle finds you are missing."

Abigail nodded. "And you will help Freya? I could not bear it if—" She held Ingrid's hands in desperation.

"We will leave for Boston immediately," she said, feeling sorry for Abby. When they had clasped hands Ingrid had been able to tap into Abigail's lifeline. She saw the years of loneliness, desolation, remorse, illness, and misery ahead of her. The witches were not the only victims of Salem.

chapter fifty-one

In the Land of the Blind . . . the One-Eyed Man Is King

Freddie blinked at the tall figure standing at the end of the hallway, holding his golden trident. The man wore a tall white hat and a black patch over the eye he had sacrificed for his wife's hand—although the tales varied, some claiming the eye had been sacrificed at Mimir's spring in exchange for wisdom of the ages.

"Odin?" Freddie whispered. "Is it really you?"

Odin. The most powerful god of their kind. The head of the White Council. Not Loki, whom Freddie had been expecting all along, but Loki's *father*.

Odin's two ravens perched on his shoulders—his familiars Huginn and Muninn, Thought and Memory.

Tall, handsome, and charismatic, Odin possessed the same dazzling green eyes as his boys, known in Midgard as Bran and Killian Gardiner. His hair, once streaked with gold and fire, was as white as the hat he wore. At his feet curled and crouched his wolves Geri and Freki, or Greedy and Fierce. His eight-foot-tall steed, Sleipnir, was the only one missing, and Freddie wondered if the horse was waiting for his master somewhere in the void. He noted that Odin's infallible sword, Gungnir, hung in a scabbard by his hip, and the hand that rested on its hilt bore the ring of ancient dragon bone that allowed its bearer to travel between worlds and time.

Freya had told Freddie that Loki had stolen Odin's ring and that it had crumbled in her fingers—but there it was, whole and unharmed of course. No one could destroy Odin's ring.

What was Odin doing down here in the darkness of the abyss? Was he . . . waiting for him? For Freddie? But why?

"We're so sorry, Freddie!" Nyph wailed.

"He threatened us!" said Kelda self-righteously, striding up to Freddie.

Sven and Irdick shrugged.

Nyph yanked on his sleeve. "He said he would send us straight to Helda if we didn't do as he told. He's the one who made us steal your trident so he could destroy the bridge, and later he made us plant it on the *Dragon* so that it would give Killian the mark on his back. He was behind *everything*. And he told us to bring you here. We didn't want to but he scared us!"

"We're too young to die!" said Kelda.

"Sorry, man," mumbled Sven, while Irdick looked mournful.

Freddie turned to Odin. "What are they talking about? Why are you here? Why have you brought *me* here?"

"Welcome, my friend." Odin smiled, flashing his blazing white teeth. "Back to where you belong," he said, wagging a finger. "Naughty boy. You don't think you escaped on your own, did you?"

"Actually . . ." Freddie said, backing away and colliding into a wall that hadn't been there before. He stumbled, and Odin laughed raucously, throwing back his head, and his ravens alighted from his shoulders to flap dramatically through the empty space.

Odin held up the hand with the ring, wriggling the fingers. "Don't even try. There is no escape this time. So you noticed I have this back. Did you and your family really think Loki was behind it all? I suppose I could see how you would think that, since he was the one who unleashed *Ragnorak* and poisoned the Tree of Life. But his powers are much too weak to be able to block the passages and take away that hot little sister of yours. Oh, no. He's just a god with a touch of Munchausen. Poor kid." He shook his head. "Likes to stir things up, then fix them. Enjoys the sport of it *and* the attention. An easy mark, plus he never did get over Freya. He loved her, poor delusional fool, which made him useful for a time."

"So the bridge—that was you, too?" said Freddie.

Despite his age, Odin had a youthful, blithe quality, a swagger even as he stood. "Yes, yes, I destroyed the bridge, set you and Loki up—that son of mine was getting a little too mischievous, shall we say, and needed to be taught a lesson, so I cast him to the frozen depths and locked you up in Limbo. Of course I let him out after a while—can't have my own boy locked away forever now, could I?—but you . . . you escaped somehow. You're a hard lot to control, the Vanir." He snickered to himself.

"But why?" Freddie asked. "I don't understand." Odin wasn't their enemy. He was feared but known as a benevolent, magnanimous god.

"Why not?" Odin yawned, looked down at his sword, and clasped the handle, drawing it from its scabbard.

Freddie needed more time. He couldn't fight Odin, not without his trident. He needed to come up with a means of escape. He supposed he had the pixies on his side, but once again they had proven themselves utterly useless. "Why did you do this? Destroy the bridge and destroy my family?"

Before Odin could reply, a harsh light lit the room, revealing every smudge on the walls and the dust in the corners. Odin shielded his good eye.

"I know why!" said Norman, rushing into the gallery, accompanied by Val.

"Oh, what a bore!" remarked Odin, removing his hand but appearing to struggle with the glare. He planted the tip of his sword on the ground and twirled it.

"Dad!" Freddie gave a sigh of relief. "How did you get here?"

"Well, I was looking for your mother at first," Norman explained. "Then I ran into this little guy, who confessed everything and brought me here to help."

Val nodded. "We're sorry, Freddie. Odin wiped our memories and then he threatened us."

"Yeah, your friends already told me," Freddie said.

"Stand back, son, this is not your fight but mine," said Norman. "He destroyed the Bofrir to hoard all of the gods' powers. The Vanir had become too powerful, so he decided to stop us and punish his sons, who had grown too rebellious and hard to control. He certainly doesn't discriminate. No nepotism there, eh, Odin?"

Odin smirked. "I try to be fair."

"But that's not the whole story, is it, old friend?" said Norman. "This is about you and me, isn't it?"

"Why I suppose it is, Nord."

Freddie looked to Odin, then his father. "What's going on? You've lost me, Dad."

"An old grudge. It's all very petty, really," Norman said. "Odin didn't lose his eye for Frigg's hand, nor did he give it up to gain wisdom. Since as you can see he has none. No. This is a personal story . . ."

A long time ago, at the dawn of the worlds, Nord, god of the sea, fished along the shores of Asgard. There on the beach, he spied a goddess more beautiful than the sun. She had fallen asleep in the sand in the shade of a large rock: Joanna, or Skadi, the goddess of earth, mother goddess. No sooner had Nord laid eyes on her than he knew she would be his immortal mate, his love for all eternity. And when she looked at him he knew she felt the same.

But another had already claimed her, not just another god but the very ruler of Asgard, Odin himself. When Odin learned he had a rival, he challenged Nord to a duel. As immortals, the object was to deprive the other of something vital. He who did so would win the goddess's hand.

It was a fair fight, and Odin lost his eye to Nord, who won both the battle and the goddess.

Norman stepped forward, unfurling his fisherman's black net. "I'm sorry I won her hand, Odin old pal, but really—destroying the bridge? Destroying my family?" Norman said. "It stops here. It stops now."

"It's too late," returned Odin. "Your daughter is dead." He smiled, studying his sword. "Her sister and my insubordinate sons, Bran and Killian, will join her in the underworld soon enough, along with your silly wife, while you and your own re-calcitrant son rot in this abyss."

"Val!" ordered Norman.

Val lifted a mirror, catching the light, directing it into Odin's one good but sensitive eye, so that the god had to crouch and lift his hands to protect his sight.

Odin screamed and fell to the ground.

"I believe this is ours," Norman said, taking Freddie's trident and wrapping his rival in the fishing net.

chapter fifty-two

Goose Chasing

B y the time Ingrid and Troy arrived at the jailhouse in Boston, Freya, Nate, and James were long gone.

"Looking for them, are you?" the gaoler asked. "I might know a thing or two as to their whereabouts," he said with an expectant look.

Ingrid nudged Troy, who removed a velvet pouch of gold. Troy glared at the shifty-looking man as he placed it in his palm.

The gaoler, his tongue finally loosened, informed them that an examination of three prisoners had been conducted the night before in Boston at a private home of a magistrate, prominent ministers and officials present. The governor himself had been in attendance. Along with two constables, the gaoler had delivered the three accused and remained in the room where the examinations took place to keep an eye on the prisoners, then transport them back to the jailhouse afterward. Thus, the gaoler had overheard all the testimony against the allegedly wicked threesome.

Being of the utmost urgency, these examinations had taken precedence over all others, conducted on that holiest of days, the Sabbath, so that the trio's trials could be expedited. If enough evidence against them were gathered here, the three would be tried on Monday in the court of oyer and terminer in Salem Village.

The triumvirate, Freya Beauchamp, Nathaniel Brooks, and James Brewster, were believed to be the leaders of the witches in Salem Village, those responsible for spreading bewitchments across New England. Mr. Thomas Putnam had filed the complaints and gone so far as appealing to the governor for speed and vigor in convicting all three. It appeared he had convinced those in the highest positions of authority that the sooner these three were brought to justice, the sooner the blight would reach a swift and conclusive end.

When Ingrid and Troy questioned the man further, he told them that Mr. Thomas Putnam and Reverend Samuel Parris had been present to give depositions. Mrs. Ann Putnam Sr. and the afflicted girls also testified against the lethal three, whom they had witnessed sharing covenant with the Prince of Darkness. Mercy testified that Freya was chiefly responsible for the evil hand besetting the village. Sobbing, the maid confessed she would have denounced her sooner, but she had been silenced with threats of being drowned or decapitated.

With a leer, the gaoler described the rituals the afflicted testified they had been made to endure in the forest outside Salem Village, where they had been given wine for blood to drink and ordered to dance in the moonlight without a stitch of clothing. "Those three are the devil itself," he said.

When Mercy was brought into the presence of the three accused, she commenced to shake and mumble and toss her head around wildly. The judge requested Mercy to place a hand on Freya Beauchamp, and when she did, the girl's fits stopped immediately, which meant that the evil had flowed back into the witch. The touch test was solid evidence Freya was guilty as charged.

Once Judge Stoughton had gathered sufficient evidence against the accused, the gaoler brought the trio to the prison in Salem Town. There, they were manacled, chained, and placed in cells for the night. Today they would be transported to the village to stand trial. This trial would be held at an undisclosed location, kept under wraps so as not to create a stir and keep the village under control.

"Everything Abby said was true, only the examinations had already taken place. She lied to us so we'd leave and not stop the trial," said Ingrid, deflated. She had believed in Abby's sympathy, but the little girl was a lying monster.

Troy shook his head as he walked to Courage and gave him a pat on the neck, as even the horse seemed pained by all this.

"We must hurry, perhaps there is time yet." She mounted the carriage and took a seat, fixing her skirts.

Troy climbed in beside her. They decided the next best course of action would be to head straight to Salem Town, where they would attempt to buy Freya's freedom. They planned to tell Mr. Putnam he could keep Mr. Brooks's money, and more besides. The sun had already begun to dip, flooding the cobblestone street with a golden light. By now, the secret trial in the village was long over. All three would have been found guilty. They would most likely be back at the Salem Town prison to be held there until the next hanging at Gallows Hill.

Troy shook the reins, and Courage took off at a trot. "So, if I gather correctly," he said, "as we were driving into Salem Village from Salem Town this morning, the three accused were being shuttled along that same road. But were they ahead of us or behind us? Do you think they could have already been in the village when we arrived?"

In her mind's eye, Ingrid combed through the events of their arrival in the village. The atmosphere had certainly been bizarre. She remembered how Mercy and Abby had suddenly crept on them. In hindsight, it was clear the girls had been antsy and looking for a way to get them to leave. They had glanced out at the entrance of the village several times. They had been so close! They had fallen for Abby's lies and had gone away.

Ingrid remembered the men coming out of the parsonage: somber, fretting, shifting on their feet, letting the girls talk to her and Troy for a bit. The men had seemed nervous and impatient. She recalled how they had inspected her and Troy but also looked in the direction of the road that led into the village. They must have been waiting for the cart that would be transporting the prisoners back to the village.

By the time she and Troy had returned from checking the woods, the village was a ghost town. By then surely Freya, Nate, and James had already been brought to the secret location for their trial—maybe Mr. Putnam's house. His farm seemed likely, being on the outskirts, two miles from the center.

283

They headed toward the Putnam farm. Ingrid worried the pendant at her neck as they drove onward, winding out of Boston. Her thoughts turned to Abby. Why had the girl lied to facilitate this Putnam coup? Somehow Freya had managed to entangle herself with two very angry girls and now was the recipient of their wrath, which coincided perfectly with Thomas Putnam's agenda.

Troy reached over and squeezed Ingrid's knee. He smiled— or perhaps it was more a flinch. "We'll find her, I promise," he said.

WHEN ENTERING SALEM Town, it is impossible not to see Gallows Hill. It rises ominously on the horizon as one swerves into the port along the peninsula that eventually forks into two fingers reaching into Salem Sound. As the carriage approached, beneath a strawberry moon, the dusky sky was tinged pink.

At the hill's summit, a small crowd had gathered, its dark,

amorphous silhouette shifting slowly. People were tilting their heads upward to watch as a body dangled from the branches of the sprawling oak: a girl whose skirts billowed in the breeze.

Freya Beauchamp was hanged on Monday, June 13, 1692. In the twenty-first century, her name appeared permanently on the pages of history books.

Ingrid screamed as Troy pulled at the reins and Courage neighed, rearing on his hind legs.

chapter fifty-three

The Death of Spring

F reya was dead. She had been hanged in Salem. When she arrived in the underworld she still had a shimmer to her skin, an apricot flush and pinkness in her lips, a bounce in her curls. She ascended to the top floor of the gray skyscraper dressed in the garb she had been hanged in save for her cap, which she had ripped from her head before the noose was slipped over it. She had refused to wear the cotton mask for the hangman. She wanted everyone watching to see her face as she died; she wanted them to be aware of the monstrosity of their crime.

As the elevator rose, she unfastened the bow of her apron, removed her bodice, and stepped out of the heavy skirt and petticoats, kicking all of it into a corner. Smiling, she stood in her plain shift, which she had embroidered herself with colorful flowers. She waited to reach the top floor.

The receptionist pointed to Helda's office, hardly lifting her gaze. As Freya approached the door, she heard music. She recognized the abrupt changes in the movement's dynamics, the silvery notes of the violin and cellos, the thrilling crescendo: Vivaldi's *Four Seasons*. This was "Spring," her very own concerto, airy but unequivocally sexy and dramatic. She opened the door when no one answered her knock.

The music, louder inside, washed over her.

"Aunt Helda? Hello?" Freya called.

The Vivaldi concerto ended, and the room went silent. Then Freya heard muttering, and someone stepped out of the broom closet.

Freya started. *"Mom?"* she said, stunned. "What are you doing here?" Immediately she understood. Her mother was in the underworld.

A soul for a soul. A life for a life. Death for death. That was the rule of Helda's book.

"No!" insisted Freya. "You can't! This is *my* fate!"

Joanna released her sweet girl. She pushed Freya's curls out of her face, kissed her girl on the cheek, the brow. "It has already been done, darling." She took Freya by the hand, guiding her to Helda's desk. She began searching among the stacks of messy papers until she came upon a thick black ledger, whose pithy title read BOOK OF THE DEAD in fading gold leaf. She opened it, ran a finger down the column of latest entries, and pointed to her name engraved on the current line.

"Mothers are not supposed to outlive their daughters," Joanna said.

Freya shook her head adamantly. "Mom, *no!*"

"I'll always be with you, my dear." Joanna cupped her daughter's face in her palms. "Always!"

Joanna felt her heart fill with love for her girl. Here she was at last—still so alive, stunning in her little shift, like Vivaldi's "Spring" itself.

There were sounds outside in the lobby—the receptionist protesting—and when the door opened, Joanna could not believe her eyes. "Norman!" she said. "What are you doing here?" He seemed to be with some sort of prisoner trapped in a fishing net. "Is that Odin?"

"Yes. It's a long story." He smiled.

"But how did you get here? This far down in the glom?"

He moved toward her. "Don't you know?" Tears brimmed in his eyes, the color of a tempestuous sea. He had seen her out on the beach that day and had followed her into the water. "Wherever you go, I go."

Joanna was speechless, befuddled, seeing that storm within him. "But . . . you can't! You don't belong here . . . You can't stay! You love mid-world!"

He smiled. "So do you! But I love you and our children more."

Joanna fell into his arms, sobbing. "I thought I would never see you again."

Norman smiled. "We have a lifetime together, here."

"Freddie!" Freya yelped, spying her twin behind her father. "You're here, too? What happened?"

"The path to Hell is paved with good intentions." Freddie smiled. He had killed the serpent, but it appeared he had killed himself as well. Helheim demanded a death, so his father had given him his. He and his twin were so alike it was ridiculous.

"Come on, sis, let's go home," he said, steering her gently away from their parents before everyone got too sad or hysterical. Freddie hated saying good-bye.

chapter fifty-four

The Love of
a Lifetime

ᴕ⚓ᴕ

Ingrid and Troy returned to the North Hampton shores through the passages of time at the same moment Freya and Freddie burst through the portal from the underworld. Ingrid cried as she hugged her sister. "But how?"

"We'll explain later . . ." Freya said, smiling wistfully as Freddie hugged the two of them close. She didn't want to tell Ingrid about what had happened to their parents just yet, didn't want to tell her the extent of their loss. "But did I take a wrong turn in the glom or is that really who I think it is?"

"Yeah, hey, Freya," Troy said.

Freya looked at Ingrid and Troy with a curious smile, but Ingrid shook her head.

"No—it's okay. We're just friends," she said firmly. She put her hands on her sister's shoulders. "I'm so glad you're home."

"I'm here because of you." Freya smiled.

"And Killian?"

"I don't know," Freya said, her smile fading a little. "He was with me in Salem . . . with Bran, too . . . but I think it's okay."

She thought of that dream she'd had of the very first time she had encountered both of them. They had made magic that night, the three of them. "I think I'll see them soon enough."

They said their good-byes to Troy.

"Coming, Ingrid?" Freddie asked as he and Freya turned to head home.

"Not just yet," she said.

Ingrid said good-bye to her family and made her way to a familiar, architecturally modern house in the hills. Matt was in bed when she slipped inside his room.

"How'd you get in?" he asked sleepily.

"Magic," she whispered. Her powers had returned in full force, and she could feel the strength returning to her body, how electrified all her senses were, how alert, but it was not just magic that was making her feel this way, she knew.

"So, is everything okay?" he asked.

"Yeah—I think so. As much as it can be," she said. Freya didn't have to tell her. She knew as soon as she saw their faces that something terrible had happened, and she could guess that it involved Norman and Joanna. In her grief, Ingrid found she could only find comfort in the arms of the man she loved.

"When you left with him, part of me thought you might never come back to me."

"Matt," she said. "I'm here now."

He reached up and pushed her hair out of her face and didn't answer. There was nothing to say. He knew she knew what he wanted, what they both wanted, when it came down to it. Now it was just the two of them, alone, together, in bed . . .

She stared back at him, wondering when he was going to kiss her. What was he waiting for? Her heart pounded through her chest, or felt as if it did.

She was tired of being shy, so she lowered her face to his and kissed him, throwing her arms around him as she hiked up her skirt and straddled him, their kisses growing deeper and more breathless, and his hand inching ever upward. She bit his lips and began to kiss his neck, tracing his jaw, as he writhed beneath her, groaning softly. Matt struggled with the zipper on her skirt until he gave up and it bunched against her waist, while Ingrid couldn't unbutton his pajamas fast enough.

He pulled her blouse over her head and pulled down her bra, and he was kissing her, kissing her all over, and it was her turn to moan. This was as far as they usually went, as much as she would dare, but this time she closed her eyes and reached down, slipping her hand under his boxers. She trembled from desire, from wanting him so much. She wanted him inside her . . . *now.*

He groaned louder, breathing heavily into her ear, holding her above him, and he whispered, "Are you sure?"

In answer, she lowered herself upon him, taking him inside her, gasping at the pain as he broke through her slowly, so slowly, and then all at once, and she cried in pain and pleasure of being filled, and her hands were on his shoulders and his were on her back, holding her as she rocked on top of him, until she could take his full length. He bit her shoulder and flipped her on her back, a surprise attack, and he withdrew, only to slam back inside her, and this time she gasped.

"Oh!"

"Am I hurting you?"

She shook her head and wrapped her legs tighter around his torso, thinking, *This, this, this, this is what I have wanted—have needed for so long—this* . . . And he was rocking against her, tenderly, then so fast, and hard, and she wanted it harder and faster, and then he was pulling her up to him again, so that she rocked on top of him, and then she was nothing but sensation and stars and she was lost, and cresting, and then a wave, crashing on the beach, and it was all white bright and pleasure, and Matt was groaning and roaring, and calling her name, crying out his love as he came inside her.

And they were shaking, still shaking . . .

Why had she waited this long?

Because she had been waiting for him . . .

They fell back on the bed, panting, slick and tingling, twitching like fish on deck. Ingrid rested her head on his chest. Matt sighed. "Mmm. I'm glad you're back. Never leave me again, Ingrid," he whispered in her ear as they drifted off to sleep.

THE NEXT DAY Ingrid woke up to the feel of his kisses, and soon they were right back where they started. It was even sweeter the second time. Afterward they wandered to the kitchen in a daze, looking for breakfast. There was a package of frozen blini and a tin of caviar in the fridge. Matt didn't remember buying either. A miracle—or magic? It didn't matter. They ate their meal, naked, standing at the counter, with crème fraîche and champagne. They couldn't stop touching each other. He ran his hands along her slim, strong arms.

She put her head on his shoulder, content.

The joy was worth the pain.

the present
easter

chapter fifty-five

Left Behind

I nside her Mini, Freya sang along to Dan Auerbach's wistful "Goin' Home" as she drove up a winding hill. Like the narrator in the song, she had spent too much time away. It was good to be back in North Hampton this last month.

She had come home.

She found comfort in the warm embrace of the familiar. But her homecoming was bittersweet and incomplete. She belted the words, glancing out the window, trying to convince herself she'd done the right thing.

This area, on the outskirts of North Hampton—hilly, woodsy, open in spots—offered a view of the ocean and Gardiners Island. It was perfect, she thought. Spring had arrived, bright and beautiful as her mother's garden.

Freya parked the car on the side of the road, grabbed the flowers and a bottle of water from the passenger seat. She squared her shoulders as she stood before the opened wrought-iron gates, took her time strolling up the shady tree-lined path. A warm, moist breeze caressed her cheeks and bare limbs. Winter had finally gone. The grass was lush, a vivid green, the cypresses creaked, and the oaks whispered. There was a peaceful hush.

She wasn't sure what had happened to Nate Brooks or James Brewster, but their names were no longer among the names of those who had been hanged during the Salem witch trials. Somehow they had escaped the noose, and for that she was glad. She had a feeling she would see them again soon.

But she was not thinking about the boys today. She saw there were a few other visitors, walking along the twining paths or standing at the grave of a loved one. Some of the tombstones dated to the late 1800s. There were angels, cherubs (for children), elaborate crosses, stoic mausoleums, and simple pink, gray, and white marble stones. The cemetery hung on the hill overlooking the sea, and at a far end one could glimpse down and see Joanna's house in the distance along the shore. It was near this spot, in the shade of three leaning evergreens, that the bodies of Joanna and Norman Beauchamp had been buried side by side. They had been found in the sea, the two of them drowned, their arms around each other, and had been buried in the same coffin.

Freya removed the dead flowers from the urn by the headstone and refilled it with water. She replaced the old with new yellow roses, which meant she missed them. She knelt on the grass in front of their grave.

The Beauchamp children had ordered the simplest of markers for their parents, and knowing Joanna's distaste for epithets had forgone them. "How can one even begin to encapsulate oneself in a single, pithy sentence?" their mother had once said. But the siblings had added a little touch: beneath JOANNA BEAUCHAMP was engraved GODDESS OF THE EARTH; beneath NORMAN BEAUCHAMP, GOD OF THE SEA.

Freya pressed her hands in the grass on her parents' grave. She knew they were content now that they were together in the underworld. They had promised to visit in her dreams, but so far, she had not seen her parents. She wondered when she ever would again. Her memories of the underworld had already begun fading.

She felt a hand on her shoulder, and when she turned she saw her twin, her grief mirrored in his eyes. Ingrid was with him. "Sorry we're late," her sister said as she added their flowers to Freya's. The siblings huddled in, holding on to one another. They only had each other now. They were orphans, but they were still a family.

More than a need for words was the need to just hang on.

chapter fifty-six

One Wedding among
the Funerals

ᴄᴄ 𝜓 ᴇꜱ

It was May. The bridesmaids' dresses rippled against their legs in the wind, and their hair flew against their cheeks. They held bouquets of violets, asters, and irises, while the ocean waves crashed majestically behind them. Ingrid and Hudson had decided on no awful pastels, no embarrassing peach or citron. Instead, the dresses were a rich, dark ocean blue.

Ingrid beamed, not realizing that Freya had managed to change her neckline so that it curved a little lower than the designer had intended. Tabitha stood next to Freya, looking especially svelte, just a few weeks after giving birth.

The ceremony was being held on the beach below the terrace of the French restaurant La Plage, where the reception would take place afterward. Despite the wind, it was a beautiful summer day, dramatic white clouds billowing across a blue, blue sky. The North Hampton Golden String Trio, sisters wearing little white blossoms in their hair, began to play Schubert's "Serenade."

Ingrid felt a bit overcome by the stately beauty of it all, the joy and gravity that they were about to witness. Freya winked at her, and Ingrid instinctively searched for her parents' faces among the seated guests before she realized her mistake. She kept doing that—wishful forgetfulness. With each instance came the dreadful realization all over again, no less painful.

The guests quieted, shushing each other. The handsome young mayor of North Hampton, Justin Frond, stepped forth and everyone turned expectantly toward the shore. Ingrid felt her eyes brim with tears as Scott walked down the aisle with his parents. His father had the same broad shoulders, and he had his mother's sweet smile.

She turned back to the audience, where Freya and Freddie were sitting with Matt. She gave him a fluttering wave, and the sunlight caught her engagement ring, sending a dazzling light into the crowd. She flushed with pleasure at the small but lovely ring on her finger.

They would be married in the fall. Their time together would be short, brutally short, in contrast to the long life she had ahead of her, but Ingrid had learned that there was no joy without sorrow, and that she would be able to bear the pain of losing him if she could have the joy of being his wife for however long they had together. She would not worry about the future, but live in the present. A baby, she wanted a baby so badly. Someone new to love, someone to fill the ache in her heart from the loss of her parents. The passages of time marched forward. It was time for new life, new loves.

Ingrid studied the crowd. It seemed the entire little town sat on the beach. Even the most awful and repellent Blake Aland had somehow landed on the guest list. How had that happened? She would have to ask Hudson once he was married. She spotted Freya's boss, Sal. Freddie's girlfriend, Kristy, with her kids, Max and Hannah. Gracella, Hector, and Tyler were there, too, since

Gracella worked for Scott part-time. Maggie sat with her father and mother. Ingrid had asked Hudson if she could invite both of them. "Bring it on!" he had said. Mariza had visited the library the other week, to bring a coffee cake and condolences. She had told Ingrid how she had lost her parents to a car accident when she was a teenager. "No one understands what it's like to be an orphan, even when you're grown. It's very hard." Ever since then, the two had become friends. Mariza even introduced her to her boyfriend, a banker from the city.

The music swelled. Freddie caught Ingrid's eye and gave her a smile and a little wave. He had a new ring on his finger as well. Matt motioned to her with a nod, and when she looked Hudson was walking down the aisle, dressed in a dashing linen suit, walking hand in hand with his mother. Mrs. Rafferty wore a transparent pale pink kerchief to match her pink Chanel suit over her blond coif.

A sudden gust of wind swept across the beach, so that Mrs. Rafferty had to place a hand to hold on to her scarf, and a few petals from Ingrid's bouquet flew into the crowd, landing on Freya's and Freddie's shoulders.

Mother, Freya mouthed. Ingrid agreed. It had to be. She'd loved peonies.

Hudson took his place across from Scott, Mayor Frond standing between them with a huge grin.

Little Tyler, looking somber and grown-up in his black suit, walked up with the rings on a pillow.

Ingrid smiled.

Tyler had been accepted into the Carlyle School off the waiting list, and Joanna's will had provided for his education. Her mother would have been pleased. Ingrid kept the envelope from her mother in her purse like a talisman. Joanna's last words. Joanna's instructions. Everything orderly and practical. Ingrid had inherited the house. "I think you will need it, my dear, for your children." *How did Mother know?* Ingrid could see into the future, but she had never been able to predict her own.

Finally, the last strains of Schubert faded as the trio set down their violins. Hudson and Scott held hands. Mayor Frond cleared his throat and began the marriage rites.

chapter fifty-seven

The Longest Journeys
Begin with a Single Step

Kristy turned to Freddie with a rueful smile. It was the day after the Wedding of the Season, which is what everyone in North Hampton was calling Scott and Hudson's nuptials. The North Inn bartenders were sitting on the top of a sand dune, some distance apart, out on the little beach at the back of her place.

Freddie stared out, playing with the ring on his finger. He twirled it around as he watched the waves. Finally, Kristy spoke. "We had a nice run, didn't we? I can't say I'm not sad."

"Me neither." Freddie winced.

Kristy's ex hadn't brought Max and Hannah back yet. They still had a little time. The sun had begun to set, silver and blue streaks running through pink and orange. It had grown chilly, and she shivered in her oversize sweatshirt. Freddie wanted to tug her to him, hold her, reassure her, tell her it would all be okay, but he knew it wouldn't be appropriate.

After all, he had just broken up with her.

He was leaving tonight. Leaving North Hampton. He was going away for a while with his old pal Troy.

Freddie wasn't ready to settle down, no matter what his heart told him now. He wasn't ready to be a husband or a father. He had been cutting ties all morning. Tragedy had a way of putting it all into perspective. He had given his marriage with Gert an earnest shot but it was over. The contract was null and void. He was a free man again. She had been weepy and apologetic, but he had already been down that road with her before, and he knew where it led. Maybe one day they would find each other again—it happened that way with their kind. He would be glad for it, even; perhaps by then he would be ready.

"I'm really sorry," he told Kristy. He meant it, but he couldn't stay.

Kristy nodded. "I knew you wouldn't stay. It's all right. Like I said, we had a good run."

He had spent too much time in Limbo, five thousand years, and he needed to roam free, there were nine worlds in the universe, and he was intent on exploring each one. He had wasted too much valuable time on nothing—video games and living online—it was time to live his lives . . .

"You're making this easy," he said.

She laughed softly. "Yeah! Maybe too easy, Freddie."

Freddie looked down at the ring on his finger. After they had defeated Odin, his father had given him the ring. "The nine worlds are yours, my son." Freddie had taken the ring made of ancient dragon bone and used it to travel to the underworld, where he had been able to say good-bye to his mother one last time.

With the trident returned to its rightful owner and the passages of time flowing once more in the right direction, the Bofrir had been restored as if it had never been destroyed. The bridge between Midgard and Asgard stood once more, and Odin would stand trial with the White Council. Even the pixies had returned to *Álfheim*. Freddie missed them a little.

Perhaps he and Troy would visit them on their journey.

chapter fifty-eight

The Loves of Her Life

J eans. Freya had acquired a special appreciation for jeans since her return to the twenty-first century, especially the kind that hugged like a second skin, that she could run and jump in. She was wearing her favorite pair along with a tight black tank, motorcycle boots, and a buttery black leather zip-up jacket.

She was back at work. Kristy had taken the day off, and Freddie had already left town. She was alone. When she walked in, the stale smell of liquor and beer filled her with affection. She leaned against the counter. Elton John's "The Bitch Is Back" pounded through the speakers.

The place was strangely dead for a summer night. Sal was in the back. Poker night with the boys. There was no one to talk to save the usual set of barflies congregating at one end, already sloppy, teetering on their stools, repeating the same exaggerated tales she had heard last time she'd been here. A young couple was all over each other in a booth, too cheap to pay for a room at the Ucky Star. Their beers were probably warm by now. This was her crowd.

Freya dusted the bottles, wiped the counter and tables till they shone, sliced too much fruit, swept and mopped the floors. There was nothing left to do. It had been about an hour, her standing there, itching for a distraction. Arms crossed over her chest, she glared at the door, focusing her witchy powers onto it, willing it to open. She threw off the jacket and stared at it some more. The old axiom about being careful what one goes wishing for holds true, especially if one is a witch.

The door swung open, and a man swaggered in, staring at her. Faded blue jeans. White T-shirt. A slow smile formed on his lips as he strode up to her at the bar. He took a stool, tossing back his dark hair away from his smoldering eyes. Killian Gardiner. James Brewster. Balder the Beautiful. She knew all his incarnations. She had left him, when she had plunged to her death, hanged by the noose, but he had been saved somehow. A governor's pardon had arrived just in time. The noose had not taken him, and with the passages open once again, his magic and power had returned, and he had been able to journey back to the present, alive and unharmed.

Freya smiled. "What can I get you?"

"You know what I like," he said with that easy, slow smile again. She poured the bourbon and set it in front of him.

He raised the glass and she poured herself a shot, downed it, and exhaled, tossing her head. She poured another round.

While they finished it, the door to the bar swung open.

Her heart bounded into her throat.

Killian turned to look and shrugged.

The tall comely fellow ambled toward them, his suit slightly rumpled, tie swung over a shoulder: a businessman home from a long trip, out for a nightcap before setting home to Gardiners Island. This was *the* Branford Gardiner, the most eligible bachelor in North Hampton. Branford Dashiell Lion Gardiner. Nathaniel Brooks. Saved from the hangman's noose as well, and free to make his way back to whatever time appealed to him. There was no time but the present. He was still the same soft-spoken, debonair man with the soul of mischief. The god Loki. He leaned against the bar. "Hi there," said Bran, making those shy green demon eyes at her. What had he said to her once? *You are more like me than you think, dear Freya.* Maybe it was true. What she had done was just a little bit wicked now, wasn't it? Certainly the Puritans would never approve.

"Hi yourself," returned Freya.

Killian handed Bran a shot glass. Freya poured the three of them a round of drinks.

Freya remembered her dream once more. The three of them, naked in the woods, alone, together, and she made love to them then, to *both* of them that night . . . In her dream she had woken, wedged in the middle between the two of them, with Killian's hand on her hip and Bran's mouth on her neck. Would it always be this way? The two of them in love with her and she in love with both of them? It had happened so very, very long ago, was all she could remember.

In the beginning, back when the world was young and so were they, and they were still innocent and in love. She had been given another chance, and she understood that whatever she did, their fates were forever entwined, in darkness or in light. She had chosen light. She had chosen joy. She had chosen love.

It was all such a haze.

But Freya knew something had happened that night.

Something that would bind the three of them together forever—or release them into the wind?

Who knew?

What was a witch to do? Maybe she would leave both of them and find someone new. The future was wide open, unwritten, the games about to begin.

She loved Killian. But she loved Bran, too.

One day, she would have to choose.

But not today.

Today she would pour the drinks.

The Nine Worlds of the Known Universe

༄

Asgard—World of the Aesir

Midgard—Middle World, Land of Men

Álfheim—World of the Elves

Helheim—Kingdom of the Dead

Jotunheim—Land of the Giants

Muspellheim—The First World

Nidavellir—Land of the Dwarves

Svartalfheim—Land of the Dark Elven

Vanaheim—Land of the Vanir

The Gods of Midgard

The Beauchamp Family Tree
(The Vanir)

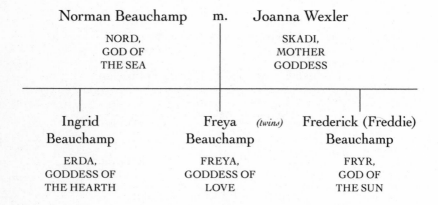

Norman Beauchamp   m.   Joanna Wexler

NORD,
GOD OF
THE SEA

SKADI,
MOTHER
GODDESS

Ingrid
Beauchamp

Freya *(twins)*
Beauchamp

Frederick (Freddie)
Beauchamp

ERDA,
GODDESS OF
THE HEARTH

FREYA,
GODDESS OF
LOVE

FRYR,
GOD OF
THE SUN

Jean-Baptiste Mésomier (MUNINN, GOD OF MEMORY)

Arthur Beauchamp (SNOTRA, GOD OF THE FOREST) *(Norman's brother)*

Anne Barklay (VERĐANDI, NORN OF THE PRESENT)

The Gardiner Family Tree
(The Aesir)

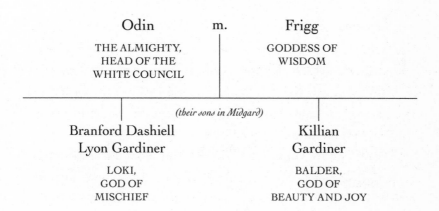

Odin   m.   Frigg

THE ALMIGHTY,
HEAD OF THE
WHITE COUNCIL

GODDESS OF
WISDOM

(their sons in Midgard)

Branford Dashiell
Lyon Gardiner

Killian
Gardiner

LOKI,
GOD OF
MISCHIEF

BALDER,
GOD OF
BEAUTY AND JOY

The Liman Family Tree

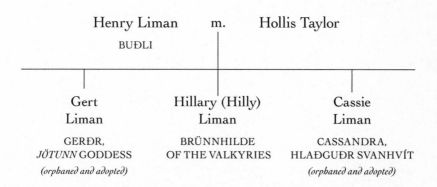

Henry Liman   m.   Hollis Taylor

BUÐLI

Gert
Liman

Hillary (Hilly)
Liman

Cassie
Liman

GERÐR,
JÖTUNN GODDESS
(orphaned and adopted)

BRÜNNHILDE
OF THE VALKYRIES

CASSANDRA,
HLAÐGUÐR SVANHVÍT
(orphaned and adopted)

Acknowledgments

◇

Thank you to Richard Abate, Erwin Stoff, Maggie Friedman, Jane Francis, Morgana Rosenberg, Ellen Archer, Elisabeth Dyssegaard, Kerri Kolen, Marjorie Braman, and everyone at 3Arts, Hyperion, Fox 21, and Lifetime for believing in the witches and the power of magic.

Thank you to Margaret Stohl, Alyson Noel, Deborah Harkness, and Rachel Cohn, the wonderful writing women in my life, who have taken the witches into their hearts. You are all goddesses in my book!

Thank you to Gabrielle Danchick for the research and care into the Salem story. All mistakes are mine alone.

Thank you to my loving family and friends who make it all worthwhile.